EISENHOWER PUBLIC LIBRARY

3 1134 00365 2195

Y0-BDJ-062

The Bench

The Bench

Linda Rawlins

Copyright © 2011 by Linda Rawlins.

Library of Congress Control Number:		2011904160
ISBN:	Hardcover	978-1-4568-8652-3
	Softcover	978-1-4568-8651-6
	Ebook	978-1-4568-8653-0

All rights reserved. No part of this book may be reproduced or transmitted in any form or by any means, electronic or mechanical, including photocopying, recording, or by any information storage and retrieval system, without permission in writing from the copyright owner.

This is a work of fiction. Names, characters, places and incidents either are the product of the author's imagination or are used fictitiously, and any resemblance to any actual persons, living or dead, events, or locales is entirely coincidental.

All quotes from the Bible are taken from the New International Version, 2010.

This book was printed in the United States of America.

To order additional copies of this book, contact:
Xlibris Corporation
1-888-795-4274
www.Xlibris.com
Orders@Xlibris.com
94402

To Rev. James McFarland, a great priest who carried God's message forward. Love one another always.

I love books. I love to read them, own them, and I always dreamed of writing one. The dream has now come true, but I have to thank some very special people who helped me. First, I'd like to thank my father, Ray, for telling me to "write the book" in a most ethereal conversation. Next would be my mother, Joyce, for encouraging me, guiding me, spending many hours reading, initial editing, and most of all, for being my greatest cheerleader.

I would like to thank my husband, Joe, for enduring all the conversations, answering endless questions, offering support, and running advice.

Matthew, you are the greatest tech designer that I know, and your help was invaluable to producing this book. Krista, you provided great ideas, tech support, and encouragement as well as enduring challenging meals. I know that you can write.

To my first readers' circle (Lorraine R., Carol M., Joyce R., Linda G., Helen B., Marie F., Joe L.), your insights, feedbacks, and suggestions were priceless.

Christopher, you are my favorite graphic designer, and, Ryan, thank you for all the information on airplanes.

John, Steve, Donna, Jesse, and Brianne, you always add color to my life.

To Helen B., hopefully you can start uncrossing things soon.

Anita, the final read was great. Thanks for your insight and friendship. The best is yet to come.

Marie F., you gave me wonderful support throughout the whole process.

To the real Florence and Ted, thanks for being so good natured.

I would be remiss if I didn't honor the memory of Father Charles O'Connor. He was one of the priests that made quite a positive difference in my young life.

To all my friends and readers for their support, encouragement, and faith. Trust in the Lord forever (Isaiah 26:4).

Chapter One

"Bless me, Father, for I have sinned."

"Yes, my child?"

"It's been three years since my last confession," she said after a small, silent pause.

"Go on," the priest whispered softly through the small screened window.

She felt cold, very cold. She began to shake as tears started to fall from her eyes, spilling over her cheeks. She tasted the salt on her lips. "I need forgiveness, Father." Her small sobs were gaining strength.

"Please continue, my child. What do you need to confess?" the priest asked softly.

"It's bad, Father, but I didn't intentionally do anything. I was trying to help. My intentions were good, but I think I made it worse." She was crying harder now. The walls of the little confessional were starting to spin, and she had trouble catching her breath. She tried to slow her breathing as her head began to swim. *Please, God, don't let me pass out,* she thought as she grabbed the wall.

"Are you all right? Do you want me to call someone?"

"No! No, Father, there's no one to call." Panic started to seep into her voice. "I just need a minute, please?" The confessional was still spinning. She practiced her breathing rhythm. *Breathe in through the nose, out through the mouth, in through the nose, out through the mouth. Count one, two, three, four. Keep your eyes closed, hang on, this too shall pass.*

He waited, listened, and realized that this was not a normal confession. "I can come out if you like, if you need help?"

"No, Father! I mean, please no. I just need to calm down. I haven't told a soul about this, and I'm afraid all the time. Every day, I think today is the day someone finds out. Today will be the day that they know."

The priest listened to the panicky female. "Can you tell me what's wrong?" He thought he almost recognized her voice.

"I thought I could, but I don't think I can now," she stammered as sweat trickled down her back. She thought going to confession would help, that she would be calmer, her anxieties pacified for a while, but this was much harder than she thought. She could barely breathe; she was so scared and light-headed.

"I can't give you penance if I don't know your sin," he whispered.

"I'm afraid to tell you. I don't know what to do anymore."

"Do you want to pray together? Perhaps we can find an answer?"

"I'm not sure, I guess we can try," she replied as she nodded her head slightly. She tried to swallow, but her mouth had gone dry, and there was a large knot in her throat. She knew she had to do something. If not, she would resort to drastic measures to stop the fear and the anxiety.

Father Michael started to softly pray, "Our Father, who art in heaven, hallowed be thy name . . ." She murmured the familiar prayer with him. His deep, soothing voice calmed her. She felt warmer, more relaxed, and sleepy.

"Excuse me, Father. I have to go now," she whispered.

"Are you okay?" He knew her voice was vaguely familiar.

"No, not really, but I can breathe better now. I have to make an important decision, Father. Thank you for praying with me."

Father Michael's stomach clenched. "You aren't planning to do anything reckless, are you?" The last thing he wanted to hear about was a female suicide in the area. "We could meet at the rectory and talk more if you want. Perhaps I can help you."

"No, Father, no meetings. I have to think about all of this."

"About what, my child? What could possibly be so bad that your Heavenly Father wouldn't forgive you?" After a long pause, so long that he wasn't even sure if she was still there, he heard her faint whisper.

"I think I killed someone." Minutes went by, but she said nothing more. He waited, trying to be patient, holding his breath. He was afraid of what he would hear, afraid of what he would have to do.

"Are you sure?" he asked softly. There was no answer. He waited a few more minutes. "Are you there?" He started to get nervous himself. He had heard of situations like this. What could have happened on the other side of the confessional window? Her fear had been obvious. What if she took an overdose of pills and was dying? What if she had just passed out? What if someone lay dying elsewhere and needed help? What if she had a gun and they both wound up dead? He didn't have a choice; he had to check on her. He slowly got up from his chair, opened the confessional door, and stepped out. The pews were empty, and there was no one in the vestibule. He was sweating now, feeling a little shaky himself. He walked to the other confessional door and slowly started turning the doorknob. The church was deathly quiet. He cautiously pulled the door open, afraid of what he would find. He crossed himself and quickly looked inside the confessional. There, he saw no one. She was gone.

Chapter Two

Dr. Amy Daniels closed her eyes and rested her head against the large old oak tree. The warm sunshine penetrated the tired muscles of her face, neck, and shoulders while she let her thoughts drift freely. In front of her was a small river known as the Divide, which flowed with a noisy ferocity toward a waterfall approximately a half mile down the road. Amy had recently moved to Rocky Meadow, Vermont, a calm town and a decent place to escape the harsh realities of life. At times, when she needed to vent her anger and collect her thoughts, she escaped to a small bench she had found by the river.

The bench had been placed in front of the oak tree years ago and faced the Divide. It was made of varnished wooden slats that were worn smooth and secured on the sides by black iron rails curled into hand rests. Opening her eyes, Amy took in the tranquil scenery. In front of her, a manicured dark green lawn ended at a rocky bank that slipped into the flowing waters of the Divide. Beyond the river, there was a vast meadow boasting blooming spring flowers that added beautiful dots of color to the landscape. In the distance, the Green Mountains of Vermont accented the scene with rolling hills and dense forest.

Amy had moved to Vermont hoping that a beautiful, quiet place would stop the nightmares. The dreams had gotten much worse after the tragedy. She tried medication, but to no avail. Counseling had helped for a while, but she just couldn't stay in that house. There were too many ugly, painful memories. The nightmares had become too severe, especially after she worked the trauma shift. Moving to Vermont was the only option to rest, sleep, and perhaps heal her broken spirit. Time would tell. For now, she would meditate by the water. The power of this particular river touched something in her soul. The energy of the forceful water was never affected by the problems going on in the world. It just continued to flow and move, rise and fall without recourse, always moving forward, cleansing its path. That was the same advice that she had been given by her psychologist: Just continue to move forward. Your path was your journey. As painful as your journey was, it would eventually make you stronger, more enlightened. Restart and forge ahead.

Watching water was pleasant during the day, yet the water in her dreams terrified her. Whether it quietly blocked roads or rampaged in the distance, Amy knew it signified danger. Perhaps dream analysis could tell her why water was a recurrent theme when she was stressed, but Amy had never wanted to pursue it. Lately, her dreams held a lot of storms, but she couldn't always tell whether they were dreams, memories, or premonitions.

As her gaze traveled across the mountains, she took note of the heavenly blue sky filled with white puffy clouds. It was a gorgeous Monday afternoon. Spring had finally arrived, and the shining sun provided beautiful warm weather. Sparkles of light danced on top of the river as it flowed noisily by. Since moving to Vermont, Amy came to this place as often as possible to relax and sort her thoughts. As a child, she had spent summer vacations in Vermont, and the peaceful memories of nature had drawn her back to heal. The sounds of the river and the nonchalant cries of the birds added to the ambience. The cool vapor that lifted from the flowing water provided a clean breeze as it blew her hair. Amy loved the smell of the flowers and the freshly mowed lawn as well as an occasional wood fire. Listening to the white noise of a tractor laboring in the distance made her feel sleepy. Her bench was the only place that afforded her the reflective peace she so desperately craved and hoped would heal her.

The bench was on the edge of the property that belonged to the St. Francis Retreat House. Behind the bench was a large church built in the nineteenth century of magnificent stone and stained glass windows. The church and surrounding property included a large rectory and a private graveyard encircled with an elegant black wrought iron fence topped with gold posts. Toward the edge of the woods was a prayer walk surrounding a large statue of St. Francis of Assisi. Amy remembered that he was the patron saint of nature, the environment and the animals. The location of the retreat house had been dedicated to his beliefs and was well chosen from what she could see. Although the area was usually very quiet, each afternoon, the church bells rang out a melodious reminder that God was in his house and admiring all his work.

Amy wondered if she felt more peaceful at this bench because of the church. She had been raised a Roman Catholic and used to enjoy the inspiration she felt after she attended mass. Her daily prayer books had ensured that her day started on an uplifting note. She hadn't been back to church or her spiritual reading since the tragedy. There were too many questions and too many doubts. For now, she would watch the river.

As a child, Amy had sat on a similar riverbank with her parents. Laughing and clapping her hands, she spread her dolls around her.

"Froggie will go here, and Teddy will go there. Froggie is the daddy, and Teddy is the mommy." Amy giggled.

"And you're the baby?" her dad had asked with a large smile on his face as he watched his daughter play.

"No, silly. Ducky is the baby. I'm the doctor. I help them when they get sick, and I never, ever hurt them."

"That's wonderful, honey. You're a very smart girl," her dad said proudly.

"Maybe you could help with our new baby too," her mom said as she rubbed her swollen belly.

Amy had just giggled. Using her plastic doctor's kit, she took Froggie's blood pressure and checked Teddy for a fever.

That had been years ago. Tears flowed down her face as Amy realized how much she missed her parents, but thankfully, they had died before the murder.

Amy had been a good student and graduated from college summa cum laude. She went on to attend medical school, and by the end of her training, she had become an accomplished board-certified trauma surgeon. Her reputation and skills grew to the point that she had been courted to work in a prestigious hospital in Boston. She accepted the position and enjoyed her work for years, until the tragedy. In order to leave Boston, she had applied to Rocky Meadow General Hospital for a position working in the emergency room. The small hospital in Vermont had been growing steadily but was still painfully understaffed and jumped at the opportunity to have Amy join their team.

Working in the emergency room usually resulted in a hectic day. Today had been worse than usual. Having an epidemic of intestinal virus spread through the neighborhood was challenge enough, but the addition of two motor vehicle accidents, including multiple lacerations and fractures as well as a young woman in premature labor, was just about all she could take. Amy leaned back and closed her eyes.

She had been working in the trauma suite, suturing one of the patients from the motor vehicle accidents, her vinyl gloves covered in blood, when

Brenda, the emergency room charge nurse, walked in. "Excuse me, Dr. Daniels?" The nurse smiled apologetically as she quietly observed Amy suture the deep laceration with relaxed, expert skill. Brenda felt as if she were watching a graceful artist finish a masterpiece that inspired respect and awe. The laceration continued to grow smaller as Amy smoothly passed the needle through the bloody skin and tissue. It was obvious that Dr. Amy Daniels had a lot of surgical skill, but beyond that, Brenda knew very little about her. It was rumored that she was single and had worked at a large hospital in Boston prior to moving to Vermont. There was some hearsay that she was running from adversity, but no one really knew. What was evident to Brenda was that Amy had a wary edge to her that made most people respect her privacy.

"Yes, Brenda? How can I help you?" Amy asked as she looked up at the efficient, friendly charge nurse and noticed that Brenda had a bevy of freckles on her smooth skin to complement her red hair.

"I'm sorry, but we need you at the front desk when you're done. The director of nursing wants to introduce you to the new candy stripers and volunteers. I told her that you were involved with a surgical repair and weren't immediately available, but she said it was important."

"Does she know they're going to have to wait a while? I still have to finish this closure. Broken glass tends to make a real mess of things, doesn't it?" Amy asked as she cautiously surveyed her handiwork.

"Well, it's certainly not pretty, but thank God you're here. Before you started, we had to ship most of our trauma patients out. I loved Doc Benson, but he was getting on in years, and it was definitely time for him to retire."

"I'm sure he did the best he could," Amy replied.

"Maybe, but we were in desperate need of new blood. Oh"—Brenda chuckled—"excuse the pun. At any rate, I told her they would have to wait until you're done."

"Okay, then I'll get to them when I'm done," Amy replied.

"That's what I told her. I think she's giving them a tour of the ER while they're waiting. By the way, those x-ray reports are back from radiology. We'll have to call in an orthopedist for the other car accident patient, unless you like to treat fractures?"

"No, thanks, I have my hands full as it is. I think Dr. Weber is on call for ortho. Go ahead and get him in here," Amy directed.

"Of course, Doctor. You should also know that the infectious-disease nurse is coming down to the ER to start tracking all the diarrhea patients.

They want to make sure that we don't have another salmonella outbreak on our hands," Brenda complained.

"Sounds like a crappy job." Amy laughed and couldn't help but remember all the stupid medical school jokes about diarrhea. "But then, someone has to do it. Sorry about that. I'll be done shortly. Maybe you can get the med tech to come in here and dress this wound for me? That certainly would move things along."

"Yes, Doctor. I'll go find him. He's probably out back, smoking."

"I wouldn't be surprised. Be sure that he washes his hands first, especially if he's smoking. I don't want this wound to get infected."

"Of course. If I can't find him, I'll come back and do it myself."

"Thank you, I'd appreciate that. Also, I'm going to order an antibiotic. Check the patient's chart for allergies first, okay?"

"Certainly," Brenda said with a smile.

After washing her hands, Amy approached the nurses' station and saw a group of nervous people surrounding a large officious nurse. Amy offered them a warm smile and introduced herself to the group, "Hi, I'm Dr. Amy Daniels."

"I'm Mrs. Russo, the director of nursing," the nurse stated sharply while offering her hand to Amy. "I know we haven't had a chance to meet each other yet, but I wanted to introduce the new group of volunteers. They'll start tomorrow at their assigned places. You may see some of them on a regular basis and others not at all, but I thought you should meet them at any rate."

"Thank you. It's always nice to see new faces," Amy replied with a smile, but inwardly bristling at the nurse's brusque attitude.

Mrs. Russo took the time to individually introduce each of the volunteers to Amy and indicate where they would most likely be assigned. "Dr. Daniels, you'll probably be seeing our new candy striper, Willow Davis, quite a bit. She'll be helping in the emergency room as well as our outpatient clinic."

Amy greeted the teenager with a handshake. "I'm looking forward to working with you." Willow took her hand and nodded but didn't look overly happy about the arrangement. Amy turned back to Mrs. Russo and gently said, "I really have to get back to the patients. Is there anything else?"

"I guess not. I just wanted you to meet the volunteers. They play an essential part of the care that we offer at Rocky Meadow General."

"I'm sure that they do, and I'll enjoy speaking with each of them on an individual basis, in the future," Amy responded, looking at her watch. "Is this the only group?"

"Well, yes, actually it is. We also have a few chaplains, but they haven't contacted me yet. I believe that St. Francis will be sending new representatives within a week or so," Mrs. Russo answered efficiently.

"Ah, excellent." Turning toward the group with a quick wave, Amy said, "It was nice meeting all of you, but I really have to get back to work. If you'll excuse me?" Amy leaned over, picked up a chart, and walked to the next exam room. When she emerged ten minutes later, the small group of volunteers was gone.

Chapter Three

Father Michael Lauretta stood as he prepared to end the daily mass. "In the name of the Father, the Son, and the Holy Spirit," he said as he made the sign of the cross and blessed the congregation.

"This mass has ended, go in peace to love and serve the Lord," intoned Deacon Eddie Miller as he stood at the side of Father Michael.

"Thanks be to God," the parishioners murmured as they crossed themselves and genuflected. They picked up their purses and cell phones and prepared to leave their pews. Father Michael and Deacon Eddie crossed to the center of the altar, bowed to the crucifix, turned around, and left the altar of St. Francis Church. As the organ music escalated, played by Sister Margaret Mary O'Connor, better known as Sister Maggie, Father Michael led the small procession down the center aisle of the church. He was followed by Deacon Eddie, who raised the Book of the Gospels high as he walked so all could see. Pew by pew, the parishioners left their seats and followed the clergy out the main door of the church and into the bright morning daylight. Monday morning mass at St. Francis Church in Rocky Meadow had attracted the usual group of daily churchgoers. Most of the parishioners lingered on the church steps for conversation and to socialize after mass. Lunch dates were set, appointments were made, and committees were born. There was always a new bit of gossip, and of course, you couldn't consider it gossip if your intentions were in the right place. One was simply expressing concern for one's neighbor, and that's what good parishioners did.

There was another group of parishioners that left the church as soon as they received communion. Despite the fact that these worshippers always left mass early, they were still in attendance for part of the mass, and partly present was better than not at all as far as Father Michael was concerned. He wondered if they would be satisfied with only part of their paycheck or part of the new movie in town. He never seemed to see people running out the back of the local theater before the end of the film.

Father Michael's stomach growled as he stood on the steps and greeted his congregation as they left the church.

"Wonderful sermon, Father. Are you coming to the meeting for the carnival tonight?"

"I'll try to be there. Your hair looks lovely today, Florence," Father Michael said.

"Oh, Father, really." Florence feigned humility as she touched the back of her recently coiffed hair but was secretly charmed that Father Michael had noticed her new style. She thought he was charming even when he didn't notice; after all, he was a very handsome man. Sparkling blue eyes danced in a face that was crowned by dark, wavy hair, and at five feet ten, his trim, muscular physique was barely hidden by his clericals. Father Michael's disarming smile and relaxed demeanor added to his allure. In his late thirties, he simply radiated vitality and was a true commercial for living an honorable life.

After greeting the parishioners, he returned to the sacristy and removed his vestments. He carefully hung up his chasuble and alb, put away his stole, and checked the church to make sure the candles were extinguished and lights turned off. As he worked, he mentally reviewed his goals for the day. The first thing he wanted to do was to have breakfast. He looked forward to some hot coffee and a serving of Mrs. Novak's fresh banana bread. When she wasn't looking, he was able to slather a decent amount of butter on the bread as well. If the bread was warm and the butter melted, he would experience a little slice of heaven. Michael loved his daily bread with God and his follow-up bread with Mrs. Novak. To offset his indulgence and spend some quiet time with God, he looked forward to several miles of trail running each morning. His daily run was the only way he kept himself conditioned and in shape. He carried an active schedule and was prone to getting overstressed despite his outward appearance.

As a priest experienced in counseling, he knew the importance of forestalling that kind of condition. Michael had attended a seminary close to home in New Jersey and had done well in his courses of scripture, theology, spirituality, and especially Christian ethics. He loved connecting with people and exploring their philosophy in life. As a result, he decided to major in psychology. He was ordained a priest with an innate ability to provide spiritual comfort and support.

Initially, Michael was assigned to a parish in an inner-city neighborhood where he was instrumental in helping parishioners find the spiritual enlightenment and courage necessary to face the troubles of today's world. Many were strengthened by his insight and wisdom. In addition to spiritually hungry parishioners, he would also help his fellow clergy. At dinner with his colleagues, the conversation would initially start with comments about the parish and eventually turn to issues suffered by spiritual leaders. Father Michael spent time counseling his brethren with results so positive that they were noticed by the archdiocese. Eventually, Michael's reputation grew to a point that he was asked to head a special program for clergy who had extreme difficulty performing their assigned duties for a variety of colorful reasons. He had been called by the bishop and told that he was being transferred to the position of pastor at St. Francis Church in Rocky Meadow, Vermont. Prior to his working there, St. Francis had enjoyed a reputation of being a desired retreat for clergy in need of solitude. The quiet, beautiful location helped to calm frayed nerves and realign priorities. However, once Michael was installed as pastor, an active counseling component was established for a steadily growing body of working spiritual leaders in need of fortitude. Michael hadn't been sure if he'd like Vermont, but out of respect to his vow of obedience, he accepted his position without question.

Michael finished locking the church and headed toward the rectory where he met Katie in the kitchen.

"Father Michael, good morning." Her cheery smile lit up her face as she handed him a steaming cup of coffee. Katie Novak, a middle-aged woman with dimples and brown curly hair held in place by a headband, was a hard worker. She had been the resident cook and housekeeper for St. Francis Church for several years. Before that, she had lived with her husband on a little farm until he passed away from cancer. Although she was a fantastic cook and dedicated wife, she didn't have the ability to care for her husband and the farm by herself. When her husband finally passed on, she prayed that she'd be able to find a way to pay her bills and stay near her husband's grave. Father Michael knew of her wishes and offered her the housekeeping position at the church. Katie had jumped at the chance to sell the property that she and her husband had tended for the last thirty years. After all the arrangements were made, she moved into the rectory to help care for the clergy, staff, and parishioners of St. Francis. She would ride by her old farm from time to time with wistful memories and dreams, but truth be told, she wasn't happy there without her husband. God could not have answered her prayers any better than he did, and Mrs. Novak was happy to be alive and working. "How was mass this morning, Father?"

"It was fine, Katie. I had an interesting homily today. I started with that little joke Elmer told me about God playing golf."

"Father, you didn't," squeaked Katie.

"I did. Of course, I added my own little details to make the point of the homily obvious. Practice makes perfect regardless of what we do in life, and we shouldn't expect to make a hole in one every time we do things. We are not God, only God is God, and he even hits one off the fairway on occasion."

"Well, I hope it helps people to be more tolerant of others as well as themselves. My lord, it seems everyone is so high strung these days."

"So true, so true," Michael said as he sighed and sipped his coffee.

"Father, what can I get you for breakfast? Would you like some eggs and bacon or perhaps pancakes?" Katie asked while wiping her hands on a dish towel.

"Thanks, but I really don't have a lot of time, and I want to go out for a trail run. I have some thinking to do before our new brethren arrive tomorrow. Do you have any banana bread left?"

"Oh, I may have a piece or two. But you know as well as I do that you need some protein if you're going to be off running through the woods. Otherwise, you'll lose your energy and pass out. We won't find you until some poor hiker trips over you at the end of summer."

Michael burst out laughing. "Now there's a morbid thought."

"Realistic is more like it, Father. It won't take me but a minute to make you a decent breakfast. I'll call you as soon as it's done," Katie offered.

"All right, you win," Michael said as he held up his hands. "I'll be in my office when it's ready. As usual, I have paperwork."

"Why don't you start by researching one of those fancy tracking phones that they have now so we can find you if you don't come back?"

"Katie, really, I'll be fine out there. Right now, I have to go over the files of the new priests that are arriving tomorrow."

"How many priests do we have coming?" Katie asked. "Just so I can plan for meals."

"Well, we have four new priests arriving tomorrow and me, of course, so that makes five."

"Yeah, but you eat for two sometimes."

"Ouch, that hurt."

"Not likely, what about Sister Maggie? Will she be having dinner?"

"Not the first night. She gets a little nervous when the new groups arrive and likes to wait until they're settled in first. From what I've been told, this particular group is a little rougher than usual, so she may be smarter than we know."

"Well, I'm planning on having six at each meal. We always have a little extra as well, so there won't be a problem if I have to add another plate here or there." Katie noticed that Michael looked at her with a small smile on his face. "What? What now?" she asked.

"You know, you're a special woman, Katie Novak. I know that this parish is never easy to cook and clean for. We always have different people with different problems moving in and out, not to mention the staff. Yet you never complain or seem to tire. I just want to thank you for the wonderful job that you do here."

"Oh, go on, Father." Katie blushed. "I'm happy to be where I am and doing what I'm doing. You know that. I only hope that I get to stay at St. Francis, helping you and those poor other priests that come here, until I see my husband again one day. Now, really, go on. I have work to do. And don't worry. I'll put the extra butter on the banana bread just like you do behind my back when you think I'm not looking. I'll let you know when it's ready."

Laughing, Father Michael turned and went to his office.

Chapter Four

Willow Davis shuddered as she passed the rusty gates attached to the low stone wall that surrounded the cemetery. It was a beautiful spring day, but she felt cold inside. The wind was blowing in gusts, and rain would eventually be on its way. Grandmother had taught her that rain was coming when the leaves on the trees turned upside down. Willow had been visiting her grandmother's grave every week for a year now. The visits were never very rewarding or insightful, but she went anyway. She would always pause on her way toward the back of the cemetery and read the grave markers. She wasn't procrastinating; it's just that some of the gravestones fascinated her.

The Rocky Meadow cemetery was approximately three hundred years old. Many of the older graves were grouped by families or professions, but there were single graves as well. Most of the headstones were the same, a slim white limestone marker that stood at the head of each grave. Most of the headstones were straight, a few were crooked, and some had fallen over completely. Occasionally, they were broken, which made them very difficult to read. Older grave markers memorialized the dead more than modern ones, but having the deceased's history on the headstones was fascinating. How they died, the year they died, whom they were married to, and who their parents were were all spelled out on the headstone. Some of the wording had been washed away by years of acid rain and harsh weather, but you could make out most of the letters. The grave markers shaped in ornate ways interested Willow the most. She wondered what the cemetery would look like if the headstones of people who were killed were shaped in a special way. What configuration would they choose to represent murder? She thought visitors might avoid those graves in case the dead wanted revenge.

Willow always stopped at the areas that held families. She noticed that children had smaller headstones as if their little lives had smaller significance. Only the children of wealthy families had large grave markers, and they were shaped like angels or saints. The dedication would always start with wording like "Our Angel" or "God's Little Lamb." The poorer families just had tiny little gravestones. Once, she found five small white limestone markers lined up side by side. Each one was for a child that had died from an infection in the early 1900s. She tried to imagine how a mother could endure losing five of her children to an epidemic at the same time. Willow didn't have any children, but if she did and they all died together, she imagined that she'd want to die with them. Her little babies, how could she let them go into that cold, dark ground by themselves? Willow started to cry at the grim, thought.

Her own mother wouldn't care if she were dead. It was apparent that her mother didn't care that she was alive. Willow was fifteen years old with virtually no parents. Her mother, Martina Sharpe, with a nickname of Marty, had gotten pregnant under a willow tree where she lost her virginity to Bobby Davis, and so she named her daughter Willow. How imaginative was that? Raised by her grandmother, Elizabeth Sharpe, Willow was told that her mom was happy when she learned that she was pregnant until she realized that Bobby didn't want the baby. As a matter of fact, Bobby didn't want Marty either. He told her that she was just another stupid girl that let him get lucky, and Marty cried for a full week after having her heart broken. Luckily, Grandmother arranged the proper medical care so that Willow was born safely.

When Bobby realized that Marty wasn't going to have an abortion, he had a change of heart, and two months later, Willow's parents were married. Despite the legal document, their marriage was not a happy one. Grandmother couldn't remember if Marty started drinking while she was pregnant or after Willow was born, but apparently, Marty spent all her time in a bottle, and Bobby spent his time in any woman he could. Not long after, he took off for good.

Willow used to look in the mirror to see if she looked weird. Reading about babies with fetal alcohol syndrome, she was worried she might be affected, but she looked okay, and no one ever told her she was mentally retarded. She didn't think of herself as pretty, but she wasn't ugly either. Grandmother told her how beautiful she was every day. Even so, she didn't like herself much. Why should she? Her parents decided they didn't like her before she was born, and it wasn't because of her looks, so something else must have been wrong. Grandmother Elizabeth said that they were just damn fools who didn't know anything about children or life.

Years ago, Grandmother Elizabeth had been a schoolteacher happily married to Grandfather for years. When he died, Elizabeth was left with a broken heart, a beautiful daughter, and 1,500 acres of farm and woodland in Vermont. She became a wealthy widow who continued to teach and raise her young daughter as best as she could. She worked as a single mother and did well until Marty became a teenager. Elizabeth tried very hard to discipline and guide her daughter, but Marty was rebellious and hung out with a bad crowd. Hooking up with Bobby Davis just made everything worse. After Marty gave birth but showed no interest in the baby, Elizabeth retired from her job and devoted herself to care for her granddaughter, Willow. Marty continued to drink and eventually moved out to live with the bar crowd.

Elizabeth had taken Willow and raised her as best she could. Willow felt grateful and safe until Grandmother died. They had done almost everything together. Willow was homeschooled after which they would sing, bake, and cook. Late at night, Grandmother would brush Willow's hair until it shone. Then she would read her a bedtime story and cover her with blankets of love.

It was bad enough that Grandmother had to die, but watching it was worse. Willow couldn't forget how Grandmother's face contorted. Willow had just given her the insulin needle when Grandmother started to sweat and get shaky. Grandmother said that her heart was racing and she felt very strange. The bad headache and shortness of breath came next. Grandmother was struggling to breathe. She started to grimace, and her eyes rolled up to the top of her head before she just fell and died. Screaming into the phone, Willow dialed 911. The operator had told her to keep talking as Willow was attempting to give CPR. By the time help had arrived, Willow's shoulders were aching, and she couldn't breathe herself.

As the paramedics tried to save her grandmother, Willow found the needle she had used lying on the floor. Afraid that she had done something wrong, she simply placed it in her pocket. Later that day, she put the needle and the insulin bottle in a fruit jar and buried it in the backyard. Willow told the paramedics that Grandmother had a spell and just died, and technically, that was the truth.

Even so, the coroner spoke to Grandmother's cardiologist, Lou Applebaum. Grandmother had been on medicine for sugar, high blood pressure, and high cholesterol. It was possible she had a heart attack even though the latest stress test result was normal, but Dr. Applebaum didn't think so. Sometimes, stress tests weren't always accurate for women.

Grandmother had watched her diet and her weight and was an exercise enthusiast, especially after she started to care for Willow. Her death was a shock, to say the least.

Willow had watched as they performed CPR, used a defibrillator, and put a tube into her lungs. Next, they transferred her to a stretcher and moved her into the ambulance. The ambulance peeled out toward Rocky Meadow General Hospital, and Willow just stood in the driveway, shaking and staring after them with tears running down her face. She stayed there until a female officer, Jaime Brand, threw a blanket around her shoulders despite the fact that the temperature was seventy degrees and placed her in the back of a patrol car. Willow didn't remember being driven to the hospital.

Willow thought of that night every time she visited Grandmother's grave. She would trace Grandmother's name on the grave marker and cry. Lastly, she would tell her how much she missed her and that she was sorry she had killed her.

Chapter Five

The blood shot up in a graceful arch that landed on the other side of the surgical table.

"Clamp that artery, now," Amy yelled.

"Pressure's dropping!"

"Open the lines, get more fluid in," Amy directed as her hand in a surgical glove covered with blood, reached up to adjust the bright light shining into the wound.

"What is that?" the intern asked with a worried look on his face.

"A piece of intestine, I think. Scalpel," Amy said as she put her hand, palm up, toward the scrub nurse. Huddled together over the narrow green-draped surgical table, the OR team worked for two hours, repairing the organs that had been damaged by the ricocheting bullet. The respirator created a white noise that gave a surreal feeling to the OR suite. Finally, the surgical repairs were complete.

"He's stable for now, get him to post-op, the poor bastard. What's his story again?" Amy asked as she peeled off her gloves.

The nurse looked down quickly as she answered uneasily, "He was shot during a home invasion."

Amy jumped up from her dream with sweat pouring down her face. The dream again. She hated that dream. She had saved the bastard's life, but who knew it would ruin hers? It was already early morning, so there was no chance of getting back to sleep. A hot shower helped her refocus, and after getting dressed and drinking a hot cup of coffee, she was ready to go to the hospital. She had promised herself a prison sentence in medical records today followed by volunteering in the hospital clinic. What did it matter? She was living in hell anyway.

The commotion in the ER got Amy's attention as soon as she walked through the doors. Looking up from the chart he was reading, a handsome man in an expensive suit noticed her. "Hey, Amy? Got a minute?" Dr. Louis Applebaum was one of the attending cardiologists at the hospital, single, and wanted by most of the nurses on staff.

"Hi, Lou, what's up?" Amy asked with a curious glance toward the cubicle.

"We just coded one of my patients, but it looks like we got him back already. What are you doing here? I thought Ernie had the ER today."

Amy shrugged. "He does, but I have to go across the hall and catch up on my pile of charts in the record room."

"Sounds like fun," Lou said with a grin.

"Actually, it sucks and you know it." Amy smiled. "So who coded?"

"A patient of mine by the name of Ben Lawrence."

"I assume that Mr. Lawrence has a bad heart?" Amy asked.

"Not really, that's why we were taken by surprise."

"Why? What's the problem?"

Lou leaned back in his chair, sighed, and crossed his arms. "This code of his is curious because we didn't see it coming. He just passed his physical with flying colors. Maybe you can offer us some insight having come from such a prestigious hospital."

"Well, I'm all ears, but I don't know what I can offer. I'm a surgeon, not a cardiologist," Amy said with a grin.

Lou looked at Amy with a warm smile. She was an attractive woman, in her early thirties, and with long legs and light brown hair that she kept in a twist at the back of her head. She was of medium height with a medium build. Lou knew that she had gone to medical school in New Jersey and had been an emergency room physician specializing in trauma surgery in Boston. Although she was perfectly calm with a steel blade in her hand, she seemed a little nervous and on edge at times. She had transferred to Rocky Meadow General approximately four months ago, but he wasn't sure why she had come to Vermont. She wasn't married and didn't seem to have any family in the area. As he told her about the case, he thought it would be interesting to get to know her better.

"I realize you haven't been in these parts very long, but Mr. Benjamin Lawrence has been here forever. He's been the proud owner of the Rocky Meadow Apothecary for fifty years now."

"Is Ben the local pharmacist?" Amy asked in a surprised voice.

"Well, yes, although he doesn't fill many prescriptions these days. He hired a couple of pharmacists who were working in the national chains to fill the scripts. He still owns the shop and oversees everything, I guess."

"Do tell," Amy chided.

"Just think, when he started working in the pharmacy, he was still compounding various meds and ointments by hand. In those days, the doctors didn't write a prescription as much as a recipe for medication."

"Well, that was certainly before my time," Amy said with a large smile. "Has he been ill recently?"

Lou paused for a few seconds. "Actually, no. That's why we're a bit perplexed here. He had a heart attack two years ago. His angiogram showed some atherosclerosis with two vessel disease. We told him his arteries were clogged, placed a couple of stents, and started him on a statin, and he stabilized quite nicely. We talked him into taking a little time off, which he did to focus on disease prevention. Like I said, we just saw him for his checkup and he was fine."

"You did a stress test and an echo?"

"Just did them last week, and everything was stable. He didn't mention any problems. No complaints of angina and no failure symptoms either. The only thing is that his friend said he seemed very stressed lately. She asked him what was bothering him, and he told her not to worry, he would take care of things."

"Meaning?"

"Who knows? She didn't know what he was referring to. As a matter of fact, she asked me about the tests because she thought they might have been abnormal, but he didn't want to worry her."

"Is he married?"

"No, and he doesn't have any children either. That's why his friend worried about him. They've worked together for many years, but they're not close enough to get married or share secrets."

"Maybe that's why they stayed close," Amy suggested with a raised eyebrow.

"Actually," Lou said through a chuckle, "she thought he was hiding something."

"Perhaps he was."

"Could be, but here's the weird part. When he first got to the ER, Ernie called me to tell me that he was here. Apparently, Ben was bleeding all over. Ernie thought he coded just because his blood count dropped. His hemoglobin was so low they had to start a transfusion just to keep him alive."

"That can certainly do it."

"Ernie asked me how much blood thinner he was on. He was getting ready to administer vitamin K once he got the lab work back."

"That sounds right. So what's the problem?"

"Ben wasn't on any blood thinners."

"Did he have bone marrow or liver disease?"

"None, so we have no clue as to why he was hemorrhaging."

"Is it possible that he was taking something from the pharmacy without telling anyone?"

"Anything's possible. Who knows? But why risk something as dangerous as that if you're in relatively good health?"

"People do it all the time," Amy said with a shrug.

"I know, but he didn't seem like a patient that would do that without telling me." "Hopefully, he'll stabilize and you'll get a chance to ask him."

"God willing. With any luck, I can get him up to the intensive care unit soon."

"In the meantime, why don't you run the lab to make sure he wasn't taking something he shouldn't have?"

"Good idea, I'll let you know." Dr. Lou winked at Amy. "Thanks for the curbside consult. Maybe I'll see you at the medical staff meeting this week."

Amy couldn't help but smile back. "Sounds like a winner, but I have to go work on my charts." Leaving the ER, she headed to the small medical record room and on to the free clinic where she promised to volunteer for a couple of hours. Later, she had a date with her favorite bench. It was supposed to be a beautiful spring day.

Chapter Six

Father Michael inhaled the cool, clean air as he got ready for his morning run. He'd already presided over the morning mass and enjoyed another delicious breakfast made by Katie. He was looking forward to using the new trail running shoes he'd received as a gift from one of his parishioners, and Devil's Peak would be a perfect run to break them in. He had changed his clericals to proper running gear and pulled a water bottle from the fridge. The trail to Devil's Peak began at the edge of the woods to the side of the church. It followed several miles of original horse trails to the top of the closest mountain range. The first mile was fairly flat, which gave him time to ease into his regular pattern of breathing while he ran. His muscles also needed time to warm up so that he wouldn't cramp during the run. The next two miles were uphill, which required a bit more effort. After curling around the mountain, the trail continued downhill and exited the woods next to the Divide in front of the church.

Devil's Peak was longer than his usual run, but Michael was looking forward to the challenge. As he stretched near the entrance of the trail, he imagined himself running with ease. He had always been taught that mental fortitude was more than half the battle in order to achieve success. When he had a great run, he would first concentrate on his form. Eventually, as he became more comfortable, his thoughts shifted to his surroundings. The cool, tree-lined paths pierced by shafts of sunlight provided a beautiful backdrop as he listened to small animals skittering through the woods. The smell of the fresh pine needles enhanced by the morning dew was always refreshing. Various birds would call out a warning as his presence was announced to the natural inhabitants of the forest. At times, he heard the flowing water of various streams and small waterfalls heading toward the Divide. On the days he was tired, he would listen to music with a heavy downbeat to energize his run. Today, he just wanted to enjoy the stillness of the trail. As his body continued to fall into a relaxed rhythm, his thoughts turned inward to achieve clarity and focus. Michael had worked out solutions to many problems during his runs in the past, and now he needed to plan for the new group of priests arriving today.

Michael wondered why the trail was called Devil's Peak. He could understand if the trail traveled downhill into a canyon, then the name Devil's Peak would have been appropriate. The trail should have been named God's Summit since the climb was extraordinary. There were areas where the trees broke open and offered an astonishing view of God's country that showcased expansive views of mountains, farms, green meadows, and acres of woods. From that vantage point, the church and the town looked like toy versions of themselves. Beyond that, there were simply open blue skies with white fluffy clouds floating past. When he first began to run in this area, the landscape was so beautiful he wasn't able to get into his normal introspective thinking pattern. As time had gone by, he had become more adept at letting his inner thoughts float forward while enjoying his run.

As he reached his routine pace, he started to think about last evening. The carnival-planning meeting had gone well. Florence ran the meeting with her usual efficiency and challenging attitude. Her demeanor reminded everyone that the carnival was her project. While she pointed out that she needed help, she maintained that she would be in charge of all the final decisions. Earlier in the year, the carnival committee picked a week to hold the event, and Florence signed a contract with the traveling carnival company. In addition to rides, they would have booths for games, charities, and their respective committees. The local stable agreed to have horses available for old-fashioned carriage, trail, and pony rides. Michael had lost count of the number of food tables that were reserved but realized he would have to do a lot of running the week after the carnival. They had even planned to have several nights of stage entertainment with local bands and comedians. Florence was a bit of a control enthusiast, but she produced impressive results.

When Michael approached the hand-carved watering trough for horses, he stopped for a drink from his water bottle. Although the water in the trough looked clear and fresh, he preferred to carry his own bottle. If he was struggling to survive, he wouldn't hesitate to drink from the brook. The streams were overflowing with water from the extra spring rains. As he drank his water, he gently stretched. For some reason, his calf muscles felt tighter than usual. He had worn the new running shoes for a few short runs to break them in, but perhaps they needed more time.

During the next couple of miles, Michael's thoughts turned to the group of priests that would be arriving soon. This particular group seemed somewhat diverse. There were four priests scheduled to arrive, all hailing from different parts of the country. The first priest on his list was Father Patrick Doherty, who needed counseling for alcohol abuse. Some priests had difficulty with alcohol, but the habit was generally very discreet. Unfortunately, Father Doherty had carried out his last homily while being noticeably intoxicated. Due to his lack of inhibition of speech, he made some personal remarks about several parishioners that should not have been said in public.

The next priest scheduled to visit the retreat house was Father Juan Ramos Cordoba. Father Juan was an avid priest in his thirties who loved to work with young people. After getting dizzy and passing out during a pickup basketball game, he was taken to the local emergency room. He hadn't been feeling well prior to that. He told himself that the stomach pains and fatigue were just from working too hard. When he received the news that he had widespread stomach cancer, he became very depressed and disillusioned. He was a devout Catholic priest who ran a very successful program that kept kids out of trouble. Why would God bring him home now? Why not let him continue his ministry? As his illness progressed, he continued to lose faith and became more depressed. He needed to find an answer to rationalize his premature death sentence, and the archdiocese thought that Father Michael might help.

Father Anthony Lomack was also destined to be part of the new group. He had taken a vow to be celibate as a priest but had met someone he cared for very deeply and found himself more drawn toward the intimate side of a personal relationship with a woman. Not wanting to break his vows, he had asked to be sent to Vermont, where he could explore his feelings and possibly make a life-changing decision.

Another priest that was expected to arrive was Father Victor Cerulli from Chicago. Father Cerulli was a big priest with an exceptional talent for boxing. He used to spend time in the ring to work off his frustration. Managing a large parish was an enormous, stressful responsibility. However, over the last several years, his time in the ring was not enough to purge him of all his disgruntlement, and he began to have a noticeable problem with anger management. After an encounter with a long-term parishioner, Father Cerulli asked his archbishop to help him before something serious happened. Father Michael was most interested in hearing the details of that encounter.

Jack Moore, the custodian for St. Francis, had left for the Burlington airport this morning to collect the new priests. They were all to be aboard a direct flight from Newark, New Jersey, to Burlington, Vermont. However, that flight had to be coordinated with Father Cerulli's flight from Chicago, which was also scheduled for stopover at Newark International Airport. Once they all arrived, Katie would provide them with rooms and much needed refreshments until they had dinner that evening and got acquainted.

Michael broke his reverie as the trail curved downward, and he needed less effort for his breathing. When he slowed down so that he wouldn't fall off the mountain trail, he noticed that the extra strain on his legs was painful. Muscle spasms started grabbing at him. He looked over to the side of the trail as some of the drop-offs were quite sheer and would result in serious injury if he was to slip. After swerving around a large boulder, a sharp, stabbing pain sliced through his calf and forced him to stop immediately. The piercing pain shot down to his ankle. He bent forward and exhaled sharply as the agonizing sensation climaxed. Michael limped a few yards to the closest boulder and sat down to stretch his leg. He was upset about the injury, but at least it was near the end of his workout. He had to finish the trail and get back to the rectory for some ice. Gingerly massaging the muscle, he recited one of his favorite passages from the Bible.

> Those who hope in the Lord will renew their strength. They will soar on wings like eagles; they will run and not grow weary, they will walk and not be faint. (Isaiah 40:31)

Michael also prayed that he wouldn't limp for a week.

Chapter Seven

Bobby Davis checked his watch and then stepped into Hasco's Bar and Grill. He took a few minutes to let his eyes adjust to the dimly lit room. It was early afternoon, and he knew that she would be there. He just hoped that she wasn't already tanked. He wanted to have an actual conversation with Marty and hoped she could focus long enough to participate. He needed to talk to her about Willow. It had been one year since Elizabeth, mother-in-law from hell, had happily died. Every time he went to the bar, it was late, and Marty was too drunk to talk. He hadn't been privy to all the legal arrangements after Elizabeth had died. The lawyer, Mr. Bradford, kept him away from the will reading at the direction of Elizabeth herself. That damn woman was still controlling things from the grave.

Hasco's was one of the oldest bars in Rocky Meadow. It was an old building filled with cigarette smoke most of the time. The remainder of the time, it smelled like beer. On the left, there was a bar running down the length of the wall. Behind the bar was a large mirror that had been hung fifty years ago. In front of the mirror, the liquor bottles were lined up, giving a decorative look as well as respite to the thirsty. The bartender was a tall beefy man with salt-and-pepper hair named Tony. If he wasn't actually pouring a drink, he was busy drying a glass or wiping the bar. He would keep a towel in one hand with an extra thrown over his left shoulder. He was a kind man who simply wanted to make a living. He watched over his regulars and made sure they had a cab when they needed one. Tony was their therapist when they felt like talking and their bodyguard when unwelcome friends came to visit. He kept a bat behind the bar at all times, and when he had to come out and use it, there was always a good show. When he didn't have time to leave the bar, he kept a loaded 9mm handgun within reach.

In his previous life, Tony Noce had been a cop with the NYPD. An undercover case went wrong, and his partner, Jim Hasco, died as a result. He felt responsible even though it wasn't his fault, and he traveled to Vermont to offer his personal condolences to Jim's father. They talked for a while about how Jim's mom had passed away years ago and all Jim ever wanted to do was to be a good cop. Jim's dad was grateful for the visit, and when he passed away from cancer, he left his bar to Tony as he had no other family. Tony had to make a choice to either sell the place or move to Vermont and run it. He had owned the bar for five years now and never regretted leaving the city. Even though it was only early afternoon, his spine started to tingle when Bobby Davis walked into the bar.

Bobby walked into the room, planted his feet, and looked around with a sour expression on his face. To his right were tables and chairs for clients who wanted to feel like they were in a real eating establishment. In the far right corner was a pool table with a low-hung light casting enough illumination to see the pool balls. Directly in front of him, against the wall, were a series of booths that were virtually in the dark. That was the area you chose when you didn't want to be seen. He was pleased with himself as he moved toward the booths and realized she was already there. Just as he had expected, she didn't look well. Her face was pale and sallow. She looked gaunt with unkempt, dry hair, and her eyes were bloodshot. Her frame looked thin under the cheap clothes she had purchased from the local consignment shop. In front of her was an untouched plate of ham and eggs along with a steaming cup of coffee that Tony had just finished making. As Bobby sat down, he was relieved that she didn't have any body odor. She looked up from playing with her eggs and realized that he was just sitting there staring at her.

"What do you want?" Marty asked as her head pounded from last night's binge and recognition dawned on her face.

"Just to talk to my lovely bride of fifteen years," he responded with a sarcastic smile. "After all, today is our anniversary."

"Screw you," she responded, noting that he looked as good as ever. He was still trim and wore a tight-fitting black T-shirt tucked into tight jeans. His hair was clean cut, and although it was just spring, he had a fairly decent tan. She noticed the little scar on his cheek. Always the charmer, he was just dripping with sweetness. The same way a viper drips saliva before delivering his fatal bite.

"You did, sweetums, fifteen years ago. That's what got us into this mess to begin with. If you had kept your legs closed, like your mother told you to, we wouldn't be having this conversation right now," Bobby said arrogantly.

Marty flipped him the bird. "Once a jerk, always a jerk. If you were able to keep it in your pants once in a while, it wouldn't have mattered. What the hell do you want, Bobby?" Marty noted that Tony was standing at the bar watching them talk.

"I want to talk to you about Willow. You remember her, your daughter? Our daughter?" he said with a plastic smile on his face.

"What about her? Is she okay? You didn't go near her, did you?" Marty started to look anxious.

"Actually, I haven't seen her since your lovely mother died. That brings me to one of my questions. How much was the bitch worth anyway?"

"I don't know," Marty said as she shrugged her shoulders. She held her temples as a result of her pounding headache with her head cocked to the side. She knew that Bobby wouldn't be asking about Willow because he missed her. Marty was devastated when Bobby had rejected her and the baby. She really thought that Bobby loved her as much as she loved him. When he changed his mind and married her, she hoped that they could work things out. They hadn't been married more than a month before she caught Bobby in bed with her best friend. At first, he tried to tell her that he was uncomfortable having sex with someone who was pregnant. It wasn't long until she realized that Bobby was actually comfortable having sex with anyone who was willing. She immediately regretted the marriage but never divorced him, thinking that the baby would change his mind. She had been wrong. Once the baby was born, Bobby ignored both of them. She became depressed, and her mother dragged her to the doctor's office again. They couldn't tell if the marriage was the problem or postpartum depression, but either way, she refused to take the pills. Elizabeth took over complete care of Willow. Marty started drinking full-time, and Bobby finally took off. She always wondered why Bobby hadn't divorced her, and now her suspicions were coming around. He had married her for the money. Thank God Elizabeth had headed that fear off at the pass. "Why do you want to know? You're not getting any of it."

"Well, I recently ran into a lawyer friend of mine." He looked her straight in the eyes. "He told me that since we're still married, I'm entitled to half of everything you got and as the legal parents for our daughter, we can challenge her current guardian."

"You suddenly want to be a papa?" Marty asked sarcastically.

Bobby slapped his hand on the table. Marty felt like she jumped about three feet in the air; her heart was pounding. "I want to be rich," he screamed. "Filthy, stinking rich. Your tightwad mother should have been worth over fifteen million dollars, and I want some of it."

Tony suddenly appeared at the table with a pot of hot coffee in hand. "Marty, you need some fresh coffee?" Marty knew all she had to do was say the word and Tony would probably smash the hot glass pot against the side of Bobby's face. Instead, she took a deep breath.

"Thanks, Tony, I'm okay, for now. I may need some in a few minutes, though."

"You got it, babe." Tony gave Bobby a dirty look and stormed off, his knuckles white on the coffeepot handle.

"Thank God I didn't want anything in this dump," Bobby complained.

"The only thing that you're going to get from here is thrown out on your ass," Marty yelled. "First of all, the only lawyers you ever talked to were the ones who caught you in bed with their wives. Second, my mother's lawyer went to extra lengths to write us out of the will because we abandoned our daughter. He even threatened to file criminal charges if we ever saw her again. I get a lousy stipend each month to use for booze or food as I choose. Neither one of us is getting anywhere near that money. It's in a trust fund for Willow, and the lawyer controls all of that."

"Well, what if you straightened out your act and tried to be a mother to Willow? She could share anything with you that she likes, now couldn't she?"

"And you think that I would naturally share it with you?" Marty's laugh was deep. "If that's your plan, why don't you get close to Willow?"

"Because she barely knows me. I don't know what that lousy lawyer told her, but she looks like she's going to faint every time she sees me."

"Good, the girl's got brains."

"Well, let me ask you this. What happens if our little dumpling turns eighteen and has a tragic accident? When someone isn't married, doesn't their estate automatically go to their parents?" Bobby asked with a sarcastic grin.

Marty's stomach heaved. Whatever color she had drained out of her pale face, and she started shaking. Her voice was low and breathy. "Listen, you bastard. You stay the hell away from my daughter. If you lay a finger on her, I swear I'll hunt your ass down and kill you myself." Marty turned to the bar and yelled, "Tony, I need coffee, right now." She turned back to Bobby and said, "I'm sure that the lawyers have all of that covered. If not, I'll call Mr. Bradford and make sure you rot in hell before you ever see a dime of my mother's money. You leave Willow alone and get the hell out of here. Now."

Bobby's fist was clenched on the table. Tony appeared with a bat in his hand and a mean look on his face. "The lady asked you to leave, get out."

Bobby spit in his face. "Believe me, pal, she ain't a lady. I've screwed her."

Tony used his sleeve to clean his face. He then turned to Bobby and rammed the bat into Bobby's stomach. When Bobby doubled over, Tony grabbed the back of his shirt and half carried him out the door to the sidewalk. As Tony threw him into the street, he yelled after him, "Don't make me regret letting you live today, and don't ever come back."

When Tony returned to the bar, Marty was sobbing in the corner. She was shaking and looked like she was going to vomit. Tony sat next to her and wrapped his bare arms around her. She leaned into his shoulder and sobbed harder. She tried to talk, choking on her words. "Tony, I am such a failure. I can't believe I was ever in love with that piece of garbage. First, he leaves me and Willow, and now, he's going after the money." Another long spasm of sobs broke out. "What am I going to do? He said he'd kill her." The tears ran down her face and onto his shirt.

"Marty, let me ask you a question," Tony said gently. "Do you love your daughter? I mean, what's up with this arrangement anyway?"

"Yes, I love her. I sometimes watch her when she doesn't realize I'm near her. She looks like I did at her age. So scared sometimes." Marty started crying again.

"Did you ever talk to her?"

"I'm afraid."

"Of what?" Tony asked.

"I'm afraid she'd tell me to get lost. I wasn't there for her. I left my baby." She choked on snot dripping from her nose.

"Here, use this," Tony said as he handed her a clean handkerchief.

"Thank God my mother took care of her. I wasn't there for her. I was always feeling sorry for myself."

"Well, your mother's been gone a year now. What's Willow doing now?" Tony asked.

"She lives out on the farm. She has a guardian, and I think someone cooks for her. She gets homeschooled, and the lawyer makes her do community work at the hospital, and the church, I think," Marty said while she sniffed.

"Any friends?"

"Not that I know of. I really managed to screw her up, didn't I? I don't even know what her favorite color is," Marty said as she looked up at Tony. "That bastard threatened her. What should I do?"

"Well, we have to tell the police and the lawyer so he can make some arrangements. If she's worth a bundle, she may need protection from a lot of people."

"The lawyer's going to think the same thing about me. He'll think I'm just getting close for the money," Marty said with a sad look on her face.

"Look, a threat is a threat. You're not asking for anything, but if you want him to believe you, clean yourself up. Stop drinking and start taking care of yourself. You know I've tried to help you before, but it's really important now. You have to do this for yourself, her, and for me. I hate to see you killing yourself like this."

"I know, but what if I can't?"

"For once, just do this. You have to if you want to protect her. The best way to keep an eye on her is to be with her as much as possible."

The tears started falling again. "You've been such a good friend to me. I don't know where to start. I don't even know what to do."

Tony held her away from him. "For one thing, your drinking days are over. Let's take you to the doctor, and we'll get some help. With a little healthy food, you'll be better in no time."

"I don't have enough money for the doctor. If you weren't letting me stay here, I would have been on the street long ago. I don't get it. You've helped me and never asked for anything in return."

"I've had my share of people help me when I needed it most. When you're better, you'll pass it on to someone else. Besides, I like you," Tony said awkwardly. "Look, it's time for you to take some responsibility and stop feeling sorry for yourself. Come on, go to the bathroom and clean yourself up. We're going on a road trip."

"Where are we going?" Panic started to seep into Marty's face.

"Well, it's still early. We have two places to go. First, we'll notify that lawyer of yours that Bobby made the threat. He didn't actually do anything except flap his jaws, but it wouldn't hurt to have it on record. After that, you and I are going to the free clinic at the hospital. Now go, get washed up," Tony said as he pulled her up and steered her toward the bathroom.

Chapter Eight

After finishing her medical charts, Amy placed them on the rolling cart in the medical records' room. Dictating medical reports was tedious, but she would hate being suspended from the hospital as punishment for not having done them. The information was vital when the patient was seen for follow-up treatment. Electronic medical records were easier than old-fashioned paper records as long as you knew how to work a computer, your passwords worked, you understood the software, and your hard drive didn't crash. Would it still be called paperwork?

Amy left the medical records' room and headed toward the outpatient clinic. She had promised to volunteer for a couple of hours and she was eager to get started. The program director, Kathy Wilson, was standing in the hall, sipping her coffee, as Amy rounded the corner. She looked as though she had the weight of the world on her shoulders. Grinning, Amy greeted her with a wave and asked, "Hey, just how bad is it?"

"What makes you think it's bad in there?" Kathy asked with a sarcastic smile on her face.

"Well, let's see. You're standing out here, leaning against the wall as if you're single-handedly holding up the building. You look tired, and you're sucking down that coffee as if it was the elixir of life." Amy pointed to the empty beverage cup.

"Anything else?" Kathy asked tiredly. "Okay, I'll admit that it's a tad crazy in there. But then again, I wouldn't want to discourage you before you get started."

"So in other words, you'd lie if you had to in order to get me in there?" Amy asked.

"Like a rug, baby, like a rug," Kathy replied.

Amy started to laugh and shake her head. "You got me here, and there's no going back, so you might as well bring me up to speed."

Kathy took another long sip of her coffee and said, "Well, you have the usual array of patients scheduled for blood work and physicals. The lab is running about two hours behind. You're the only doctor that showed up today despite the fact that three doctors were on the schedule, and there's a large group of patients gathering in the conference room to hear a diabetes lecture. Unfortunately, I don't have a nutritionist to give that lecture since Becky started having stomach cramps and left for home."

"Is that all?" Amy raised her eyebrows. "Does the administration have a clue that you need help down here?"

"Yeah, they have a clue. The hospital budget has been cut to bare bones. They still want to offer clinic services because a lot of people don't have insurance. The good will is there, but we don't have the resources, so I'm told to just do the best I can. If I begged you to stay until we're under control today, would I stand a chance?"

"Who else is here?" Amy questioned.

"We have two nurses, a lab tech, a secretary, and a candy striper."

Amy burst out laughing. "That's ridiculous. I don't believe it." Amy was lost in thought for a moment. "Well, I would need at least one nurse with me to perform procedures. The lab tech can draw the blood. You and the other nurse would have to triage the remaining patients until I get to them."

"Really? You'll help me out? Bless you. Bless you, big time."

Amy shrugged. "What else can we do? If anything serious comes in, send them to the emergency room."

"I would be more than happy to," Kathy said as she smiled. "What about the lecture? You have any ideas about that?"

"Well, do you have a tech guy?" Amy asked.

"Who?" Kathy asked with a confused look.

"I don't know the official term, you know, a tech guy. Do you have a person who's in charge of audio-visual stuff? When I was in Boston, we would teach a lot on the Web. Haven't you ever watched a webinar?"

"Not really, but we have a diabetes tape," Kathy offered hopefully.

"Wow." Amy shook her head. "Well, get the tape running for the lecture group, have the volunteer pass out some diabetes literature, and I'll answer questions for ten minutes when they're done. You can schedule a follow-up lecture when Becky feels better."

"Sounds like a plan." Kathy tossed her coffee cup into the garbage pail, took a deep breath, and said, "Let's go."

For the next several hours, the team of women busied themselves in the clinic. They concentrated on registering patients and escorting them to the exam rooms. The patients were examined and treated according to their various ailments. Amy made time to give a quick lecture on the importance of diet and exercise for diabetic patients and entertained several questions.

In the early afternoon, a lunch cart was wheeled into the clinic from the hospital cafeteria. The hospital administration had been kind enough to provide lunch for the staff and volunteers. When the final patient left, they all sat down to share chicken soup, cold sandwiches, and standard hospital-issued chocolate pudding in the small conference room attached to the clinic. Nestled next to several different bottles of soda and water was a large bowl filled with ice. The remaining cart was filled with paper napkins, plates, cups, and plastic utensils to enhance their dining experience.

"At least we got lunch today," Kathy mumbled as she opened a plastic-wrapped tuna fish sandwich. She held up her soda in a mock toast. "Well, ladies, we made it. I couldn't do it without all your hard work, and I really do appreciate the effort. I would especially like to thank Dr. Amy, who is officially now my hero."

"You're welcome," said Barbara, one of the nurses. "Do we have to leave a tip for the lunch cart?"

The volunteer med tech spoke up and said, "I'll leave them a tip. Don't eat here." The ladies all spontaneously broke out into laughter.

Amy looked at the small medical party assembled around the conference table. "How does this clinic work? I mean, how does the hospital keep it running?"

Kathy shrugged her shoulders and answered her question, "Lord knows. I'm the only person who gets a meager salary. I find volunteers from other departments in the hospital that are willing to come in and see patients who don't have insurance. The only problem is that we don't have any resources anymore. It's hard to get test kits, gloves, or meds when I need them. I can hardly get human help."

"So why do they keep it open?" Amy asked.

"Well, it does show some community support, and the minor problems we can treat here actually do take a burden off the emergency room. Otherwise, the ER docs, as you are well aware from working over there, have to stop working on more difficult patients just to order strep tests. Sometimes, the ER gets jammed with routine patients sitting around for hours. Some of the patients have insurance, but the reimbursement from that barely pays for our supplies. I just wish that we had a more organized approach to the staffing," Kathy said as she sighed heavily.

"Do you mind if I talk to someone in administration about it?" Amy asked.

"Would you?" Kathy couldn't believe her ears. "Maybe they'd actually listen to you."

Amy looked pensive. "Well, I might have some ideas to coordinate the care between the emergency room and the clinic."

Kathy bowed to Amy in mock salute. "May the force be with you."

The rest of the ladies started to chuckle. Amy took a few minutes to officially meet the other members of their makeshift team for the day. Most worked for the hospital and enjoyed giving back a couple days a month. They pointed out that they would be more excited about working in the clinic if it were more organized or if they received a small stipend or a better lunch cart for that matter. Amy turned to the young volunteer.

"Hi, I met you in the ER the other day. Your name's Willow, right?"

"Willow Davis, like the tree," she replied as she made a sarcastic face.

"Willow is a pretty name. Are you interested in medicine?"

"No. I don't mind helping people, but I don't like medical things," Willow said flatly.

"Then, why are you working in the hospital?" Amy asked curiously.

"Because I have to," Willow stated bluntly.

Amy shook her head in surprise. "What? Why do you have to?" Amy was confused.

"It's a long story," Willow said. "Basically, I have no real parents. My grandmother raised me until she died, and then her lawyer took over as my guardian. He thought it would be a good idea if I did some volunteer work at the hospital and the church, you know, to explore my options." She said this as she made quote marks with her fingers.

"I take it that you aren't considering a future in medicine then," Amy said awkwardly. She felt bad for this young girl who looked so sad and angry.

"No, I like to help people, but needles make me nervous." Willow stared down at her feet.

"What do you do with your friends for fun?"

"I don't have any friends, and I don't have fun," Willow said as she swallowed hard.

After an awkward silence, Amy cleared her throat and said, "Willow, please remember my name. It's Dr. Amy Daniels. If you ever need anything, call me. I hope we can work together in the clinic again someday. I promise, you'll never have to go anywhere near the needles." Amy made a vow to herself to look after this poor girl. There was more to her story, and she needed some help.

"Thanks, Dr. Daniels," Willow whispered.

"Call me Amy, please. We can be friends." Amy extended her hand for a handshake. "Okay?"

"Okay, Amy." Willow took her hand with a small, embarrassed smile.

Clearing her throat, Kathy jumped up from the table. "Well, ladies, I guess that wraps up the day. Go and enjoy the sunshine while you have some afternoon left."

"You don't have to tell me twice," the med tech murmured as they left the table to collect their things.

Chapter Nine

Father Victor Cerulli shifted in his airplane seat as he gazed out the window to his right. He always enjoyed watching the miniature view of the landscape speed by when he was flying. Victor was happy that his seat was in the front of the plane, so he didn't have to spend the entire trip staring at the wing. He had transferred to the smaller plane after his layover in Newark, New Jersey, from Chicago, earlier in the day. Flying from Chicago, he had been seated in the middle of three seats of a Boeing 737. As he was a tall man, he had some difficulty with the cramped space and was surprised that the airline hadn't charged him extra money for his height. Perhaps they showed mercy when they saw his clericals. At least, he could enjoy the view from the window on this flight. He was still cramped, but he was distracted as well. At that moment, overhead static interrupted his thoughts.

"This is your captain speaking. We are beginning our descent to the Burlington, Vermont, area. The temperature is currently fifty degrees on the ground, the winds are northeast at fifteen miles per hour, and the sun is shining brightly." The Fasten Seat Belt sign lit up with a loud ding. "We want to thank you for flying our airline and hope that your trip was pleasant. Please place your seat and table trays in an upright position and stay seated until we have come to a complete stop. Have a great day and we'll see you again soon."

Victor started to collect his garbage for the stewardess walking down the aisle with a refuse bag. Once his tray was clear, he pushed it toward the back of the seat in front of him and turned the clips to the proper position. He could hear the landing gear being lowered in the middle of the plane. He sat up straight, raised the back of his seat, readjusted the carry-on bag at his feet, and fastened his seat belt. As he gazed out the window once again, he noticed that the trees were much closer and looked larger than several minutes ago. He always got nervous when the plane was ready to land, as if the wheels would touch down and the plane would explode on impact. The ground rushed by faster than ever, and Victor gripped his armrests while he steeled himself for the landing bump. He resisted the urge to cross himself and simply took a deep breath and closed his eyes. Within seconds, the plane hit the ground with a small bounce, and the roar of the reverse thrusters sounded. Victor's stomach clenched in a knot until the plane speed slowed to a reasonable pace. Most of the passengers breathed a sigh of relief and started to applaud appreciatively.

As the plane came to a stop, the travelers jumped up and started pulling their bags from the overhead compartments. The aisle was already jammed with commuters eager to depart the cabin. Victor had noticed two other priests board the plane in Newark. They had been seated in various parts of the plane and were waiting in line to disembark. There might have been additional priests, but these two were the only ones who wore their clericals, so Victor assumed they were on business and wondered if they were headed to the same destination.

Eventually, the travelers in the aisle line, as well as the passengers standing in nearby seats, began to exit the plane. The cabin began to slowly empty as everyone filed out past the stewards and pilot.

Victor had several pieces of luggage as he had traveled from Chicago and planned to stay in Vermont for several months. Heading into the main terminal and looking for the luggage pickup area, he noticed a man standing at the end of the escalator holding a small white sign. Written on the white placard in black magic marker were the words "St. Francis Church." The man was shifting uncomfortably from one foot to another as he eagerly watched the passengers who filed past him. He appeared to be in his sixties with short peppered gray hair. On his nose were glasses, and he was dressed in black work pants and a warm flannel shirt. Father Victor approached him directly.

"Excuse me," Victor asked. "I'm headed to St. Francis Church in Rocky Meadow, Vermont. Are you by any chance going that way?"

A large smile spread over the man's face. "Yes, yes, I am. Jack, Jack Moore," he said as he extended his hand. "St. Francis's taxi at your service."

Victor reached out to shake Jack's hand. "It's nice to meet you. I'm Father Victor Cerulli from Chicago."

Jack shook Victor's hand as he greeted him. He noted that Father Cerulli was a big man. He wasn't overweight, just tall and strong. If he hadn't been a priest, Jack would have guessed he was a professional linebacker. "Well, it's sure nice to meet you. I hope you had a good flight. You've come a long way over the past day or so."

"That's for sure," Victor responded. "I feel like I've been in a sardine can all day. I can't wait to stretch my legs and take a nice long walk."

"Well, Father, don't get too used to stretching just yet. I'm supposed to drive four priests back to the church. I have the minivan, but it'll still be cramped with five people and luggage."

"Well, we all have crosses to bear. I suppose I can wait a little longer. Is it a long trip?" Victor asked.

"Not really, it's about thirty minutes from here," Jack answered as he glanced behind Father Victor. Another priest approached the little gathering. "Are you headed to St. Francis Church?" Jack asked the priest.

"Yes, I'm supposed to be meeting a driver to Rocky Meadow, Vermont," he responded.

Jack Moore extended his hand to the thin cleric and said, "Welcome to Vermont. My name is Jack, and this is Father Victor Cerulli from Chicago. What's your name, Father?"

"Doherty, Father Patrick Doherty," he replied as he extended his own hand.

"Nice to meet you, Father Doherty. Where are you from?" Jack asked.

"Pennsylvania, from the Allentown region," Patrick answered as he greeted both men.

"Well, again, Father," Jack responded with a smile, "welcome to Vermont. We're waiting for two more priests, and then we can be on our way. This may be another one of our guests now."

All three men turned as they watched Father Juan Cordoba descend down the escalator. He looked kindly, but very tired. Sitting on the step in front of him was a small rolling suitcase. Jack held up the placard so that Father Juan could see it as soon as he stepped off the escalator. As his descent came to an end, Father Juan had a brief struggle lifting the suitcase before the last step disappeared underground. A small, tired grin played on his face when he saw the sign, and he gave a half wave. He placed the suitcase on the ground and began to stroll over to the group. "Are you from St. Francis Church in Rocky Meadow?"

"That we are. Welcome to Vermont, Father. I'm Jack Moore." Jack shook the priest's hand and introduced him to the other priests.

"Hi, I'm Father Juan Cordoba," he replied as lines of fatigue played on his face.

"One more guest and we'll be on our way," Jack announced. Beaming, he felt he was doing a great job assembling his guests. After greetings were returned all around, Jack repeated they were waiting for a Father Anthony Lomack. Once they connected, they could retrieve their luggage and proceed to the van.

Father Juan turned to Jack, "Oh, wait a minute. I'm sorry that my head is in such a fog, but a fellow priest approached me in the airport while I was waiting to board the plane and asked me if I was going to St. Francis Church in Vermont. He said that he was supposed to be going as well but that he had decided against it. He gave me an envelope and asked me to give it to Father Michael Lauretta." As he explained, Father Juan pulled a letter-sized envelope from the inner pocket of his black jacket. The envelope was sealed and addressed to Father Michael. He started to give the envelope to Jack.

Jack glanced at the front of the envelope, marked Personal, and said, "Father, why don't you hold on to that until we get to the rectory? Perhaps it would be better if you give it to Father Michael yourself."

"If you think that would be best," Father Juan said as he nodded his head and put the envelope back in his inner coat pocket.

Jack stood up straight and said, "Okay, I guess we're all here then. Let's pick up the luggage and be on our way." The small party of four walked over to gather their things. Their suitcases were among the few items that were left in the pickup area, rotating in a continuous circle around the luggage chute. Jack searched the area for a rolling rack, but they had already been claimed by other passengers, so each priest bent to gather their belongings.

As Jack turned toward the exit doors, Father Victor leaned toward Father Juan and said, "Why don't you let me get those suitcases for you?" Before Father Juan could respond, Victor had scooped up both their bags and was following Jack toward the exit. He looked at ease despite the fact that he was carrying two suitcases in each hand. Juan whispered a silent prayer to thank God as he was already clearly exhausted from his short journey.

Once the passengers, as well as their luggage, were safely tucked inside the van, they left the airport. Jack navigated the van onto Route 89 south toward Rocky Meadow, Vermont. As the new guests watched the restful scenery glide by, Jack began to tell them about the history of Vermont and St. Francis Church. He finished by saying, "Vermont has some of the greatest coffee and ice cream in the world, and I hope you all like warm banana bread."

Chapter Ten

*T*he clear bubble of fluid balanced precariously on the tip of the sharp needle. It would be so easy to walk around the hospital bed and push the needle into the IV port. One second and it would all be over. He deserved to die; he was a scum. The only problem is that the bastard would never know. The injection would provide a peaceful death, much too kind for his sort. He needed to suffer. He should feel pain and beg for mercy. The sound of the door broke her thoughts, and she hurriedly capped the syringe and thrust it in her pocket. Yes, the bastard needed to die, but not today, not now.

Amy sat on the bench, staring at the view across the Divide. Instead of taking in her surroundings, she was lost in her memories. Once again, she found her thoughts back in Boston, to the events that changed her life and those around her forever. She wanted to make sense of it all; she wanted God to tell her why it had to happen. So far, she had no answers. Amy was told she might never know the why of it; she needed to put it behind her and move on. She hadn't made much progress. It didn't matter how many times she reviewed the past; nothing changed.

*   *   *

Father Michael slowly limped down the trail from Devil's Peak. He had just spent the previous hour rubbing his calf and trying to stretch. The pain would subside for a few minutes and then crescendo again as the cramp grabbed his leg. He needed ice, his favorite balm, some tape, and an elastic wrap. First, he needed to get to the rectory and avoid running into Katie in the process. She was already on his nerves about running alone in the woods. Seeing that he was actually injured while away from the church wouldn't help his credibility, but at least she cared.

The sun was warm today, but the woods had stayed cool and pleasant. Looking up, Michael was relieved to see the end of the trail in sight. He knew there was a bench near the exit, and he planned to stop and rest there. The bench was located on the lawn, in front of the church, near the water. The breeze from the Divide frequently brought pleasant relief to those who stopped to pause and enjoy the view. He would often finish his runs in that area, and although the bench looked tempting, he didn't sit as he needed to complete his cool down. Today was different. His leg was painful. He imagined himself limping down the aisle at mass tomorrow and the rest of the week for that matter. Then, he would have to answer a litany of questions from Florence. At least she would be properly informed when she told the other well-meaning members of the parish why he was limping. *Mea culpa, Mrs. Katie Novak.*

As Father Michael hobbled into the clearing, he looked up and saw an attractive young woman sitting on the bench. She had been there several times before, always alone and deep in thought. She wore casual work clothing and never smiled, used a cell phone, or listened to music. She sat on the bench and watched the water as if she had a thousand thoughts flowing along with the current. Expressions would play across her face and give her a mysterious look as if she held many secrets. Most of the time, she just looked sad. He never saw her at mass, so he didn't think she'd come here for the solace of the church grounds, but then you never knew. A new cramp in his calf disturbed his thoughts, reminding him to stop staring and move on. As he approached the bench, she looked up and noticed he was injured.

"Are you okay?" she asked with a concerned expression. "Do you need help?"

"Thanks, I'm okay, but would you mind if I shared your bench for a few minutes?" Michael said with a small, embarrassed laugh.

"Not at all," she answered as she shifted to the left. "Technically, it's not my bench. Are you sure you're all right? You look like you're in pain."

"That I am. I was running through the woods, and my leg cramped up," he said as he rubbed his calf. "I tried to walk it off, but it didn't help. I had to walk down the trail, and I limped the last hundred feet or so."

"Sorry to hear that," Amy said.

"Me too. Maybe it'll help if I just sit for a minute," Michael said.

"Have you stretched it out? Maybe it'll help if you point your toes toward your face," she suggested as her medical experience kicked in.

"I'll give it a shot," he said as he complied. "I've been rubbing and stretching it for a while now. It feels a little better, and then it cramps up again. Hopefully, it's just a muscle spasm."

"Maybe you should call your doctor," Amy said.

"I will if it doesn't get better soon."

"Do you run a lot?" she asked as she noticed the new running shoes and appropriate clothing. Amateur runners usually wore the wrong clothing and wound up getting overheated, blistered, or chafed as a result. He was also trim, muscular, and attractive.

"I try," he said. "You?"

"I used to run. It was a great way to work off stress, but then I had an injury and never quite got back into it." Amy shrugged.

"What do you do for stress now?" People who exercised regularly just always assumed that other people who exercised simply migrated from one activity to another. If you couldn't run, you biked, and if you couldn't bike, you swam, and so on. "If you don't mind my asking," he added.

"Well, I enjoy visiting this bench. It's a very peaceful place," Amy said as she indicated the river and the scenery.

"That it is, there's nothing like God's natural beauty."

Amy nodded her head as she agreed with his thought. "Feeling any better?"

"It's starting to lighten up," he said. "I'll just have to walk for a while until it's healed."

"Sounds like a plan," she said.

Trying to draw her out, Michael continued, "Do you like to walk?"

"As a matter of fact, I do. Since I moved to Vermont, I've started looking for hiking trails," she replied.

"There are some very nice trails in this area. Anything from flat horse trails to rock climbing, depending on your preference."

"Well, I'm not up to rock climbing yet. Besides, I have a hectic work schedule and don't always have a lot of time."

"Well, that makes things a little more difficult then. Some of these trails are fairly long and can take a lot of time to explore," he replied gently. "Some can be dangerous if you don't know exactly where you're going."

"Thanks, I'll keep that in mind."

As he extended his hand, he said, "My name's Michael, Father Michael Lauretta. What's yours?"

"Amy, Amy Daniels," she replied as she shook his hand.

"Nice to meet you, Amy Daniels."

"You too," Amy said, feeling a little confused.

"Have you lived in Vermont long?"

"About six months now," she answered as she looked out toward the Divide. Amy knew where this conversation was headed, and she tried not to encourage a barrage of questions. Her whole purpose in moving to Vermont was to keep under the radar and avoid talking to anyone for a while.

"How about you?" she politely asked in return.

"About three years. I moved up here from New Jersey, and it took a bit of getting used to, but eventually, you don't want to leave. It's beautiful up here, not like the rat race in Jersey."

"I know what you mean. I grew up in New Jersey," Amy offered with a smile. "But it's very different now. Between 9/11 and the taxes going up, it's changed quite a bit."

"What part of Jersey are you from, or should I ask what exit?" Michael asked. He remembered that most people who lived in New Jersey described where they lived by stating what exit they used on the Garden State Parkway.

"One-four-five," she answered with a laugh.

Michael laughed with her. Maybe he could get her to relax and open up. "Good old Jersey, I do miss some of it. By the way, you have a wonderful smile."

"Thanks," Amy said self-consciously.

"I have a confession to make," Michael said sheepishly. "I've seen you here a couple of times when I've been out running. Are you part of St. Francis Church?"

Amy shook her head. "No, actually, I . . . ah . . . haven't gone to church in a while. I'm kind of working out a couple of issues with that." Amy's face turned red as she finally realized she was talking to a priest.

Michael chuckled and said, "Isn't everyone? I didn't mean to pry. It's just that I've seen you on this particular bench a lot, and I thought maybe you were considering joining the church." *Great,* Michael thought. Now he looked like he was stalking her. He couldn't believe that he was doing such a lousy job of meeting someone. To cover his embarrassment, he stood up and took a couple of steps. He placed both hands on the back of the bench, stretched his leg out behind him, and placed his heel flat on the ground.

"How's the spasm going?" Amy asked gingerly.

"I think it's better, thanks. I need to throw a little ice on it when I get back to the rectory."

"That sounds like a good idea," she said awkwardly, clearly at a loss for words. Her peaceful meditation was apparently over for the day. Amy pointedly looked at her watch. "Well, I'm sorry, but I really have to be going. Are you okay? Can I give you a lift somewhere? My car is on the street near the bridge." Amy stood and held her car keys.

"No, I'm fine," Michael said. He felt embarrassed, and he didn't know why. "The spasm is less, and it'll be better if I walk some of it off. The rectory is right over there."

"Okay, then I guess I better get going." Amy tried to keep herself from sprinting toward her car.

"It was nice to meet you, Amy," Michael said as he extended his hand once again. "I appreciate your help."

"You're welcome," she replied shyly as she took his hand. She noticed he had a firm handshake, but soft hands. "Nice to meet you too. Be careful on those running trails."

"Thanks for the tip," he said with a smile.

"You're welcome," Amy said as she turned and started walking toward the covered wooden bridge that crossed over the Divide.

"Keep smiling," Michael called after her.

Amy turned back and offered a wave with a small grin.

Still smiling, Michael turned toward the church and began to limp back to the rectory. He didn't know what her story was, but she certainly looked like she needed someone to talk to. He was hoping that he would run into her again although he wasn't exactly clear on why he felt that way.

Chapter Eleven

Dr. Louis Applebaum paused at the bedside of Benjamin Lawrence and watched the cardiac monitor intently. Ben's heart was in normal rhythm. After being stabilized in the emergency room, Ben had been transferred up to the cardiac intensive care unit. His vitals were holding nicely, but he hadn't woken up yet. Then again, if he had a cerebral bleed, he wouldn't mentally be himself even if he did wake up. The whole scenario didn't make sense. From a medical standpoint, Lou knew that a major piece of the puzzle was missing. Once he figured out exactly what happened, he would be able to treat Ben more efficiently. For now, all Lou could do was wait and hope he could ask Ben himself at some point.

Lou reviewed the completed test results that had been placed on the chart. There was no trace of toxins, infections, or an oral blood thinner. Ben's case was clearly a mystery, but not the first. The suddenness of this event reminded him of the way Elizabeth Sharpe had died.

Elizabeth had been healthy when she died. She had just had a normal stress test, and after several years of depression following her husband's death, she was finally enjoying life again. Elizabeth tried desperately to help her daughter, Marty, with her alcoholism, to no avail. Thankfully, she had a great relationship with her granddaughter, Willow. Elizabeth was in the process of making plans for her and Willow to reopen the stables since they both loved to ride horses. Unfortunately, Elizabeth had died suddenly, and all the plans were thwarted. Lou felt sorry for Willow and occasionally saw her working in the hospital. He wanted to reach out to her but she seemed frightened and tried her best to avoid him.

Lou finished signing his current orders and placed the chart on the nurse's desk. The staff of the cardiac intensive care unit would continue to monitor Ben's condition throughout the evening, and he'd get a call immediately if there was any change. With luck, it would be a positive change. If not, he needed to find out why his patients were dying.

Chapter Twelve

Using an elastic wrap to secure an ice bag to his calf, Michael leaned back in his office chair. As his gaze traveled out the window to the grounds beyond, he allowed himself a deep sigh. The lawns around the church were well manicured, and the distant vision of the mountains and green hills of Vermont was beautiful. As he relaxed, the throbbing in his calf seemed to diminish. He had enjoyed the challenge of Devil's Peak but wouldn't be able to return to that trail for another week. He had also enjoyed meeting Amy Daniels. She was a lovely, attractive woman, yet she seemed extremely guarded and didn't let her defenses down easily. Sitting on the bench deep in thought was clearly a daily habit for her. Michael had wanted to reach out to her for a while and was trying to gauge her reaction to finding out he was a priest. Hearing that she had issues with the church, he thought his title might be better left unsaid, but honesty was the best policy after all. Michael received different reactions from people when they found out he was a priest. Sometimes, the conversation turned polite and veered away from worldly matters as if a priest never read a newspaper or had an opinion of life situations. Occasionally, a stranger would want to unload their emotional burdens as if a curbside confession would free their soul. Either way, he was there to serve.

As Michael continued to look out the window, he saw the church minivan pull into the parking lot. After a minute or two, Jack Moore hopped out of the driver's seat and headed toward the rear of the car. The remainder of the passenger doors opened, and three men exited the vehicle. They were all dressed in clericals, and Michael knew they were part of the new group of clergy to be counseled. One priest was missing, and Michael hoped he wasn't lost at the airport. Perhaps their guest had missed his plane. Michael would find out. These priests were assigned to him for counseling and obliged to attend if they wanted to continue their ministry. If someone decided not to show up, Michael was compelled to make the archbishop aware of the situation.

Jack opened the hatch of the car and removed the luggage. The guests picked up their bags and moved toward the front of the rectory. There was a very large priest, who, without any apparent effort, scooped up four bags at once. Michael guessed that was Father Victor Cerulli. He looked like a boxer. It would be interesting to meet his new guests, but in the meantime, he needed more ice for his calf.

Chapter Thirteen

Marty and Tony quietly walked out of Mr. Bradford's office. They had spent the last hour sitting at a table, speaking openly with the lawyer. Luckily, Mr. Bradford had agreed to see them immediately. He spoke fondly of Elizabeth as she and her husband had been friends with him for many years before their deaths.

"Marty, you know that your mom was always very worried about you," the lawyer explained. "She tried to do everything she could to help you stop drinking. All the arrangements she made were there to protect you and Willow in the event of her untimely death."

"Thank God for that," Marty cried. "I know I haven't been a great mother, and I guess I was a lousy daughter. I've apparently spent the last fifteen years having the biggest pity party known to man," Marty said with tears spilling down her cheeks. "I don't even care about myself anymore. I just want to make sure that Bobby can't hurt Willow."

"Apparently, Elizabeth was worried about the same thing," Mr. Bradford replied. "She never liked or trusted him, and she was always afraid for you as well. She wanted you to be happy and healthy. Marty, let us help you. Your mother made provisions for you to take care of your health and live a normal life. Tony seems to be a good friend to you. Let him take you to the hospital so you can register with the clinic. It's never too late to start recovery."

"You think so?" Marty replied. "I've lost everything. I'm thirty-two years old. I've lost my daughter, my mother, my health, and my self-respect. I have no home or independence. I don't even have a driver's license."

"That's been your choice, but you can work to get all that back," Mr. Bradford encouraged her. "It won't be easy in the beginning. You'll have to see a doctor and go to Alcoholics Anonymous meetings. You'll need to live a healthier lifestyle, but like I said, all the arrangements have been made. Just make the commitment, and we're there by your side."

"I don't think I can do it. I've been drinking for too long. I feel horrible every day. I swear to myself every night that I won't touch another drop of alcohol. As soon as the next day rolls around, I'm reaching for the bottle," Marty cried dejectedly.

Tony gently took her hand. "Marty, you're living with an addiction. Your body starts to go through withdrawal when you don't drink. That's why you reach for the bottle, to stop the shakes. Look at your hands now, you can't keep them still. We either have to get medicine for you soon or you'll have to take a drink just to avoid having a seizure."

"Well, right now, I'd rather have to the drink," Marty responded with a weak laugh.

"Your mother had a will of steel," Mr. Bradford comforted. "Just try to channel her energy and you'll be fine. Don't worry about Bobby. We've had our eye on him for a long time. Right now, Willow is protected legally, and she has her appointed guardian taking care of her at the house. However, I'm sure she'd really appreciate having a mom to take care of her as well. First, you've got to take care of yourself. All the bills will be covered. Your mom was adamant that the finances always go through my office. To be honest, even when you've reached a decent level of sobriety, I'll still be handling the money, so Bobby can't hassle you for it. When you've reached ninety days of sobriety, we can talk about you moving back to the farm with Willow."

Marty looked at Mr. Bradford. She had an awful headache, her hair was a mess, and her clothes were rumpled. "Thank you for helping us. But most of all, please watch out for my daughter. Despite the fact that I wasn't there for her, I love her more than anything in the world," she said with fresh tears falling down her face. "Bringing her into the world is the only thing I've ever done right in my life."

"Marty, let's go." Tony gently took her hand. "We need to get to the hospital before you change your mind. I'm sure Mr. Bradford has many other things he has to attend to."

"Okay, just give me a minute to go to the bathroom," Marty said as she got up. Before she left the conference room, she shook hands with the lawyer and thanked him for his time.

"You're welcome, Marty. We'll meet again when you're well," Mr. Bradford assured her.

When she had left the room, the lawyer turned to Tony. "Thank you for looking after her. Let me know what she needs and I'll take care of it. That includes clothes, food, medicines, whatever. I knew her when she was a little girl and had the privilege of watching her grow up. I hate seeing her like this. Elizabeth will rest more peacefully if Marty is able to straighten herself out."

"I'll try my best," Tony replied.

"Let me know if you see Bobby again. I'll get the police involved if I have to."

"Thank you, sir," Tony said with a handshake. Two minutes later, Marty and Tony were heading out the front door on their way to the hospital.

Chapter Fourteen

Katie opened the door to the rectory and ushered the new guests inside. She waited while Jack followed them in and closed the front door. "Welcome, welcome to St. Francis. We've been expecting you," she said with a large smile on her face.

Jack smiled back and then introduced her to the three new guests. "Everyone, please meet Katie, housekeeper extraordinaire. She'll be taking good care of you while you're here. I promise you that."

"Jack, stop that," Katie said with a slight frown on her face. She turned to the new priests. "Hello, everyone. You must be tired and hungry from your trip. I'll see you to your rooms so you can relax for a few minutes. When you're ready, come back down to the library for some refreshments before dinner. The library is over here on the right." Katie pointed to a large room off the main hall.

The entrance hall was modest in decor. There was a table that held a nice arrangement of spring flowers. The walls were dark, and the floors were laid with carpeting. There was a beautiful wooden staircase ascending to the second floor. When the three priests turned to locate the room Katie had just referenced, she said, "If you need anything at all, please let me know, we'll get you settled in a jiffy. If everyone is ready, you can follow me upstairs and I'll show you to your rooms."

Katie turned and started walking up the staircase. The new guests grabbed their luggage and followed her to the second floor. When they reached the landing, Katie turned to the right and started down a long hallway. "Okay, let's see," she said, somewhat deep in thought. "Father Cordoba, you will be staying in the St. Francis de Sales room. That's this first room to the right. As I'm sure you know, St. Francis de Sales is the patron of editors and writers." Katie laughed. "Perhaps, you'll feel like writing your experiences in a journal while you're here. At any rate, I think you'll be comfortable, and if you need anything at all, please let me know."

"Thank you, Katie. I'm sure I'll be fine," Father Juan replied with a wink, but not before Katie noted how exhausted he was. Father Juan entered the room with his bags in hand. Once inside, he placed his luggage on the floor. Within minutes, under a warm comforter, he was sound asleep on the bed.

"Okay, next we have the St. Patrick room for Father Doherty. I don't want you to think I'm profiling you, Father Doherty, but I think that you would rather like this room," Katie said with a smile.

"Well, we'll see, won't we?" Father Doherty said as he thanked Katie and stepped inside. Katie thought she heard a distinctive clinking noise as he passed her with his luggage.

Katie and Father Victor Cerulli were all that remained. As they traveled further down the hallway, Katie stopped at a room on her left. "Father Cerulli, you'll stay in the St. Vincent de Paul room. This is a lovely room and a bit larger than the others. You have a particularly wonderful view of the Divide and the mountains beyond. But please, Father, don't brag in front of the other priests."

"Don't worry, Katie. This will stay our little secret. It's a beautiful room indeed, and the view is quite inspirational," Victor said as he looked out the window. "By the way, Katie, I'm sure that you know that St. Vincent de Paul is the patron of charitable groups. I appreciate your consideration. I'll see you in a little bit."

Katie smiled and said, "Enjoy, Father. I must attend to the dinner now." She turned, and closing the door, she headed down the back stairs that led to the kitchen. When she reached her destination, she noticed Jack standing near the stove looking into the pots and pans.

"Jack, why do we only have three priests? What happened to Father Lomack?"

Jack shrugged. "He didn't show up at the airport. He gave one of the other priests some sort of letter for Father Michael. I don't think he's coming."

"Oh." Katie looked disappointed. "Okay then. Well, I guess that'll be one less dinner plate. Jack, it's late. I made enough food for a football team. Would you like to eat with me in the kitchen?"

"What did you make for tonight?" Jack eagerly looked around.

"I made a delicious eye round with green beans, mashed potatoes, and gravy. We have chicken soup to start, and there's apple cobbler for dessert."

Jack's mouth was already watering. "Katie, my girl, I'm ready when you are."

"Well, we should have a bite now. Once our guests come downstairs, I'll be busy serving refreshments and dinner. First, I have to tell Father Michael that everyone is here. Go wash your hands and I'll be right back." Katie hurried off to find Father Michael and deliver the news.

After an hour or so, Father Michael approached the library. He was still slightly limping, but the ice had quelled much of the pain, for now. He had gone to his private quarters, freshened up for dinner, and was now prepared to meet his new guests. Katie had told him that Father Lomack had not been at the airport but that one of the priests had some information for him. As he walked into the library, he saw two of the new priests engaged in conversation. Katie had laid out fresh iced tea and cheese appetizers. One of the priests, Father Doherty, was drinking wine.

"Good evening. Welcome to St. Francis. I'm Father Michael Lauretta," he said as he introduced himself. "We've been awaiting your arrival. I see that you've already been getting to know each other. 'For where two or three gather in my name, there am I with them.'"

"Evening, Father." Victor reached out a beefy hand. "Father Victor Cerulli from Chicago."

His other guest reached over as well. "Father Pat Doherty, nice to meet you, Father."

"Same here, as soon as we hear from Katie, we can go have dinner." Father Michael continued to speak to the two new priests. He asked about their trip and welcomed them personally to St. Francis. After a few minutes, Father Juan anxiously walked into the room. Father Michael greeted him warmly and smiled.

"Good evening. I'm Father Michael, Welcome to St. Francis. It's nice to meet you."

"Hi, I'm Father Juan Cordoba, and I'm really sorry that I'm late. I put my head down for a moment and must have fallen asleep," he admitted anxiously.

"Not a problem, except that all the appetizers are gone. We're about to go have dinner, so you can relax," Father Michael said with a smile as he remembered that his case files indicated that Father Juan had been diagnosed with terminal cancer. Juan looked tired and pale. His retreat at St. Francis was more for spiritual restoration than any other reason, and Michael expected him to have more physical problems than his other guests.

Katie appeared in the doorway and nodded to Michael from the hall. He turned and announced, "If you're ready, we can all go into the dining room and enjoy a delicious dinner from our housekeeper, Katie. I believe that you've all met her. Her cooking has a reputation for miles, and I'm sure that you'll be pleased. Once again, if any of you have special requests, please let her know." Michael then turned to face Katie as did all the guests in the room.

Katie smiled. "If you'd all follow me to the dining room, we can get dinner started. You must be starving." She turned and started down the hallway with four men trailing along like ducklings following their mother. Once they arrived in the dining room, they arranged themselves for dinner, leaving the seat at the head of the table for Father Michael. He entered the room last and sat down. Tucking his napkin over his lap, he smiled at his guests and said, "Shall we pray?" They all quieted and bowed their heads. "Heavenly Father, we welcome our guests today, who have safely traveled a distance to be with us. We thank you for their presence and for the graces you have given us in our lives. We ask that you continue to watch over us, that we may continue to offer our blessings to those around us and bring love to them as well. We remain in you as you remain in us. Amen."

The group all murmured, "Amen." Father Michael looked up and said, "Could someone please pass the potatoes?" They all chuckled and began to pass the food that had been laid out on the table. Katie bustled in and out of the dining room, clearing dishes and refreshing their drinks. As the group enjoyed a sumptuous meal, they began to relax and engage in conversation.

"So, Father Michael," Victor said, "tell us about St. Francis."

"Well, our St. Francis was named after St. Francis of Assisi who you all know is a patron of ecologists, animals, and florists. The original church and grounds were built with private donations, and the property was used for years as a retreat house for religious personnel and troubled parishioners. As a matter of fact, it was first called the Rocky Meadow Retreat House. The original retreat house, which now serves as the rectory, had twenty guest rooms installed that were dedicated to visitors searching for spiritual enlightenment and welcomed all religions and backgrounds. The National Forest, as well as the river and mountains, provide a very tranquil place for people who need respite. After a while, the local congregation grew to the point that they needed a community parish, so the archdiocese decided to devote the church to the community. It was renamed St. Francis. We now serve approximately three thousand parishioners with three weekend masses and one daily mass. We never opened a school, but we do offer religious education. In addition to the regular parish business, St. Francis still serves as a beautiful haven for fellow brethren to heighten their spirituality and help with the parish since I am the only full-time priest. Every three months, the archdiocese sends us new priests to work with. We occasionally still have guests from other religions and disciplines as well. We miss the guests who leave us, but they come back to visit, and we have Katie and Jack full time, and that is truly a blessing."

"I haven't seen much, but what I've seen is beautiful so far," Father Doherty said as he reached for more wine from a bottle he himself had supplied.

"St. Francis is truly an awe-inspiring property," Father Michael replied as he watched the priest fill his glass for the second time. "You'll see for yourself when you get to explore the full grounds. We have a beautiful prayer walk in the forest that overlooks the mountains and valley in various spots and is divine. I'm sure that you'll be pleased as you get to walk around a little more in the next few days," Father Michael replied.

"What else can we expect?" Victor asked guardedly.

"Well," Father Michael said slowly, "we have morning mass at nine o'clock daily. After we celebrate tomorrow's mass, I'll be meeting with each of you to assign your duties and firm up your schedules." Michael didn't want to fully elaborate as he didn't want to breach confidentiality. Some of the visiting priests came simply for vacation and respite; however, others, such as this group, had been assigned for counseling as well.

Katie then scurried into the room with a cart laden with coffee, tea, and the apple cobbler. She served each priest according to their desire and whisked the remaining dishes from the table. As she prepared to leave the room, she gently announced, "In the morning, breakfast will be served buffet-style in the dining room. If you happen to miss the meal for any reason, come see me in the kitchen and I'll take care of you."

"Thank you, Katie. Your reputation is well deserved," Father Victor stated. "I'm afraid that I'll be gaining weight during my stay here." The gentlemen all laughed and attended to their dessert.

Father Michael caught Katie's attention on the way out and whispered, "You did a wonderful job tonight. The meal was delicious. If you need any help, let me know. I'm good at dishes."

"Father Michael, you know that we have a dishwasher," Katie replied. "Thank heavens for that. I think I'll be just fine. But if you want to come to the kitchen, you can get more ice for that leg of yours." With a wink, she pushed her cart from the dining room.

As each of the priests finished their dinner, they began to stand and stretch. One by one, they said good night to their host as they left the dining room to return to their rooms for prayer and relaxation. As Father Juan said good night, he paused for a few seconds. "That was a wonderful meal. I thank you for your hospitality."

"You're welcome, Juan. I'm just glad that you enjoyed it."

"That I did. Father, when I was at Newark Airport, I was approached by another priest. His name was Father Anthony Lomack. He asked me to give you this envelope and to tell you he was sorry," Juan said as he handed the envelope to Michael.

"Did he say anything else?" Father Michael inquired.

"That was it. He said you'd understand when you read his letter. I promised him that I would give it to you. He didn't want to mail it. I hope that everything is copacetic. Good night, Father."

"Good night, Juan. Sleep well." As Father Juan left the room, Michael glanced at the envelope. The contents would provide interesting reading for sure.

Chapter Fifteen

Standing in the empty room, Amy stared down at the open mahogany casket. The overwhelming silence pressed in on her causing her heart to pound. Resting in a bed of soft ivory satin, her younger sister looked beautiful. In death, the look of horror on her sister's face from a few days before had been replaced with one of peace. An overwhelming sense of loss gripped Amy as she stood there, touching her quiet sister's face. Amy started to cry as she realized that her sister was gone, physically lost to her forever. She had been murdered by that scum. He had taken her only sister away from her, and now, he would pay.

Amy jumped up from her dream, heart pounding and chest constricted. Her breathing remained labored as beads of sweat dripped down her face and into the creases of her neck. Flinging the covers aside, she sat up on the side of the bed, put her head in her hands, and sobbed. The gut-wrenching pain of that dream was as bad as the night she found out her sister had been murdered. As a wave of nausea washed through her, she remembered her niece was still alive, for now. The neurological institute had not given her an update in a while. Amy would have to call them. Now was not the time to falter. *Stay strong and forge ahead. Keep hope alive.* This was all part of the plan, but why? One day, she hoped she would find out why this had to happen to her family.

Knowing from experience, the best thing to do was get ready for the day and distract herself from obsessing. Amy took a hot shower and got dressed to go to work. As she drove through the woods, she smelled the clean, fresh air. She wished her sister could see how beautiful Vermont was. The earthy, clean smell of nature was pure and relaxing at the same time. Life didn't seem as frenetic in Vermont, yet she was still having dreams about the tragedy. Someday, she would figure it all out.

Amy was scheduled to work in the emergency room today. After her shift, she had an appointment with the CEO of Rocky Meadow General

Hospital. She had been thinking about ways to help Kathy energize the clinic. A full working clinic would certainly take some of the burden off the staff and resources of the emergency room. The biggest issue was the financial support. She was willing to work in the clinic and spend less time in the ER if the hospital would allow it. She had only signed a contract to work with Rocky Meadow General Hospital for one year. Not sure if she could even complete the year, four months had already passed and she was still working. She was still broken inside and taking one day at a time, but she was functioning. There were days when things seemed to be a little easier and some days that were not. She told herself again, *Just keep moving forward, like the river.*

Amy parked her car in the physicians' hospital parking lot, picked up her travel mug of hot coffee, and made her way to the emergency room. She had a clean change of clothes in her work locker. For sanitary reasons, she wore scrubs when she was working in the ER. She had learned her lesson the hard way after tossing out mounds of clothing stained with various body fluids over the years. As she approached the central nursing desk, she saw Brenda adjusting the charts on the board. Brenda did a great job of organizing the patients and doctors. Keeping track of tests that were pending, results that had returned, as well as which patients were being admitted or discharged kept Brenda fairly occupied.

"Brenda, good morning," Amy greeted her with a smile. "What have we got going today?"

"Hi, Dr. Daniels," Brenda responded. "So far, things are not too bad. We have a patient in room 1 with stomach pain. We're waiting on the results of a CT scan. Room 2 has a patient with an exacerbation of high blood pressure and a pounding headache. We called her private medical doc, and he ordered some medication. We're watching her and waiting for the meds to kick in."

"Good, keep going," Amy coaxed her along.

"The patient in room 3 has a fishhook stuck in his forehead."

"What?" Amy laughed for the first time that day.

"Apparently, he was standing behind his fishing buddy who isn't very talented at casting," Brenda replied with a half smile.

"That's a first for me. I'll have to remember that if I ever go fishing," Amy stated bluntly. "What are we doing about that?"

"Actually, Ernie should be done removing the fly by now, and of course, the patient wants it back because it was expensive."

"That's too funny," Amy said with a grin.

"Don't ask me how, but Ernie always gets funny cases." Brenda laughed.

"I'll look forward to that. What else do we have?" Amy asked.

"Room 4 has a patient that's here for alcohol abuse. We're waiting for a substance abuse counselor to see if we can admit her for detox or transfer her to another facility."

"How's she doing? What's her blood alcohol level?" Amy asked.

"It's low. She came in late yesterday afternoon. Apparently, she was trying to go to the clinic, but it was already closed for the day."

"I know, I was the only doc there, so we could only work morning hours," Amy explained.

"Oh, that's a real problem here. Anyway, her friend, a big guy named Tony, brought her to the ER instead. She hasn't had any alcohol since yesterday," Brenda reported. "She was shaking a bit, but I just finished giving her medication for that."

"Does she have any history of seizures?" Amy inquired.

"Not that we know of," Brenda answered. "But then, I get the impression that this is the first time that she's really tried to stop drinking."

"Anything special make her hit bottom?"

"They were talking about some family situation. It sounds a bit convoluted at this point. However, I'm sure that when the counselor gets here, we'll get more information. In the meantime, that's about it for now. As far as I know, the other beds are empty and nothing is on the way in." Brenda shrugged and completed her report by placing the charts back on the rack.

"Thanks, I'm going to change. If Ernie finishes, tell him I should be back in a minute, and then I've got the helm." Amy turned and started walking toward the women's lockers at the back of the emergency room.

Chapter Sixteen

Father Michael stood at the top of the stairs in front of St. Francis Church. It was a beautiful Wednesday morning, and he was watching his new priests interact with the parishioners. They had all attended and concelebrated the morning mass. Afterward, the new brethren waited on the front steps while the parishioners exited the church. Florence waited outside with her friends until they were all properly introduced to the new clergy. Father Michael had started the introductions. "Florence, I would like you to meet our new priests for the summer."

"It's so nice to meet you," she stammered as she tried to shake hands with each of them in turn.

"Likewise. It's a beautiful day. May God be with you," Father Victor responded with a beefy handshake and a hearty smile. Florence stared up at him with her mouth hung open and eyes wide as she tried to size up the largest priest that she had ever met.

"You too, Father," she replied in a meek voice. She turned to Father Doherty, who appeared not to have slept well. "I'll look forward to seeing you again, soon. I'm glad that you'll be here for our carnival."

"Me too," Father Pat Doherty replied blandly. "It should be exciting. I'm sure that we'll have a great turnout." As he turned away, Father Doherty stifled a yawn while stretching his neck with his eyes closed to try to release the muscle tension at the back of his head. As Father Michael looked on, he noted that although Father Doherty looked tired, he had more energy than Father Juan, who stood at the top of the steps shaking hands with various parishioners. Father Juan held on to the rail with his left hand while he offered his right hand for greetings. Michael wasn't sure, but he thought he noticed that Juan's right hand was shaking. He would have to remember to check his medical report when he got back to the rectory. Father Juan had been cleared to travel to Vermont, but the trip might have taken more of a toll on him than they expected. Michael wanted to make sure that Juan registered with the local hospital while he was here in case he had setbacks to his health. As Michael continued to observe his new priests, he noticed that Father Pat's hands were shaking a bit as well, but for a completely different reason.

Once the parishioners were gone, Father Michael had asked his new charges to meet him in the library after they had changed and been fed a sumptuous meal by Katie. In the meantime, he needed to go back to his office to put another ice pack on his calf and read Father Lomack's letter.

Chapter Seventeen

Pulling on both sides of the drawstring, Amy cinched the waistband of her scrubs. Years ago, the same outfit had simply been referred to as "greens" and was worn only in the surgical suite of the hospital. Over time, "greens" were produced in many brilliant colors and patterns and worn in a variety of medical departments. As Amy left the women's locker room, she stopped for a final glance in the mirror next to the door. She had chosen a set of dark purple scrubs that nicely complemented her complexion and light brown hair. She knew that by the end of her shift, her scrubs would be stained and rumpled and her hair would be falling out of its clip. With a deep breath, she opened the door of the locker room and made her way to the central desk in the emergency room.

Ernie was sitting at the computer, busily entering information he had collected for his patients. Once the information was entered, the transition of care from shift to shift would be seamless.

"Hi, Ernie, how's it going?" Amy stopped and looked at the computer over Ernie's shoulder.

"Status quo at this point. Nothing too exciting going on," Ernie said. "Brenda's getting ready to discharge most of the patients except for room 4. We're still waiting for a counselor to do an evaluation." Ernie typed in his last sentence and hit Submit. He turned to look at Amy and gave her a big smile. "Hopefully, things will stay quiet for a while. After all, it's only Wednesday. The ER usually starts hopping toward the end of the week."

Amy laughed while she typed in her password so she could continue using the computer. "Where I came from, we were taught to never use the 'q' word. The minute you said that, things were . . . uh . . . you know, you would have a crisis a second. Let's just knock wood and hope for the best."

"Well then, my fair maiden, I offer you my head as the only piece of wood you're going to find in this room." Ernie tilted his head slightly forward in a respectable bow toward Amy.

Amy knocked once on top of his head and said, "Go ahead and get out of here before you jinx me some more. I'll take care of room number 4 since I have some time. Just tell me the patient's name before you leave."

Ernie looked at the computer. "Her name is Marty, Marty Davis. Short for Martina. Considering her situation, she's doing reasonably well. She's had a lot of support from her friend, Tony." Ernie got up from the desk and turned to Amy. "Basically, that's it in a nutshell and I am gone." He waved over his shoulder as he briskly walked toward the men's locker room at the back of the ER.

After taking a minute to review the remaining charts on the desk, Amy walked across the ER to room number 4. She stood at the doorway and noticed a small, thin woman sitting cross-legged on the gurney. Her head was bowed, and dark brown hair hung limply over her tear-stained face. She was holding hands with a big muscular man, and Amy assumed that he must be the infamous Tony. He was obviously trying to cheer her up with small talk and keep her distracted from her current situation. Amy knocked on the doorframe. "Hello, can I come in?" Marty looked up with a frightened expression and nodded. Amy offered a big smile to dispel the tension and eased near the bed. "Hi, my name is Dr. Daniels. I'm taking over for Dr. Ernie Baker this afternoon. He told me you were here, and I just wanted to check in on you. How are you feeling?"

Marty glanced up at the new doctor and said, "I'm very scared and shaky at the minute." She looked over at Tony, who squeezed her hand and smiled.

"I'm sure that you are, but you should be very proud of yourself for getting medical help. How are you feeling physically? Are you having any chest pain or headache?" Amy asked softly.

"Ah, a little headache, and my heart feels like it's jumping out of my chest. My hands are shaking, and I probably could throw up if I thought about it long enough."

"Marty, it's Marty, right?" Amy asked with a smile. Marty nodded her head a few times. "When was the last time you had a drink?" Amy asked while she picked up the chart and started looking through some of the pages.

Marty turned to look at Tony. "What's today?"

A somewhat tired Tony answered her, "It's Wednesday morning." Tony then turned toward Amy. "We got to the hospital yesterday afternoon. We tried to go to the clinic, but it was closed."

"Yes, unfortunately, the clinic does have short hours sometimes. We're trying to work on that," Amy conceded.

Tony continued, "Anyway, Marty was so upset that I thought we should go to the ER. I figured that they could tell us what to do next."

"Go on," Amy prompted softly.

"That's basically it. We're kind of in a holding pattern until we find out what's going to happen. I think that they're waiting for some kind of counselor or something."

"Okay, but let's go back to my original question. When was the last time that you actually had an alcoholic beverage? I'm trying to determine how many hours or days that it's been since you last had alcohol so I can determine if you're at risk for a medical problem."

Marty looked up. "I think it would be Monday night. I'm getting all confused. Tony, was it Monday?"

"Yes, Monday night. It's been about thirty-six hours now," Tony answered for her.

"Are you always with her when she drinks?" Amy asked Tony.

"I'm pretty sure that I am. I own Hasco's Bar and Grill. Marty doesn't really have any place to live, so she stays in the back room. I try to look out for her and make her eat. At night, I also pour her drinks," Tony admitted sheepishly.

Amy quizzically raised her eyebrows. "Do you mind if I ask what your relationship to each other is?"

Marty looked up with a strong set to her jaw. "He's the best friend that I've ever had. If it weren't for him, I'd probably be dead right now."

"Marty, I'm just trying to help you the best I can," Amy said kindly. "I need to ask you some of these questions to determine what to do for you. Apparently, when you arrived at the hospital, a counselor was called in but hasn't arrived yet. If I can get some of this information now, maybe we can get you out of this room sooner."

"Amen to that," Marty snapped. "I'm sorry. It's just that I'm feeling really cranky right now."

Amy turned toward Tony. "Let me see if I understand the situation. Marty is a friend of yours that's staying in a room at the bar. You've been watching out for her in a sense but still letting her drink at night. First, I'd like to know if you can tell me how much alcohol Marty drinks on an average day."

"Well, to be honest, and this is probably going to get her mad, I would guess about two to three drinks each night. She tends to ask for a lot more, but I've been watering them down. Usually, the first one is a real, honest vodka and tonic. As she asks for each additional drink, she gets less vodka and more tonic. By the fourth drink, it's mostly just ice and tonic. I've been trying to convince her to get help for a while now. Since she hasn't been willing to go, I've been serving her less alcohol and weaning her that way. She didn't really seem to notice the difference," Tony said as he looked at Marty from the corner of his eye. He noticed that she was making a face at him.

Amy couldn't help but smile. She liked Tony. He was trying to help even if his method was a bit unconventional.

"Have you had a lot of experience with drinkers, Tony?" Amy asked.

"Well, I was NYPD before I moved to Vermont. So I've seen my share. I own the bar, so I try to keep a close eye on the activity, if you know what I mean."

"Actually, I think I do. Okay, then my next question is, why now? What happened yesterday that you decided to go for broke?"

Tony looked at Marty. "You have to answer that one."

Marty swallowed hard. "My husband came to the bar yesterday and threatened my daughter's life, which scared the living crap out of me. He is, and always has been, an arrogant, self-centered bastard. I was never much of a mother to her because I was too busy drinking and feeling sorry for myself for the last fifteen years. I wouldn't give up the bottle for myself, but I'll stop drinking to make sure that jerk never gets anywhere near my daughter, or I'll die trying."

Small sparks of recognition went off in Amy's brain. "Marty, may I ask what your daughter's name is?"

"Willow, Willow Davis." Marty barely said her name before she started to cry.

"Is your husband her biological father?" Amy asked.

"Let's just say he's the man who got me pregnant. Beyond that, there's absolutely no relationship."

"Marty, I've worked with a teenage girl named Willow in the clinic. Does your daughter work at Rocky Meadow General?"

Marty nodded her as she started to sob some more. "My mother used to take care of her. When she died, her lawyer, Mr. Bradford, took over. He thought it would be a good idea for her to be well-rounded since she doesn't go to a public school."

"I see," Amy stated as parts of the puzzle fell into place.

"You probably know more about her than I do at this point. I sometimes look at her when she doesn't know that I'm watching. I'm afraid to talk to her because I'm sure that she'll just tell me to drop dead. All I want is to tell her how sorry I am," Marty choked out the words through an exhausting string of sobs. "I can't believe I abandoned my own daughter."

"Well, technically, you didn't abandon her. You knew that your mom was with her." Amy put her hand on Marty's shoulder supportively.

"And I knew that my mom would do a better job than I could." Marty blew her red nose on a piece of toilet paper. "I was only fifteen. What the hell did I know about raising a kid? I obviously couldn't even take care of myself. My mother tried to help me, but I wouldn't let her."

"Listen, Marty, I think we've talked enough for today. You must be exhausted. Tony, I hear that you've been here all night as well."

Marty looked up at Tony. "You were with me all night? What happened to the bar?"

"Don't worry. I got Mickey to cover for me. Everything's fine, and that's the least of my concerns right now." Tony looked down at Marty with tenderness in his eyes.

"I owe you so much, I can't believe it."

"Listen, if you want to thank me, you'll do whatever Dr. Daniels tells you to do. We've come this far, so let's finish it this time. Okay?" Tony wiped a tear from Marty's cheek as he held her shoulder with his other hand.

"I'll try," Marty said weakly.

Tony turned toward Amy. "What's next?"

"Well, I think that we'll be able to manage any detox that Marty needs right here at Rocky Meadow General," Amy answered, looking at them both. "I'm going to have Brenda come in, and we'll get you admitted to a hospital room for now. You'll have to go to a special floor, and they're going to ask you all sorts of questions about how you feel. Just answer them as honestly as you can. Sometimes, things can get very emotional when you stop drinking, especially in the face of a potential crisis. While you're there, you'll have some tests to check your heart, liver, and kidneys. We actually have a few medical things to take care of. So just be patient with us. Marty, look at me," Amy directed. "I really think that everything is going to turn out all right. So be brave for now and follow the nurse's directions. Can you do that?"

"Yeah, I'll do the best that I can."

"It may not be easy at times, but just keep plugging. I'm going to get Brenda to help you now, all right?"

Marty nodded her head again and grabbed Tony's hand. "I'm scared."

"You'll be fine. I promise. I'll stay with you or visit you as much as I can."

Amy turned to leave the room, and when Marty wasn't looking, she beckoned for Tony to follow her out of the room. She waited in the corridor until Tony was able to leave Marty's side.

"What's up?" Tony asked with a concerned look.

"You said that you were NYPD, right?" Amy asked him.

"Well, retired, but yeah, why?"

"Were you with Marty when her husband threatened Willow?"

"I was near her, but I didn't hear exactly what he said. All I know is that she went hysterical and I threw him out of the bar."

"Why would he threaten Willow? From what I hear, he hasn't had anything to do with her since she was born. I didn't want to ask Marty because she's already so upset, but I want to know if the threat was tangible enough to get the police involved."

"Well, after I threw him out, we went to that lawyer and told him everything. He was happy that we did and wanted Marty to get help. Apparently, her mother was worth a few bucks and made arrangements for Marty and Willow. We just had to convince Marty to help herself, and Willow is in a holding pattern until she becomes a legal adult. Her husband wanted to know what would happen to the money if Willow were to die after she inherited the money."

Amy's mouth fell open in shock. "Are you kidding me? What a piece of vermin he is." Amy was so angry when she heard about the threat she started shaking. "Garbage like him shouldn't be allowed to walk the streets."

Tony noted that Amy had more of a reaction than he expected. "It's not that I don't agree with you, but unfortunately, we have to wait for him to actually break the law before we can do something. Gary Parker, the chief of police, is a friend of mine. Once Marty is all tucked in, I was planning on having a little talk with him. If we need a restraining order, we'll get it done. Sometimes, that doesn't matter though."

Amy had to take a few deep breaths through her nose to calm herself, and she could feel her face getting hot. "Listen, Tony, I think you're a nice guy. I've met Willow, and I've met Marty. I can take care of them medically, but you do whatever you have to do to keep that son of a bitch from hurting them out there." Rubbing her temple, Amy turned on her heel and walked back to the central emergency room desk while Tony looked after her with a quizzical expression on his face.

Chapter Eighteen

Father Michael sat at a table in the church library with his three new charges. After an informal meeting, he would speak with each of the priests individually to discuss their duties and counseling. "Good morning. Thank you for coming. I hope you all slept well last night. Mass was very inspirational today with all of us gathered together. I wanted to let you know that we're excited about having you visit with us for a while. You'll each receive a schedule, a duty roster of sorts for the next four weeks or so. We have rotated the responsibilities for being the main celebrant for daily mass as well as visitation to the local hospital. We provide the main bereavement support for Rocky Meadow General as well as support for patients that need help with addiction or other spiritual issues. St. Francis also tries to bring communion to our local homebound parishioners. As time allows, we then get involved with helping out our religious education programs and overall community presence. At the end of the four weeks, we'll redo the schedule accordingly. I just want to point out that none of your duties will start until Saturday, so you'll have a couple days for personal reflection and relaxation."

As Father Michael spoke, the three priests watched him impassively. Father Victor occasionally held a smile while nodding his head. Father Pat simply looked at the floor as if he were contemplating the number of different patterns in the commercial tile. Father Juan looked depressed. Father Michael couldn't understand why Victor looked eager about the duties he was going to be assigned. Hadn't these same duties been the reason his anger had surged to begin with? He would find out when they met individually. Father Michael continued, "Our church carnival will be coming up in the next few days. I must say, our carnival usually proves to be an exciting community event, especially for those who love to eat."

"That's the assignment I want," Victor said excitedly while patting his stomach. "I'll humbly volunteer to go daily and test the quality of the food we're offering our community members. After all, we don't want anyone to be at risk."

Michael turned to Victor with a grin. "It's very kind of you to sacrifice yourself, Father, but we may have to ask you to stand at the back of the line if we want to make any money from these concessions."

"Ah yes, the last shall be first. I will try to control myself, Father Michael, I promise. But I must say, all this mountain air is sure giving me an appetite."

Father Michael crossed himself and said, "Lord, bless us all and stand back from the food table lest we get caught up in the cross fire." Everyone snickered for a few minutes while looking at Victor. Father Michael gathered their attention for a few more seconds. "Gentlemen, thank you for joining me. If you don't mind, I would like to spend a few minutes with Father Pat alone. But I'll be talking to each of you individually in the next day or so. In the meantime, have a blessed day." Dismissed, Victor and Juan rose from the table, nodded to Father Michael, and left the room.

Chapter Nineteen

Bobby slowly drank his coffee and continued to look over the local obituaries. He knew it had to be here, but so far, he couldn't find what he was looking for. Benjamin Lawrence had to be dead after that injection. Bobby had injected him with the whole bottle of blood thinner and then left him on the floor of the pharmacy. A simple cough would have been enough to start a fatal hemorrhage. If good old Ben hadn't kept asking questions, he might be alive today. Ben had been getting a little too nosy lately. He was anxious about missing vials from the pharmacy and, of course, immediately suspected that Bobby had taken them. He had been right, but what an insult. Just because Bobby had worked at the pharmacy years ago and knew his way around. Of course, Ben had been right, and that's why he had to die. It always came back to the incident with the stupid cat. Bobby thought back to the days when he needed work and Ben Lawrence had been kind enough to give him a job. Bobby had been fascinated with injections back then. He loved playing with the needles. At first, he would stick them in and out of oranges and bananas. The liquid he injected at the time came from an old bottle of saline he found in the back of the pharmacy. He would feel important withdrawing the medicine from the bottle, holding the needle up to the light, and tapping it a few times to feel official. Just to complete the process, he would inject the saline into a banana at the counter. Eventually, someone would eat the banana, but nothing ever happened because it was just saline.

Bobby didn't want to become a doctor; he just liked playing with needles. When Ben wasn't looking, Bobby started to sneak real medicine out of some of the vials and save it in the syringes. Then one day, he had tried to inject the old alley cat in the back of the pharmacy. Of course, the cat hadn't cooperated and scratched Bobby's face so badly that he needed antibiotics. His face had healed but left him with a scar on his cheek. Afterward, he looked for that cat because he planned to crush its stupid head with a rock next time he saw it. But the cat never came back. Eventually, neither did Bobby. Mr. Lawrence had told him that he was forced to let him go because business was slowing down. Bobby never believed him because he saw the scared look in his eye and the nervous way he kept straightening the already-immaculate counter as he spoke. Maybe Ben had caught on to his antics or saw him take the needles. Bobby wasn't sure, but Ben wouldn't make eye contact when he fired him because he was weak, and now Ben Lawrence was dead. But why couldn't he find the stupid obituary?

Bobby put his coffee down and decided to call the pharmacy. The new chain store pharmacists were the ones actually running the store these days. That's why everything was harder. After Bobby listened to the instructional recording, he pressed zero to speak to the pharmacist personally. While he waited, Bobby mused about the fact that all the vials and needles were coded and counted to the last drop. Bobby could still slip into the back window of the pharmacy with ease. He was able to prowl around at night and help himself to whatever pills and pharmacy items that he wanted. Unfortunately, due to the new electronic system, Ben received reports about what was missing on a regular basis. That's why Ben became nervous and started asking too many questions. Obviously, he hadn't called the police yet because he wasn't quite sure what was going on.

A bright perky voice broke into Bobby's thoughts. "Rocky Meadow Apothecary. This is Becky speaking. Thanks for waiting. How can I help you today?"

"Oh, hi," Bobby said in a timid voice. "Uh, I think that I have poison ivy, and I just wanted to know what cream I should use."

"What makes you think that it's poison ivy, sir?"

"Well, it looks all bubbly, and it's really itchy, and some of the bubbles are oozing clear fluid." Bobby made a face as he lied to the pharmacist. "Mr. Lawrence usually helps me a lot when I have a problem like this. Is he there today?"

"No, sir, I'm afraid he isn't here today. I'm not sure when he'll be back, but it does sound like classic poison ivy. Have you tried a cortisone cream or called your doctor?"

"I haven't tried anything yet. I was hoping Mr. Lawrence could help me. He's always been such a great friend," Bobby pleaded with a fairly convincing tone in his voice.

"Well, if you're a good friend, I suppose I can tell you, but don't tell anyone that I was the one who let the cat out of the bag."

Bobby cringed at the cat analogy, but he couldn't wait to hear what was coming next. "What do you mean? Is something wrong?" Bobby asked the question with sugar-coated concern.

"Well, to be honest with you, Mr. Lawrence is in the hospital," the pharmacist offered helpfully. "We're all hoping and praying that he gets better, but we're not quite sure what's going on."

"What?" Bobby was actually dumbstruck. Ben wasn't dead? Of course, the helpful pharmacist mistook his silence as dismay and continued to offer information. "He's currently in Rocky Meadow General right now, and I don't know when he'll be back."

"You've got to be kidding me." Bobby was amazed and suddenly panic filled. Ben knew that Bobby was the one who injected him. The police could be looking for him right now.

"Are you okay, sir? Maybe I shouldn't have mentioned it, but you said that you were a friend."

"Oh, I'm okay. I was just really surprised by your answer. Listen, I'll try the steroid cream and call back if it doesn't get better."

"In that case, you really should see your doctor, sir."

"I'll do that. Thank you." Bobby hung up the receiver with a thud. Ben was alive? That was a serious problem. He had to get over to the hospital and see what the story was. What else could he do? He couldn't just ask a whole bunch of questions, especially now that the privacy laws were in place. How the heck was he going to get into the hospital with minimal interference? He needed a disguise to get to Ben in hopes that he hadn't spoken to the police yet. And this time, he had to finish the job.

Chapter Twenty

Amy spent the next couple of hours treating patients, completing charts, and stewing about Bobby Davis. It never ceased to amaze her how deeply self-centered some people could be. Just like that scum in Boston. She realized that most of her anger was being triggered by the tragedy. It still boiled and seethed at times despite the move. She was going to have to talk to someone about it soon before it consumed her. She needed a psychologist, but she didn't want to tell her story to anyone at the hospital. *Concentrate on your work, think about it later.*

"Hey, Amy, what are you doing?" Dr. Lou Applebaum leaned on top of the central ER nursing desk.

"Just the usual stuff in order to keep the place going," Amy replied.

"Is it bad today? You're not looking very happy." Dr. Lou smiled kindly.

Amy looked up at Lou. "No, not really. It's me. I have to finish up here and then go talk to the administration about the clinic." Amy shrugged.

"Good luck with that. Why don't you try to catch some sunshine? It's a beautiful day outside. Do you have time to take a break?"

"Not right now, Lou, but thanks. I'll get to that sunshine as soon as I possibly can, believe me." Amy smiled at Lou, but she was thinking about the fact that it would never be a beautiful day for her sister again. She would never be able to step out, sit on her favorite bench, and enjoy any day courtesy of one self-centered bastard. "First, I have to escort a patient to the cardiac intensive care unit."

"Hey, while you're up there, take a look at Ben Lawrence and let me know what you think."

"How's he doing, Lou? Is he any better?"

"Well, his blood levels have all stabilized. He showed a little more activity this morning, but he hasn't come to consciousness yet. We still don't know what actually happened, but it's not your average case, I can tell you that. Even when he does start to talk, we're not sure if there's going to be any permanent damage, so we may never know."

"Well, hopefully, time will tell. I'll look at him when I go up there. Let's just hope for the best." Amy smiled. "Now, why don't you go catch some of that sunshine while you still have the chance? I hear that it's going to rain again tomorrow."

"Well, are you sure you can't take a break?"

"I really can't, Lou, maybe next time," Amy said.

"Okay, in that case, I better get going. See you tomorrow." With a wave, Lou hurried toward the exit doors.

Chapter Twenty-One

Father Michael sat with Father Pat Doherty at the small table. "Thank you for staying and speaking with me, Father."

"Call me Pat," Father Doherty offered in friendship.

"Okay, then Pat. I'm curious, what do you think of St. Francis and Vermont?"

"It's a beautiful location for the Lord's work," Pat answered with a smile but looked uncomfortable.

"Yes, that it is," Father Michael agreed. He sat back in his chair and looked at Father Doherty. "Pat, do you know why the bishop sent you here to St. Francis?"

After clearing his throat and shifting in his seat, Father Patrick Doherty responded, "I believe that there were a few concerns about my performance lately."

"Do you think they were valid?"

"Somewhat. However, I don't think they're as much of a crisis as some people would think."

"What do you think is the main problem?" Father Michael asked the million-dollar question gingerly.

"Stress. There's a lot of stress being a priest these days."

"I would agree with that." Father Michael nodded. "I guess then the question is, how do you handle your stress?"

"What do you mean?" Father Doherty raised his eyebrows.

"Well, how do you dissipate your stress? How do you blow off steam? What do you do when you're ready to punch a hole in the wall?"

Father Doherty laughed. "Why, I pray, Father. You should know that."

Michael nodded with hands folded in front of him. "What I do know is that we're all human, and handling our human reactions sometimes means engaging in behaviors that may not be spiritually rewarding. However, when our human reactions spiral out of control, we need a little help. Do you think that you need help, Pat?"

"I'm not so sure of that, Father Michael," Father Doherty answered coolly.

"Well, you realize that I can only act according to the reports that I receive from your bishop. Apparently, some of your parishioners were concerned about the amount of alcohol that you've been consuming lately."

"Since when are priests not allowed to drink?"

"Well, that in itself has been debated for years and in different areas. I don't know that the problem is being allowed to drink as much as whether you're in control of the alcohol or it's in control of you."

"I can handle my liquor," Father Doherty replied in an agitated voice.

"How many days has it been since your last drink?" Michael asked directly, knowing that Father Doherty had several bottles of liquor in his bedroom for immediate use.

"I have a glass or two each day, Father Michael. It helps me relax, sometimes."

"Do you ever crave alcohol?"

"There are times when I do look forward to a drink. Just like other people look for dessert or a cigarette."

"Most of the time, all of those habits are self-destructive. It's okay to have an occasional dessert or glass of wine at dinner, but when the habit persists, despite the fact that you suffer from physical problems or a loss of control, we enter the arena of addiction."

"I'm not an alcoholic, Father Michael."

"Pat, I'm not here to label you in any way. This is not a formal intervention. I simply want to help you. Some of your parishioners felt that you seemed to be having some difficulty. I don't know exactly what your situation with alcohol is, but I'm hoping that during your stay here, you'll be able to sit back and reevaluate your daily habits."

"What if I feel that my 'daily habits' are fine?"

"Well, I guess we'll have to discuss that later. In the meantime, when was your last physical?"

"Excuse me?" Father Doherty asked.

"I wanted to know when you had your last medical exam. One of the requirements of your stay at St. Francis is to have a medical checkup. If you haven't seen a physician in the last six months, we're going to have to ask you to have a physical at Rocky Meadow General. We just need to make sure that you're healthy enough to carry out your duties."

"I'm sorry, Father. Is this a retreat or a boot camp for priests?" Father Pat asked angrily.

"It is a mandatory retreat, Father Pat. The purpose of the retreat is to make sure that you're healthy from a spiritual, emotional, and physical standpoint. Once we've established that you are, we'll all be a lot happier and have fulfilled our responsibility to the Lord as well as our parishioners," Father Michael said kindly. "You're not in prison. We can't force you to stay here. However, we are giving you an opportunity to reassess your life situation, and if you want to return to an active parish life, you'll have to meet a few requirements. Also, while you're here, you'll be assigned certain duties and you'll be evaluated during those duties."

Father Pat flushed and clenched his teeth. "What, may I ask, do you have in store for me?"

"Well, besides helping out with the daily activities around the church, we have assigned you to be the spiritual representative for the local addiction center at Rocky Meadow General. You'll attend their meetings, lead the prayer portion of the group, and offer spiritual counseling."

Father Pat laughed sarcastically. "Will I be known as a spiritual leader or a patient?"

"You'll simply be viewed as the image that you and only you decide to set forth, Father Pat."

"I see. Will there be anything else, Father Michael?"

"I just want to remind you that your duties at St. Francis will start on Saturday and we'll meet twice a week to check on your progress. In the meantime, I might suggest that you spend some time with the Bible reading Proverbs," Michael said as he stood up. "Father Pat, try to have a peace-filled day, relax and de-stress, without the alcohol."

Father Pat stood up and nodded toward Father Michael. "Thank you for your concern." He couldn't wait to go upstairs and have a drink.

As Pat left the room, Michael sat at the table thinking about his own ways of getting rid of stress. It was true that being a priest was becoming more difficult and not giving in to temptation was a challenge. Sometimes, the only way he saved himself was being strong for the others.

Chapter Twenty-Two

Bobby stood at the entrance of the cardiac intensive care unit and looked around. There was a large central nursing desk surrounded by ten separate glass-walled rooms. On the desk were monitors that recorded each patient's heart rhythm on a consistent basis. Various nurses bustled around the unit, assigned to specific duties that contributed to the care of the heart patients. An energetic nurse brushed Bobby's arm as she ran by with medical supplies. Stopping, she turned and said, "Oh, I'm sorry, Father." At first, Bobby didn't respond.

When he finally realized that she was looking at him, he said. "Quite all right, my child." For just a second, Bobby had forgotten that he was dressed as a priest. He knew that he wouldn't be able to walk into the hospital and ask for Mr. Benjamin Lawrence due to the confidentiality laws. However, if he dressed as a priest, he would have instant access to his destination. Disguised in clericals, he arrived at the hospital and asked for Ben's room. The girl at the reception desk told him that he'd be able to find him in the intensive care unit. Unfortunately, she hadn't explained that there were different types. He had already visited the medical intensive care unit as well as the surgical intensive care unit. He had to admit that the staff had been most eager to help him find his target.

"Can I help you with anything, Father? You're looking a bit lost," the friendly nurse asked.

"Well, actually I was looking for a patient by the name of Benjamin Lawrence. I was told that he was in the intensive care unit."

"That's correct. As a matter of fact, you can find him in room 2." The nurse pointed to the left and smiled at Bobby.

"Is he okay? How's he doing?" Bobby asked with his heart in his throat.

"Well, he's stable, I guess. He hasn't really woken up yet, but you can go sit with him if you'd like."

"Has he been like that since he came in?" Bobby asked.

"I'm pretty sure that he's been unconscious since he arrived at the hospital, but you might be better off discussing it with his doctor. Do you want me to call him?" The nurse asked.

"Oh, Lord, no. That's quite all right. I'll just go pray with him anyway," Bobby said nicely.

"Okay, let me know if you need anything, Father," the helpful nurse said.

"Bless you, my child," Bobby responded with practiced charm. His heart rate slowed considerably. At least he was pretty sure that Ben hadn't talked to anyone yet. He needed to kill him before he was alert enough to talk. Bobby didn't see a police guard and thought that was a good sign. How was he going to do this? After the nurse retreated to perform her duties, Bobby walked to room 2. He had a syringe and a bottle of potassium chloride in his pocket. The only problem was that he was in full view of the staff at all times. If he used potassium chloride, death would be almost instantaneous and they would know that he was the last visitor in the room. He couldn't suffocate Ben without being seen. He would have to think of another way to kill him without being obvious.

Chapter Twenty-Three

Ben Lawrence struggled to make sense of the whirling thoughts and sounds in his head. He felt confused and couldn't orient himself to where he was or even what day it was. What had happened? Where was he, and what was this place? He knew something bad had happened. He couldn't remember what. Ben tried to move his head, but nothing happened. He couldn't feel his hands or feet. Ben wasn't even sure if he was breathing. There was no pain, but there was plenty of bright light. Was this heaven? It didn't really look like heaven. People, many different people, kept looking down at him. Some smiled and looked like they were saying something. Some just had blank expressions on their face. Sometimes he would see his mother and father, but he knew that they were dead. Later, he was riding his very first bicycle and felt free, so very free, with the wind in his face. He felt absolutely weightless. Then he was back in the very bright room, but this time he was scared. There was a man with a scar looking at him, and he didn't look very happy.

Ben felt an explosion of adrenaline flow through him. He was terrified, so very afraid. Something was wrong. The man with the scar was dressed like a priest, but that was wrong. He was a bad man. Ben was so confused; he couldn't remember. He had to warn them that this was an evil man, but Ben didn't get the chance before everything went dark.

Chapter Twenty-Four

Amy leaned against the back of the elevator and waited until they reached the fourth floor. She was standing at the head of a gurney carrying an ER patient who had come to the hospital with chest pain and shortness of breath. The patient was examined and had a battery of tests, which indicated that she was in the process of having a heart attack. All the necessary procedures were done to stabilize the patient; her private medical doctor had been called, and Amy was now accompanying the patient to the cardiac intensive care unit. The gurney had a defibrillator sitting near the patient's feet just in case her heart decided to stop en route to her new room. Once in the CICU, the patient's care would be transferred over to the medical team in the unit, and Amy would be able to pay Mr. Benjamin Lawrence a visit.

The elevator announced its arrival to the fourth floor with a small ding followed by the efficient opening of the elevator doors. A responsible elevator passenger kept his finger on the "open door" button until the gurney had completely, and smoothly, been pushed out of the elevator by a male attendant. A left turn had been made followed by a small walk down a bright sterile corridor. Once at the CICU, the automated doors opened without difficulty, and the gurney was brought to the central nursing desk until the charge nurse directed the small medical party to the appropriate room. As the nurses started to transfer the patient from gurney to bed and attached the appropriate sensors and wires, Amy left the room to search out the whereabouts of Ben.

Amy felt like she had known Ben for a while despite the fact that he had never been conscious in her presence. After listening to Lou talk about Ben's life story, he became more real to her. He was a person and not just a disease or a condition. Actually, Ben was still a mystery. They had no more information now than when he first arrived at the ER.

When Amy was in Boston, the trauma patients were easier to treat when she didn't know them or their families. She could concentrate on the patients and their broken bodies without getting emotionally involved. Once you got to know the patients, the wives, the parents, the children, and the friends who sat for hours and days with endless pain, fear, and worry on their faces, it was harder not to become personally involved. It was difficult not to feel their pain. She would cheer when they recovered, and she would cry when they died. But those emotions seemed superficial compared to what she felt after her personal tragedy. She couldn't even think about that catastrophic night without feeling dizzy and nauseous. She hadn't been able to accept it yet. Not now, maybe not ever. If she did, she would acknowledge that it really happened. She preferred to think that she was just on a little working vacation in Vermont and everything in Boston was fine. Right now, she would look for her new friend, Ben Lawrence. Amy was hoping that he would do well and his mystery illness would be revealed.

Amy walked into the room and found Ben quiet in his bed with a priest standing over him. The priest was well groomed, in his early thirties, and with a scar on his right cheek. He looked anxious and worried.

"Father, are you all right?" Amy asked him with genuine concern.

Bobby looked over at Amy. "I'm sorry, what did you say?"

"I asked if you were okay. You look extremely upset," Amy tried again.

"I'm fine, I'm fine, if you'll excuse me." Bobby turned and abruptly left the small medical room. He didn't want anyone to associate him with Ben. He didn't want anyone asking questions when Ben died.

Chapter Twenty-Five

Father Michael sat with Father Juan in the library of the rectory. He had gone back to his office after speaking with Father Pat and made an appointment for all three priests to have physicals at the clinic on Friday morning. Next, he spent a few minutes reviewing Father Juan's file as he wanted to speak to him personally about his physical and spiritual health. Michael knew that Juan was disheartened with the news that his cancer had spread and that he would have to leave his position of parish priest. Father Juan was very close to the youth of his parish, and he apparently felt like he was letting them down with his failing health.

"Father Juan, thank you for meeting with me today. How do you like our little parish in Vermont?" Father Michael asked pleasantly.

Father Juan answered him calmly and with a faint accent, "It's very quiet and beautiful, but with the most respect, it is a little too peaceful for me. I miss the youth in my city and the basketball court."

"You know that this retreat is for you to explore your feelings spiritually and emotionally. Sometimes, you need to leave your immediate environment to have enough privacy to do that."

"I understand that, Father, but I miss my people. When I die, I want to be in New Jersey. I want to be near the people I love and the people that love me."

"Absolutely, Juan. Your wishes are our primary concern. You can leave anytime that you'd like. We just wanted you to have the opportunity to consider your circumstances without interruption by all the people who do wish you well. Sometimes, it's hard to find 'alone' time when a lot of people start to surround you, admittedly to provide for you. But all too often, you wind up helping them deal with the situation instead of concentrating on yourself. Facing the limitations of your physical humanity can be difficult enough for yourself without having to be supportive of others' emotional reaction. It's better to resolve your own personal feelings before you comfort others, and I know that you'll do exactly that when you return to your parish."

Father Juan was quiet, his face reflective. His arms were on the table before him. A single tear traced the line of his cheekbone as it fell to the table next to his shaking hands. "Father"—he choked on the word as he spoke—"I am ashamed of myself. I am asking for your help and forgiveness."

Michael leaned forward and supportively clasped Juan's wrist. "Juan, you have no control over this condition. What could you possibly be ashamed of?"

"I'm afraid to die. I'm afraid to suffer. Yet my whole life has been devoted to serve the Lord. Now that it's time for me to go home, to him, I should be joyous. I should be happy, but I'm not. I'm a coward and embarrassed by my fear."

"Juan"—Father Michael peered into his eyes—"it's normal to be afraid to die, and it's normal to fear suffering. Nobody wants to die. You have nothing to be ashamed of. Fear is a normal reaction to news like this. You need to sort this out, and that's why you're here. Staying at St. Francis will give you the privacy and mental space that you need to confront your feelings."

"I see that, but I wish I was home. I'm having trouble concentrating. Instead of working through anything, I can't focus at all. When I was busy, my inner thoughts would slowly peek through, and I'd either confront them or, I'll admit, ignore them as I saw fit."

"Juan, I promise that we'll work on your return home. I have to make some calls to expedite that. In the meantime, might I suggest two things? First, I have made arrangements for all of us to go to Rocky Meadow General Hospital on Friday for physicals. This has nothing to do with you personally. We'll all have physicals done to make sure that our health is stable."

"Yes, I would welcome that. Thank you, Father."

"Secondly, I can offer you a place to start your journey. Go back to the Bible. We use the New International Version. I want you to read from Psalm 34. Can I read a part of that Psalm for you now?"

"Please, Father."

I sought the Lord, and he answered me;
He delivered me from all my fears.
Those who look to him are radiant;
Their faces are never covered with shame.

"And then," Father Michael continued reading.

> The righteous cry out, and the Lord hears them;
> He delivers them from all their troubles.
> The Lord is close to the brokenhearted
> And saves those who are crushed in spirit.

"That last part is my favorite. So many people seem crushed in spirit these days. Juan, please remember that we're all human. We all go through difficult times and become depressed or anxious, fearful and tired. That's the time to lean on your faith. You will be carried while you are weary."

Juan nodded and smiled. "Father, you have renewed my sense of peace for today."

"Good, I'm glad. Now why don't you have a short walk and then take a nice nap?" Father Michael smiled back.

"That is the best idea yet." Father Juan laughed and stood up. "Thank you, Father Michael. Perhaps I can relax a little after all." The two men embraced each other for a brief second before Father Juan left the library.

Chapter Twenty-Six

The light was becoming brighter. Ben realized that he was back in the bright room again. This time there was a pretty lady looking down at him and talking. He didn't think that she was an angel. He thought angels would wear something white and flowing like a dress. She had on scrubs and a white lab coat. Ben's eyes were barely open, and they felt dry, but he could see her.

He had to warn her about the evil man. Ben remembered that the man had done a bad thing, and it had something to do with Lizzie. Poor Lizzy. She had been so happy since she'd been taking care of Willow, like her life had new meaning again. She was a good friend. Ben always wondered about her death. He didn't think that Willow had done anything wrong, and now he knew. It was the bad man, the one with the scar on his face. The bad man even admitted it to Ben. That's why they had that big fight. Ben had been going through the records and realized that vials of medicine were missing. What was his name? He had to remember his name and warn someone. He had to warn the pretty lady. Names came to him, but his thoughts were all so hazy. Robert, he kept thinking Robert. Yes, he was quite sure that was his name. Why did he look like a priest? He wasn't a priest. He had killed Lizzie, and he would kill again if Ben didn't do something about it.

Ben did the only thing his body would allow. Grabbing the pretty lady's wrist, he screamed, "Rob Liz, Rob Liz." He saw the fear on the pretty lady's face as she jumped at his touch, but all went dark again as he let go of the lady's arm.

Chapter Twenty-Seven

Hoping to find something to help Lou with answers, Amy had been reading through Ben's chart as she stood by the bedside. Ben's vitals were stable, and his lab results were returning to normal. His brain MRI was normal as well. By all indications, he should be awake soon. She had seen her share of trauma patients and knew that healing took time. As long as Ben was stable, he should be all right. Once he was awake, they could do a neurological exam to see if he had suffered any obvious brain injury.

Amy was looking at the clipboard while talking to Ben. She couldn't be sure whether Ben heard her or not, but she always talked to coma patients as if they heard and understood everything going on around them. She was just asking Ben why he wasn't awake yet when he suddenly seized her wrist in a death grip and screamed, "Rob Liz, Rob Liz." Jumping at his touch, her heart started pounding. She stared down at Ben in shock. His eyes were wide open, yet still slightly vacant. Terror tore at his facial expressions. Slowly his eyes closed and his grip loosened as his hand fell back to the bedside. She really hadn't expected that. Amy had been so startled that she dropped the clipboard, hands shaking and stomach clenched into a knot. When she was a child attending her first wake, she had been afraid to go near the coffin. She experienced the same feeling when she started working on her cadaver in medical school and again when she attended her first autopsy. She never wanted to be too close to the body in case the deceased suddenly woke up. Obviously, Ben was still alive, but his sudden burst of activity scared her just the same. His brain was working on some level. Hopefully, he wasn't having a repetitive nightmare.

Amy quickly hit the call button to get a nurse in the room. While she waited, she rapidly rechecked Ben's vitals and listened to his heart. He must be struggling to wake up. She called out to him, but he didn't answer. What did he mean Rob Liz? Was he trying to tell them something? She had no idea, but maybe Lou would know. When the nurse arrived, Amy explained the situation. The attending physician for the cardiac intensive care unit was called, and another round of tests were ordered. In the meantime, Amy wanted to call Lou to update him about Ben's status and see if the expression "Rob Liz" had any meaning for him. Maybe they would soon find out from Ben himself.

Amy left the glass cubicle and sat at the nursing desk. She called Lou's office and was told that he was out. She then tried his cell phone without any luck. Calling his service, Amy left a message for him to call her directly on her cell. She explained that the matter was important and concerned a patient. Hopefully, Lou would receive the message soon.

After checking to make sure that Ben was still stable, Amy left the intensive care unit and headed back to the ER. She had to finish her shift and get ready for her meeting with the administration about the clinic.

Nearing the elevator, Amy was almost hit by a wheelchair that was being pushed by an aide.

"Oh, heads up," Amy hastily reacted.

"Dr. Daniels, you're just the person I want to see," Marty anxiously cried out from the wheelchair as she grabbed Amy's hand.

"Marty, what's wrong?"

"I don't know. What's going on? Why are they taking me for tests? I thought I was just here for detox," Marty questioned nervously.

"It's okay, Marty. Calm down," Amy smiled. "I ordered a few tests because you haven't had a physical in a while. I just want to get a chest x-ray since you've been around a lot of people who smoke. It's also normal for us to do some blood work to check on your liver and kidneys. Once we know that your physical is normal, it'll be easier for you to move on with your program."

"Tony went home, and I'm getting very scared," Marty said peevishly.

"Listen, the next few days are the hardest part. You have to be strong and try to get through them. Every day that you don't drink, every day that you are sober gets you closer to taking care of Willow and starting your new life. It's like going on a diet. Our motivation is always strong for the first few days, and then it starts to fade rapidly. You can do this for yourself and for Willow. Tony will be so proud of you as well. You have a few rough days coming up, but you'll get through them. We're here to help you with that, I promise." Amy tried to be as encouraging as she could for Marty.

"You promise?" Marty asked as the tears started flowing again.

"I promise. Now go get your x-ray so you can get back to your room and relax," Amy ordered playfully. She leaned down and gave Marty a quick reassuring hug.

"Thank you," Marty called out as the nurse pushed her chair toward the elevator. Neither one of them saw Bobby watching from down the hall.

Chapter Twenty-Eight

After he finished his meeting with Father Juan, Father Michael left the library and headed for his office. Now that he had a few minutes, he wanted to tackle part of the growing mound of paperwork on his desk. He usually enjoyed sitting at the polished antique desk handling phone calls and his affairs, especially in the winter when there was a heartwarming fire in the hearth. Today was a little different. His heart and mind felt heavy. His calf was still painful as well. He loved doing God's work and offering spiritual guidance, but the workload seemed to be growing on a steady basis, and the gravity of the work seemed to be increasing as well. Michael was sorry for Juan's grief. It must be frightening to be given a diagnosis of metastatic cancer after one trip to the doctor's office. Michael noticed that as he aged, he didn't have the same energy to tackle all the problems of the world. Instead, he spent a little more time focusing on what he personally wanted from life. What were his goals? What if he were told that he only had three months to live? Would he have accomplished all his dreams? He hadn't even identified them; he had been so busy helping everyone else. The problem was that many of them didn't even want the help. Michael felt a little guilty thinking about how satisfied he was with his life. He vowed to help others, but at what cost?

Michael organized his phone messages and found three from Florence. The carnival was scheduled to begin soon, and she apparently had a lot of questions. He dialed Florence's home, and a man answered the phone on the fourth ring. Michael assumed that he was her husband although Florence was always alone at mass.

"Grand Central Station. Can I help you?" the man boomed into the phone in a not-so-friendly voice.

"Hi, is Florence there?" Father Michael asked politely.

"Yes, she's here," the man returned. "Do you want to speak with her?"

"Yes, I would. I'm returning her call." Father Michael smiled into the phone.

"Who is this?"

"It's Father Michael from St. Francis Church."

"Oh, I'm sorry, Father. She's been getting a thousand phone calls about the carnival. I feel like her personal telephone operator. I didn't mean to be sarcastic."

"That's quite all right. I appreciate all the work you're both doing for the church. I'm sorry. I don't know your name."

"Ted. My name is Ted. I don't usually get to church on Sundays because I drive over to Rutland to help my mother, but I'll be at the carnival, Father."

"Well, Ted, thanks again for all you do. I'll look forward to meeting you. May I speak with Florence?" Father Michael asked again.

"Here she is. Nice talking to you."

"You too, Ted. Please send my blessings to your mother." Michael heard a lot of fumbling with the phone as it was handed from Ted to his wife.

"Father? Father Michael?" Florence asked eagerly.

"Yes, Florence. It's me. How can I help you?" Father Michael answered.

"Oh, Father. Everything is popping around here. The carnival is almost here, and I've so much to do." Florence was speaking so quickly he could only imagine how fast her mind was spinning.

"Florence, remember that we have many volunteers available to help you arrange things. We certainly don't expect you to run a one-man show." Father Michael was concentrating on the fact that Florence did not like to give up control.

"Oh, I'm fine. Besides, Ted's going to help me," Florence replied.

"Well, I'm happy about that," Father Michael replied while imagining Ted making faces in the background. "Florence, how can I help you?"

"Well, I have a question about the food tables. Everyone wants to bring food warmers, and I'm not sure how to handle the electricity issue or how to arrange the tables."

"Florence, you have to call Jack and run the electric by him. We have to make sure that everything is to the town's specifications, or they will close the carnival. That part of the carnival is his job. He talks back and forth with the inspectors."

"Okay, I'll call him. Also, we didn't know where you wanted the stage. If we put the stage in the middle of the carnival, the main music would have to be turned off every time that we have an announcement or an entertainer. If we put the stage near the woods, we may lose a lot of the visitors for the concerts."

"I thought that we decided to have the stage near the food stands. People can relax with a cup of coffee or a dessert while they are listening to the show."

"We did, but then we would have to put it near the middle of the carnival," Florence said petulantly.

"Florence, I realize that. But don't forget, we'll need to turn off the main music when we have mass anyway. Do you really want to walk all the way back to the woods when you have to announce the winners of the fifty-fifty or the food contests?" Father Michael realized that she wasn't happy with the stage placement; however, for the numerous volunteers who needed to carry music equipment and separate sound systems, the trek to the woods would be an extra burden.

"Oh, you're right." Florence was much more agreeable when she realized that she would have a turn in the spotlight as well.

"Good, I'm glad that we are all in agreement. Now, don't forget that you have to call Jack about the electricity arrangements and you need to coordinate with Katie about the kitchen. Last year, we had so many people walking in and out of the kitchen with dirty dishes and garbage I thought Katie would quit."

"Well, I can't control everything, Father."

Michael smirked as he stared at his desk. "Just promise me, please call them."

"Okay, I'll call them. Maybe we can have some of those volunteers work in the kitchen this year."

"Thank you for understanding, Florence. We couldn't pull this together without all of your brilliant plans." Father Michael said the words that Florence so desperately needed to hear despite the fact that she drove everyone else nuts.

"Oh, it's nothing, Father," Florence said brightly.

Father Michael could practically hear her beaming through the telephone. His thoughts were then interrupted by a knock on his office door. "Florence, I have to go, someone's at the door. I'll talk to you again," he said hurriedly.

"Okay, bye, Father," Florence sang out.

Michael hung up the phone and limped to the door to see who had saved him from an extended conversation about plans. Katie was standing in the hall with a lunch tray. "Katie, admit it to me. You're really an angel that was assigned to help me, right?"

"Why? What's wrong? Is Florence bothering you again?"

"How did you know?"

"Well, it's only a guess, but she's called the rectory about forty times. I don't understand it. She insists on being in charge, but then she gets anxious and angry with the burden. Why does she do it?"

"She needs to feel important, Katie. The carnival is her baby. That's the only way she can do it right now. I keep trying to convince her to delegate some of the work to other people, but she isn't ready yet, except for poor Ted. By the way, I told her to call Jack about the electricity and to make sure that she calls you about the kitchen."

"She better get in touch with me. If she keeps sending people in and out like she did last year, I'm likely to smack her."

"Katie!"

"I'm only kidding, Father Michael. I couldn't hurt a flea, but that woman is a bit frustrating, if you know what I mean."

"I know, Katie. Believe me, I know." Father Michael could see a cloud pass over Katie's face. "It'll be all right. We'll be better organized this year, Katie. Please don't get upset."

She looked over at Father Michael and smiled. "I'm okay. Sometimes, I just get inside of myself."

"Well, please don't go too far in. We need you," he said gently.

Katie laughed. "I bought you an ice pack with your lunch. How is your calf today?"

"It's better. It's not cramping as much today. It just feels very tight and sore. Hopefully, I'll be able to get back to Devil's Peak soon."

"You're lucky that you just strained a muscle and didn't fall off the side like in the old days."

"What do you mean?" Father Michael asked.

"Don't you know? That's why it was named Devil's Peak. Years ago, the kids would go up that trail to drink and fool around. After a few of them went over the side, the State Park took over that piece of property. Some of the drop-offs are pretty sheer during the day. A few have a ledge over the side, but I can't imagine what those kids were thinking going up there at night."

"I never knew that. I always wondered how it got that name."

"That trail deserved that name because there was nothing but trouble on it. It's been better since it's fixed up, but it's still a dangerous trail," Katie admonished.

"I promise that I'll pay close attention whenever I use that trail," Father Michael said while he made a cross over his heart with his right hand.

"You see to it that you keep that promise." Katie laughed as she wagged her finger at him. "I like my job."

Father Michael replied with mock astonishment, "Just think, I thought you were worried about me all this time."

"I do worry about you and all the other priests and guests that we have at St. Francis. You know that, Father," Katie said with a smile despite the fact that she looked like she might cry. "By the way, how are our new guests doing so far?"

"Katie," Father Michael said with a heavy sigh, "this particular group of priests needs a lot of support. My job seems to be getting more difficult."

"I don't doubt that. The better you are at your job, the more work you get. Maybe you should slow down some," Katie said with a shrug.

"Katie! Surely, you don't believe that."

"Of course I don't, but I love my job. It's different when you start to burn out, remember that. By the way, I found Father Doherty's hidden stash of liquor bottles when I was refreshing his room this morning. I didn't touch them, just like you said."

"Good. Father Pat has to make the decision to stop drinking on his own. It wouldn't help if we confiscated them. He could buy more liquor anytime he wanted to." Father Michael paused for a few seconds. "I really feel sorry for Father Juan. He's struggling emotionally right now. I wish that I could do more for him."

"I'm sure that you do, but as you always tell us, Father Michael, 'Keep the faith and the Lord will provide.' You'll find a way, I know it in my heart," Katie said with a smile. "Anyway, I don't want to keep you from your work. Enjoy your lunch, Father Michael."

"You're a good woman, Katie Novak. I appreciate all you do for me," Father Michael said. "Are you sure everything's okay?"

"I'm fine, Father. I'm just a little tired today, that's all," Katie said with a sad face.

"Then take a nap and get some rest. I won't tell a soul," Father Michael said to her as she smiled, turned, and closed the door to the library on her way out. While he enjoyed a delicious bowl of tomato cheese soup with a fresh ham sandwich on rye bread, he kept thinking about his new charges. He was planning on meeting with Father Victor Cerulli after mass tomorrow morning. Victor looked like a kind man but one you wouldn't want to tangle with if he was angry. After that interview, he would have to try to contact Father Anthony Lomack to see if he would change his mind about coming to St. Francis. If he continued to refuse, Michael would have to inform his bishop that Lomack hadn't arrived. He thought about the letter he'd received from the struggling priest. Father Michael had read it last night after dinner, but just to be clear, he opened his top desk drawer, retrieved the letter, and started to read it again.

Dear Father Michael,

    Greetings. If you are reading this letter, I am obviously not at St. Francis Church. I have struggled with this decision for a long time now. Several years ago, I met a special woman in my parish. We spent a lot of time together. I find that I spend as much time thinking of her as I do the Lord. I made a vow to love God through all people. However, I also feel that my love is intensified when I am with my friend. We continue with a loving platonic friendship, but I find it harder to act as a close friend to her without our relationship being misconstrued and judged. I do not wish to place shame on ourselves or the church; however, I don't want to lose her friendship and love. Although I am a priest, I'm still human and do get lonely for someone to talk to, confide in, and support me. I promised to love God and promote God, but I am conflicted about whether I want to do that alone or with someone else's help. I would like to be able to show her how much I love her without betraying my vow. I don't know if it's possible.

    I didn't take the opportunity to speak with you at St. Francis as I wanted some time to think things over for myself. I'll speak with you at some point before I finalize my decision, but I wanted to make my own decision by examining the feelings in my heart first.

    I send all my love and contrition and the many blessings that God can bring. I hope to speak to you soon with a clearer heart and conscience.

Yours in the Lord,
Father Anthony Lomack

Father Michael replaced the letter in his top desk drawer. He wished that he could go running and think the situation over; however, with his stiff calf, the most he would be able to manage would be a walk to the bench near the Divide. Father Michael felt a little pang of guilt because he knew that Amy would be there this afternoon as well. He had watched her sit there most days and wondered what she was thinking, perhaps more than he should be. Now that he had met her, he was hoping he would find out. Michael understood Father Lomack's conflict as he saw how the lines of propriety could easily be blurred, but he decided he was going to visit the bench this afternoon anyway.

Chapter Twenty-Nine

Amy walked down the hospital corridor at a fairly decent pace. She had just left a productive meeting with the administration about the clinic. Heading for her locker in the emergency room, she was looking forward to getting out of the hospital and relaxing at her bench. She was surprised by the reception her plan had received.

"If we can build up the services of the outpatient clinic, we can offload some of the nonemergent treatment in the emergency room," Amy explained.

"That sounds like a very reasonable plan, but we can't afford to hire another physician or staff for the clinic," Walter Douglas, the CEO, explained.

"Within a short time, the clinic should pay for itself. We start with minimal staff, and I'll work there as the doctor. I can still be on call for the emergency room if needed. If we take the routine cases in the clinic, we'll save money in our budget for the ER. We'll bill insurance for those who have it and maybe actually turn a profit," Amy proposed. "The rest of the patients can pay on a sliding scale according to their income determined by the social worker and billing office."

"Why don't we talk to the CFO and see what the basic cost would be?"

"I can talk to the other docs and Kathy about the staffing. We can start small in the beginning and add staff as the patient population grows."

"If it can pay for itself or even save funds from the emergency room, I'm all for it," Walter said. "Why don't we gather the info and get back together in a week?"

"That sounds great. You won't be disappointed," Amy said.

"I'm sure that I won't be." Walter smiled. "I'll look forward to next week."

"Thank you, I appreciate your time," Amy said as she left his office. She was hoping that she could get Willow to work there as often as possible. Amy could keep an eye on her, and Willow would benefit by seeing a positive result to her volunteer work. At least the CEO was open to the idea. She hoped the next meeting was a green light.

As she walked toward the emergency room, Amy didn't notice the priest following her in the halls. After getting her purse from her locker, Amy left the hospital through the side employee door and entered the parking lot to find her car. At the same moment, the priest walked quickly out the front door of the hospital.

Chapter Thirty

Bobby followed Amy throughout the hallways of the hospital. Hoping to remain invisible, he ran out of the intensive care unit when she entered the cubicle. She looked too closely at him and was now a threat. He stayed as close to her as he dared without being noticed. Seeing her with Marty near the elevator just made everything worse. He needed to know more and then decide how to handle her. When she entered one of the business offices, he sat in a nearby alcove and pretended to read the multiple magazines that were left on a small coffee table in front of a worn couch. Nearby, a half-finished jigsaw puzzle sat on an old wooden table. He wondered how many people had worked on that puzzle and over what period of time. Bobby wanted to go over to the table and scatter the pieces all over the floor. How many of the patients being prayed for during that time had lived, and how many had died? Maybe a few of them should have been lost like the pieces of that stupid puzzle. Where the hell was she anyway?

Bobby was just about to give up his watch and leave when he saw her emerge from the administrative office and shake hands with a gentleman in an expensive suit. She was smiling and didn't notice Bobby when she walked briskly past him. He raised his magazine in order to hide his face and only lowered it to the table when she was twenty yards ahead of him. He followed her toward the emergency room, and then she turned to exit the building. Bobby continued to move forward and quietly thanked the powers that be for providing parking spaces for visiting clergy in the main circle in front of the hospital. Turning over his engine, he had more than enough time to spot Amy's car as she left the parking deck. It would be better if she had an accident away from the hospital. He needed to follow her to find out where she lived. The hospital traffic was busy at this time of day as all the day shift employees were leaving at once. Conveniently, they each had to stop at that little gate to hand in their parking ticket, which gave Bobby more than enough time to spot Amy in a light green Audi convertible. As she left the parking lot, Bobby turned his rusty old car into the road and carefully blended into the traffic behind her. He followed her for a short distance toward the edge of town. After crossing over a covered wooden bridge, she pulled to the side of the road and parked. Bobby slowly continued past her car until he could park far enough away that he wouldn't be noticed. Locking her car, Amy walked along the bank of the Divide. Bobby thought that she was going to walk directly to the entrance of St. Francis Church when she suddenly slowed down and sat on a bench facing the river. After twenty minutes, she was joined by a man who had come out of the rectory of St. Francis. Bobby watched them until he noticed a blue minivan slowly drive toward him. There was a St. Francis symbol on the side of the van, and it was slowing down. Remembering that he was dressed as a priest, he jumped into his car and left before they reached him. He needed to rethink his plans.

*   *   *

"Jack, do you know who that priest is?" Katie asked as they turned into the road that crossed the wooden bridge leading to St. Francis.

"Nope, never saw him before. He's not one of the priests I picked up in the airport," Jack replied.

"Do you think that could be the missing priest?"

"I don't know, maybe just a visitor? Why would he leave if he was just arriving?" Jack asked.

"Maybe one of the locals just checking out the rectory," Katie decided. "I'll ask Father Michael."

Jack parked the van and opened the doors. "I'll get the groceries inside, why don't you go on in?"

"Thanks, I need to start cooking right away," Katie said as she hurried inside.

Chapter Thirty-One

Amy sat on the bench and watched the cool water rush by. She had spent a long Wednesday in the hot, stuffy hospital, and the cool, crisp air felt refreshing. On the way over, she opened all the windows in her car. The breeze blowing through her hair and thoughts felt great. It was incredible that her discussion with Marty and Tony was only this morning. That was just the beginning. Next, having the life scared out of her by Ben Lawrence and her meeting about the clinic, she felt like she had been in the hospital for three days. She wondered why she hadn't heard back from Lou yet. Amy had no idea if the phrase "Rob Liz" was important or not, but she wanted to ask Lou if he thought it was significant. Just the mere fact that he woke up long enough to grab her arm and start talking was important.

"Mind if I sit down?" Michael asked as he gestured to the bench.

For the second time that day, Amy started as she looked up at him with a frightened expression on her face, her hand over her heart.

"I'm sorry," he said. "I didn't mean to startle you."

"That's okay, it's been that kind of a day," she replied after blowing out a sigh of relief. "Your name's Michael, right?"

"That's right," he replied, pleased that she had remembered.

"How is your calf feeling?" Amy asked with genuine concern.

"It's stiff today, but not as bad as yesterday. I've been icing it as often as I can."

"Hopefully, you'll be able to run again soon." Amy noted that he looked quite attractive in a pair of faded blue jeans and a fitted black T-shirt instead of his running gear. She was sure that he had introduced himself as Father Michael; maybe she had been wrong.

"I've started stretching it out already. A couple of days and I hope to be back to normal."

"Let's keep our fingers crossed," said Amy, cheerfully laughing along.

"So how was your day?" Michael smiled as he asked.

"My day?" Amy was surprised at his question. "Not too many people ask about my day."

"Why not?" Michael asked curiously.

"Well, the question is generally more about what I can do for them than the other way around," Amy said seriously.

"Why is that? What do you do?"

"Nothing special," Amy said sarcastically. "It's just that I'm a physician, and generally people start to ask for medical advice when they see me."

"Like my leg?" Michael asked.

"You didn't ask about your leg, I offered," Amy said.

"That's true," Michael agreed. "Well, so much for my leg, now it's your turn. So, Amy, how was your day?" Michael asked again with a smile.

Amy thought for a few moments before she spoke. "It was typical, I guess. Stress filled and full of aggravation." Amy laughed. "It's probably a good thing that I don't often get asked about my day."

Michael looked straight at her. "The typical physician, always helping someone and never concentrating on herself."

Amy felt a cloud pass over her and thought she could easily start to cry around this man. How could he have gotten into her head so quickly? "What was it that you said you did again?" Amy asked.

Michael felt a brief moment of anxiety and stuttered. "I'm . . . I'm a psychologist. I talk to people to help them with personal issues."

"I see, now I get it." Amy started to laugh again. "Do I look like I have a lot of issues?"

"No, I was just trying to be polite. Although I will say, you do look like you're pretty deep in thought at times," Michael replied.

"Well, sometimes I need to have some quiet time after work to sort things through."

"Thinking time?" Michael chided her.

"Yes, thinking time," Amy defended her position. "My thinking time helps me process a lot of information and make decisions." Amy didn't admit that most of the time she was thinking about the tragedy that still seemed surreal to her.

"I see. And how do you feel about that?" Michael asked with a mischievous smile.

"Probably the same way my grandfather used to feel about taking his naps every day. He would call it thinking time, but he always sounded like he was just snoring to me." Amy laughed. "Don't you ever need thinking time? You know, a few moments of quiet reflection to sort out what all your patients have said to you?"

"I'm teasing you, but yes." Michael nodded his head. "I actually do try to practice some quiet reflection each day."

"Do you have a lot of difficult patients?" Amy asked pointedly.

"Difficult? What do you mean?" Michael asked.

"Well, I mean patients that you don't seem to connect with or patients you feel you're not helping enough?"

"Yes." Michael thought for a moment. "I do have a few difficult patients. It really depends on the situation. Some of them have physical problems, and some have very emotional problems."

"What do you do for them?"

"For the physical problems, I get them to a doctor, like you, as soon as possible." Michael smiled.

"And that's how I wind up sitting on a bench, staring off into a flowing river," Amy concluded her argument. Amy and Michael both enjoyed a good laugh.

"Well, it's a nice place to have thinking time. I have to admit that," Michael acknowledged.

"That it is. We don't often take the time to appreciate the beauty around us and reflect on the important things in our life," Amy said quietly.

"What are the important things in your life?" Michael asked.

Amy's stomach clenched as she realized she no longer had the most important things in her life. She was just floating through day by day. She felt her eyes start to well up and quickly countered his question as she swallowed hard, "Do you always ask so many questions?"

Michael realized that he had hit on a raw nerve and quickly apologized, "I'm sorry. I guess it's a bad work habit."

"It's probably good for work, but in the social setting, I'm used to questions about the weather and my car," Amy scolded lightly.

"Well, what would your friends ask you?" Michael asked, realizing that he hadn't socialized with anyone without acting as a priest or psychologist in a long time.

Amy smiled. "They would ask me, 'What's new?' or 'How are you feeling?'"

"Which brings us right back to where we started," Michael said. "Can we be friends?"

Amy realized that she was actually blushing. "Yes, I think that I'd like that."

"Good, at least we got that cleared up," Michael said as he grinned.

"Well, friend, I hate to say this, but I have to go and get some things done," Amy said tiredly. "It was nice talking to you, and by the way, it's a beautiful day."

Michael sported a large grin. "Yes, it is a lovely day, and I like your car."

Amy laughed as she gathered her purse and keys. She waved good-bye as she walked toward the covered wooden bridge and her car.

Michael called after her, "See you tomorrow, right here at our bench."

Amy grinned and nodded her head as she continued to walk toward her car. Her spirit felt lighter than it had for the past year. Maybe there was hope for her after all.

Once Amy had gotten into her Audi and driven away, Michael stood up and walked toward the rectory. He was happy to have a friend that didn't look at him as a priest or a psychologist. He simply enjoyed her company and hoped it would stay that way.

Chapter Thirty-Two

W illow leaned over the large machine and shoveled crystal clear ice into her sterile bucket. Her volunteer pink smock was sporting a wet spot from where she was leaning on the ice maker. It was Thursday morning. Thursday was her day to deliver ice to every patient room on the sixth floor of Rocky Meadow General Hospital. The patients always appreciated the cool, refreshing ice and some pleasant company. Some of the patients were too sick to notice, and others were so lonely and afraid they'd ask her to stay and talk for a while. A few were just bored and welcomed the distraction.

Yesterday, she had spent the entire day being homeschooled with her new tutors. They made her work much harder than grandmother had, and practice for the SAT exams would start soon as well. Despite the fact that she was practically a very wealthy woman, Mr. Bradford insisted that grandmother wanted her to finish her studies and attend college. Willow wasn't sure what she wanted to study but agreed that a good education would always be helpful besides the fact that she didn't have a choice. Grandmother was a wealthy woman but continued to read and educate herself, and Willow intended on doing just as Grandmother had done. She missed her so much. Grandmother had been her best friend. Willow thought about all the nice people she was meeting at the hospital and the church when she helped out on various committees, but she didn't really have any close friends. Hopefully, one day she would.

Willow heard her name being called and looked up to see Dr. Amy Daniels walking toward her down the long hospital corridor. Dr. Daniels had always been very nice to her. Willow thought that medicine was interesting when Dr. Amy took the time to explain what was happening to the patient and why.

"Willow, how are you?" Amy asked in a bright voice.

"Okay, I guess," Willow replied and shrugged.

"You're on the floor today?" Amy pointed to the ice-making machine.

"Yeah, Mrs. Russo has me working on the sixth floor every Thursday." Willow shifted the cold bucket onto her cart.

"Do you like the sixth floor?" Amy smiled at Willow.

"I guess so, most of the patients are nice, but some of them are a little creepy."

Amy laughed. "Some of them are very sick, but you're right, some of them are also just plain creepy." Amy watched a broad grin spread over Willow's face. "Listen, Willow, I know that you're busy with the ice delivery, but do you think you could meet me in the conference room later today? You should be able to finish all the rooms by then, and I have some important things to talk to you about."

"Am I in trouble?" Willow asked hurriedly.

"No, not at all! I have some news that I want to share with you as well as an opportunity that I'd like to discuss with you. I just want to talk in private. I know that you usually spend some time with the patients, so we can meet after lunch. Sound like a plan?"

"I guess so," Willow said as she shrugged and felt half anxious and half excited.

"Great, let's say two o'clock in the sixth floor conference room. I'll see you later." Amy smiled and waved as she walked away toward the elevator. She hoped that their meeting went well. Willow might not be happy about the fact that her parents were circling around her again, and Amy wanted her to have as much support as she needed.

Chapter Thirty-Three

Father Victor Cerulli sat in the library while he waited for his meeting with Father Michael to begin. They had all celebrated morning mass together and, once again, met with the parishioners outside of the church. Florence had been quite animated as she continued to discuss carnival plans with Father Michael. After mass, they blew out the candles, hung up their chasubles, and returned to the rectory for some delicious banana bread and coffee with Katie. Victor was glad that Katie had not been working with him for years, reasoning that he would probably weigh four hundred pounds by now. She was an excellent cook and housekeeper. Unfortunately, he hadn't had time to work out in a while, and he wanted to find a local gym with a boxing ring. Once he had his schedule and assignment, he would ask Father Michael for some help finding a place.

As Victor continued to wait, he thought about that fateful day in Chicago several months ago that led him to Vermont. As the pastor of his church, he was in charge of all spiritual and administrative business dealings. He concentrated on trying to make the best decisions for all on the advice of the pastoral council as well as the other committees in the church, but it was impossible to make everyone happy. More specifically, he could never make Concetta happy. Concetta was the one parishioner who fancied herself the grand overseer of his parish. For almost a year, he worked hard at handling the business decisions, but he became more and more frustrated, and Concetta would continue to complain. He was even more upset that he seemed to disconnect from his spiritual side to focus on paperwork, and Victor believed that was a bad thing indeed for himself and for his church.

He had been on his way to help his parish priests with the blessing of the throats, an important Catholic ritual, when he had received a call from his bishop. Apparently, Concetta had called the archdiocese again to complain about his last homily. The bishop wasn't overly upset as this was probably Concetta's thousandth call with a complaint, and by now, he realized that she was just an unreasonable person. Everyone missed the former pastor, but after all, he had died, and Father Victor had been chosen to replace him. The bishop had tried to explain to her that even calling Rome would not bring back the old pastor and traditions. Some of those decisions had been made by the archdiocese and were not the sole evil product of Father Victor's mind. Even so, hearing the report on the entire conversation only upset Victor and fueled his huge, hulking frustration.

That frustration was burning within him as he started his blessings, and there she was. He couldn't believe it. There were four priests standing at the altar delivering the blessing of the throats, and she had to be in his line. When she finally reached the altar, he carefully placed the crisscrossed, ribbon-bound white candles against her throat and started the prayer to keep her vile throat from becoming ill. He said the prayer, "Through the intercession of St. Blaise, bishop and martyr, may God deliver you from every disease of the throat and from every other illness related to the throat, even the words that one speaks, in the name of the Father, and of the Son, and of the Holy Spirit." As Victor said the prayer, he made the sign of the cross over her. When he looked up, he saw her standing there with a loathsome look on her face, and he was upset. These candles symbolized purity, and the red ribbon symbolized the martyrdom of St. Blaise to protect one from an ailment of the throat, including making unkind remarks, and she was mocking that ritual.

Victor imagined himself squeezing the candles tighter and tighter around her scrawny little neck and watching that expression change into one of surprise and fright. He imagined her neck veins begin to bulge and her face darken as black as the veil on her head as the blood supply was cut off at her neck. Finally, she would crumple to the ground, and that evil little throat of hers would never utter another complaint about anything.

"Are you having a stroke or what?" Concetta was staring hard and complaining once again. "Those candles have been around my neck for so long I feel like I'm getting my chin waxed."

Victor shook his head and came back to reality. "What? I'm sorry. I guess that I just got lost in my thoughts or something." Inside his chest, his heart was pounding. His daydream had scared him. Choking her had seemed so real and inviting.

"You must have been thinking about something really enjoyable, Father, because you had the biggest smile on your face. I'll be sure to tell the bishop about this little lapse in my next phone call," Concetta sang out with a diabolic grin.

"Yes, you do that," Victor suggested as he watched her pudgy body walk down the aisle with her cane. Victor helped the other priests administer the blessing to the remaining parishioners, and then Victor himself called the bishop as soon as he returned to the rectory and requested an immediate retreat. He wasn't sure if Concetta was just a purely diabolical person or if he was just overwhelmed with his duties, but his fantasy had scared him. What if he had truly lost control?

"Father Cerulli, are you all right?" Father Michael asked as he sat down at the dining room table.

Victor looked up and noticed that Father Michael had quietly slipped into the room during his reverie.

"Excuse me?" Victor asked politely.

"I asked if you were okay. You looked like you were deep in thought. I thought you were distressed or in pain."

"I was thinking about a pain all right, but not the physical kind." Victor chuckled.

"Would that pain have anything to do with your visit here?" Michael asked. "To be honest, I read your file before mass this morning."

"Yes, that would be the pain I was thinking of. That cranky, old, busybody, evil battleaxe that we lovingly call Concetta."

"We all have difficult parishioners to deal with, Father."

"I know, and to be honest, it wasn't Concetta that pushed me here as much as myself. I'm a big guy with a soft heart. However, a lot of people find me intimidating because of my size. I go out of my way to try to make other people feel comfortable around me, but I scared myself when I imagined choking the life out of her. I really got upset wondering if I could actually lose control like that."

"Nothing is impossible. We both know that. Have you suffered from anxiety at all since leaving Chicago?" Michael asked curiously.

"It's funny that you ask me that question. I'm not as bad as when I was in Chicago, but I am having a few moments of anxiety. I was always afraid of my anger," Victor said with a shrug.

"Don't forget that anxiety and anger can be a mere whisper of each other," Michael explained. "They are both expressions of feeling out of control or being overwhelmed."

Victor did not readily respond, so Michael continued with his question. "What do you usually do when you feel anxious?"

"Pardon me?" Victor asked.

"What do you do to get rid of the anxiety? Do you read or pray, take deep breaths, knit, exercise, or ignore it? How do you get through it?"

"I never quite thought about it like that. I guess, I try to say a rosary or pray and hope that it would just pass. Sometimes, I read the Bible. If I feel really nervous, I go to the boxing ring and work out a couple of rounds as well."

"Do you feel like you need to do that now?"

"I'd love to get in a ring now," Victor said.

"Vermont is a wonderful place to pray, meditate, and relax," Michael said.

"Father, St. Francis is a wonderful place to find time for all those things. Just the view from my room is awe inspiring. I've gone on the prayer walk at the base of the hill and plan to make it a daily exercise. But to be honest, I would also love to find a ring somewhere around here. I haven't had a chance to work out for the last couple of weeks, and I feel the difference. You wouldn't happen to know a good gym, would you?" Victor looked hopeful.

"I'm sure that we can find some place for you. Just give me a day or two to look into it."

"I would really appreciate it," Victor responded with a huge smile.

"Don't forget, part of this retreat includes a physical just to make sure that everything is okay and you're fit to box. As a matter of fact, I have us all scheduled for a physical tomorrow morning at the Rocky Meadow General Clinic."

"Friday morning?"

"Friday, that's right. Then on Saturday, you'll begin your assignments. I have assigned both you and Father Pat to duty at Rocky Meadow General. You'll help offer spiritual counseling for those in need and offer communion for those who request it."

"I used to work at a hospital in Chicago. There were times when it was a very difficult assignment."

"Why do you say that?"

"It depends on the group of patients that you're visiting. Most of the patients were very happy to pray, and it helped their fear and anxiety. Some of the dying patients begged for redemption with their eyes. But I learned the most from the faithful patients that have suffered the greatest. To witness their devotion was a humbling experience."

"Then, Father, you have truly been blessed," Michael said with a smile. "Hopefully, more people will appreciate and practice their faith and devotion. If we could only pray for more love and respect in the world and concentrate less on materialism, we may make a difference."

"Amen to that." Victor nodded.

"Father Victor, for now, I would like you to concentrate on a reading in the Bible for me. Please read Ephesians 4:25-32 and start to write a homily about that passage. We can talk about the reading in our next session."

"Yes, of course. That is one of my favorites, if I may quote the Bible," Victor said.

"Please do." Father Michael smiled.

"Ephesians 4:29, 'Do not let any unwholesome talk come out of your mouths, but only what is helpful for building others up according to their needs, that it may benefit those who listen.' And Ephesians 4:31-32, 'Get rid of all bitterness, rage and anger, brawling and slander, along with every form of malice. Be kind and compassionate to one another, forgiving each other, just as in Christ, God forgave you.'"

"A powerful message to be sure," Michael said.

"A homily on this would be interesting indeed," Victor said.

"Yes, and a learning point for you as well. Now, let's both go get some lunch. This mountain air makes me hungry." They both laughed as they left the library and headed toward the dining room.

Chapter Thirty-Four

Amy stepped inside the cardiac intensive care unit and scanned the area. She hadn't heard back from Lou last night, and she was eager to tell him what had happened yesterday. Ben had scared her when he grabbed her arm, and Amy still wanted to know if the phrase "Rob Liz" meant anything specific to Lou.

Amy approached the nurse sitting at the central desk, monitoring the heart rhythms. "Hi, have you seen Dr. Lou Applebaum?" The nurse turned toward Amy and smiled.

"As a matter of fact, I haven't. You're the new doctor here, right?"

"Well, yes, if you count a couple of months as new," Amy teased.

The nurse laughed and said, "This is the first time that I've seen you in CICU. Although sitting behind these monitors, I really don't get to see many people at all."

"Very pleased to meet you." Amy extended her arm in a friendly handshake. "By the way, how is Mr. Ben Lawrence doing today?"

"About the same, fairly unresponsive. We can see that he isn't comatose anymore, but he really hasn't woken up and talked yet."

"Has Lou come by and checked him today?"

"Actually, his partner and the resident were here to check on him. His partner is answering all of his calls as well."

"I see." Amy was a little surprised that Lou wasn't around. "Do me a favor, please let him know that I was looking for him."

"Will do. Don't worry about Mr. Lawrence, though. He's apparently in good hands. He's had a priest hovering over him almost constantly. He must have been very connected with his church or something."

"Do you know which church Ben is connected with? Is it St. Francis?"

The nurse picked up the chart and looked up the registration page. "His religion is listed as Catholic, but otherwise, his church isn't listed. To be honest, St. Francis is the only church in the immediate area, so that must be the one. Although, I haven't seen this particular priest before. I would have noticed him because he is quite handsome. St. Francis constantly has priests rotating through here, and they all help out with the community."

Amy glanced toward Ben's cubicle and noticed the priest standing next to Ben's bed. It was the same priest she saw there yesterday with the scar on his cheek. She made a note to herself to check with Mrs. Russo when she saw her. All the volunteers were supposed to register with her. The sooner they could straighten this out, the better.

Amy turned to the nurse. "Well, I have to be going. Please let me know if you see Lou or if Ben wakes up. I would appreciate it."

"My pleasure, and it was nice meeting you." The nurse waved. Amy half waved back as she headed out the CICU sliding doors.

Chapter Thirty-Five

Bobby watched as the pretty little doctor left the CICU. He had been sitting with Ben for a good part of the day. The nurses were constantly in and out of the room, so he still didn't have an opportunity to act. On the other hand, he was told several times that Ben was not responding and technically in a light coma. If he could only be sure that Ben would never wake up, there wouldn't be a problem. If not, he would have to make sure that Ben died before he was able to tell anyone who had tried to kill him. The longer he stayed in the room with Ben, the less he was noticed. The nurses didn't question his presence anymore, and that would make it easier when he decided to make his move. He was hoping to wait until Ben was moved to a different room, away from the intense observation of the CICU. Bobby still hadn't decided if he was going to use an injection of potassium chloride in his intravenous fluids or just smother him with a pillow. He doubted that a medical examiner would do an exhaustive autopsy on a comatose patient. He had to be careful, though. That pretty little doctor was always asking questions. She was a problem, and she was watching him. He caught her looking at him twice today. Too many questions would lead to an investigation, and he didn't want that. He was already surprised that he hadn't been asked what church he was with. Everyone just assumed that it was St. Francis.

Hiding in plain sight had been easy so far, and it also gave him an opportunity to watch Willow in the hospital. He had walked right past her in the hall. She showed no signs of recognition when she saw him. On the other hand, he had to hide when he saw Marty in the hall. If she realized what he was doing, she'd call the police immediately. That guy, Tony, from the bar was always here too. Both of them had been talking to that doctor. She must know about him. She was definitely a problem.

In the meantime, he needed to concentrate on Willow. He had been watching her whenever he could. He noticed that she looked exactly like Marty did when she was Willow's age. The last time she passed him, she looked right at him, smiled, and said, "Have a nice day, Father." Unfortunately, she had no idea that he was her real father. Would it have made a difference? Would she be willing to share all those millions that she had locked up in her trust funds? Maybe Marty was right. He should kill her with kindness until she turned eighteen. Once she was able to access that money without interference from that arrogant lawyer, he could manipulate her any way he wanted to. The only problem was that he really couldn't afford to wait another three years for the money. He owed people, and he owed them a lot. Besides, he should be living the good life now. Why wait? He would find a way to work this out to his advantage. He always did.

Chapter Thirty-Six

"Bless us, O Lord, for the food we are about to receive. Let it provide us with the strength to continue our mission to bring God's beautiful graces to others, especially to those in need." Michael recited the blessing with his hands clasped before him as he bowed his head in prayer. The other priests answered with a resounding, "Amen." In a synchronized motion, they all crossed themselves and looked at the bountiful meal that Katie had prepared for lunch. "Enjoy your meal, gentlemen." Michael smiled as he reached for a steaming bread basket. "I've asked Katie to make a light dinner tonight. Tomorrow morning, we have to fast until our blood work is drawn at the clinic. So feast while you can."

"It all looks delicious to me," Victor said as he surveyed the food on the table before him. Michael wondered if he should have Victor fill his plate last to ensure there would be enough food for the rest of them.

Michael watched as his guests ate. Juan chose some of the lighter fare, and Michael wondered if he was experiencing nausea from his tumor. In addition to a general checkup in the clinic tomorrow, Juan had an appointment with an oncologist at Rocky Meadow. He needed to continue his chemotherapy during his stay in Vermont with the hope that his physical, as well as his spiritual health, would be improved by his retreat at St. Francis.

Michael noticed that Father Pat remained fairly quiet and that his hands were shaking slightly as he reached for the ham. His face was drawn, and he looked tired. Michael wondered when the last time was that Father Pat had actually smiled or felt a passion for something in life other than alcohol.

"Excuse me, Michael, would you mind passing the biscuits?" Victor asked eagerly.

Michael broke from his reverie and handed the plate of biscuits to Victor. "I'm glad that you're enjoying the meal."

"It's all delicious. I wish that I had someone like Katie at my parish, but then again, I probably would have weighed a lot more than I do by now," Victor said with a smile.

"Well, next week, you'll be in your glory. Our carnival starts on Tuesday, and you'll be amazed at the amount of food that shows up here."

"Quite frankly, I can't wait," Victor replied as he took a bite of his meal.

Michael looked toward the other priests. Both were listening to the conversation but were eating their food halfheartedly.

"As a matter of fact, I wanted to ask all of you to help hang the carnival posters in town today," Michael said. "Florence will be coming by to pick them up later this afternoon, and I was hoping you'd go with her to Main Street. I think it would be a good idea to meet some of the people in the community, and Florence could really use the help."

"Of course, Father." Victor nodded his head. "Maybe I can find some info on a gym while I'm there. Is that okay with you?"

"Absolutely. You may get a workout carrying these posters. Normally, I'd go with you, but I injured my calf earlier this week, and it's just starting to come around, so I don't want to overdo it. I hope you don't mind," Michael said as he looked around the table with a questioning glance.

Father Pat nodded his head. He would go, but he wasn't happy about it. He never had to do this type of work in his parish, and he really didn't want to start now, but out of respect to his host and his vows, he would be obedient.

As the meal concluded, Victor and Pat excused themselves and left the table for their rooms. Juan remained at the table for a second longer, and Michael seized the moment to speak with him. "Juan, please stay at the rectory this afternoon. We want to include you in all our activities, but I understand you may not be feeling strong enough to go into town. I don't want you to exhaust yourself for your physical tomorrow, but the decision is completely yours to make," Michael said with a smile.

"Thank you, Father. I'm not sure what I'll do yet. I'm going to rest for a while, and then I'll see how I feel. I'm very tired lately, but I don't know if it's from all the traveling this week or the tumor." Juan shrugged lightly.

Michael thought it might also be depression as Juan looked like he was about to burst into tears. "Don't worry, Juan. Tomorrow, we'll get more information after our visit at the clinic. We have some good medical people here." Father Michael reached out and squeezed Juan's arm. "Right now, you need to pray and keep your faith."

Juan nodded as a single tear slid down his cheek. "Thank you, Father. I'd better go now."

Michael sat at the table for a moment longer and silently said a prayer asking for strength and guidance and realized that he had a bit of work ahead of him. These priests had all taken the first step and willingly agreed to attend St. Francis for the retreat. God willing, through their prayer, meditation, and assignments, they would find the love and compassion of God that had made them so eager to become priests years ago. He hoped that he could help them erase some of the bitterness that had come from years of stress. Many professionals had a high rate of burnout, and that included priests as well.

Chapter Thirty-Seven

Willow waited anxiously in the sixth floor conference room. It was exactly two o'clock, and she had given fresh ice to all the patients on the sixth floor and taken the time to visit with some of them. She had promised to come back and visit with the others after her meeting. She was nervous about her conference with Dr. Amy and had visions of finding out she was in trouble for something. But she didn't know what. Did she know about Grandmother Elizabeth?

Willow looked up hurriedly when she heard the door to the lounge swing open. Amy walked in and greeted her with a smile as she approached the table and sat in the chair next to Willow's. "Hi, Willow. Thank you for taking a moment to meet with me this afternoon," Amy said with a reassuring smile. "How is your day going so far?"

"Hi, Dr. Daniels." Willow shrugged her shoulders. "Okay, I guess."

"Good." Amy looked pensive for a moment. "Willow, I have two things that I want to discuss with you today. The first one involves your work." Amy paused for a second. "I was wondering how you liked working in the clinic on Tuesday?"

"I guess it was all right. I had fun," Willow replied.

"If you could choose, would you rather spend more time working on the medical floor or would you want to spend more time in the clinic?"

Willow seemed lost in thought for a minute. "Well, to be honest with you, sometimes the hospital floor is depressing. Some of the patients are really sick or cranky. But then, some of them really appreciate my help because they say there aren't enough nurses to help them with little things. The clinic was different because I helped more people with paperwork or showing the patients where the exam room was."

"Well, do you have any preference of one over the other?"

"I don't know, there are things that I like about both of them. Why?"

"That's a good question. The hospital has had a clinic for years, but lately, they haven't been using it very much because they didn't have enough staff to work there as well as the rest of the hospital. So what would happen is that patients with a simple ear infection or strep throat would go to the ER. The problem is that they would sit there for hours and then keep the nurses and doctors from working on the more serious patients. The whole situation really wasn't too efficient, so I had a meeting with the hospital administration. They agreed to let me reopen the clinic on a regular basis with a small group of nurses and a volunteer. If I can show that the clinic would save the hospital money in the long run, they'll let me staff it full-time. Since you were the volunteer who worked with us last Tuesday, I wanted to give you the first opportunity to be the volunteer. What do you think?"

"Well, who else would be there?"

"I'd probably be the doctor most of the time, and Kathy would still be the director. We're going to ask the same nurses who were there on Tuesday to come back and work on a regular basis. We all seemed to make a pretty good team."

"Well, I guess so." Willow shrugged her shoulders. "What if I don't like it though?"

"Then just let me know, and I'll have Mrs. Russo assign you back to the hospital floor. I don't want to push you. It's just that our first day is tomorrow, Friday morning. We actually have about eight patients scheduled, and I want things to go smoothly. You can always come up to the floor on your breaks to visit your favorite patients," Amy added hopefully.

"I'll try it," Willow said tentatively. "What time do we start?"

"Nine o'clock in the morning. We'll only work until lunchtime for now, and the best part is that the hospital agreed to send the lunch cart down each day." Amy rolled her eyes and grinned. "Just think of all that delicious chocolate pudding."

Willow smiled, a real beautiful wide smile, and she looked very pretty. Amy realized that this was the first time she had seen a genuine smile from Willow. For that reason, Amy dreaded what was coming next. "Now that we have the clinic part over, I wanted to ask you about something else. I wanted to know if you would tell me something about your parents."

Willow's smile deflated like a balloon. "My parents? Why?"

"Well, I wanted to find out a little more about you and your family," Amy said sheepishly. "You mentioned in the clinic the other day that you didn't have any parents and that you had a lawyer for a guardian."

"I don't really have any parents. I mean, they're not dead, I don't think so anyway."

"Willow, I know this is painful, but it's important. When was the last time that you saw your mother and father?"

"I don't know, a long time ago. They didn't want me as a baby, so my grandmother raised me." Willow started to get choked up.

"Are you okay?"

"Yeah, I'm fine. It's just that my grandmother died last year, and I miss her a lot."

"So who takes care of you now? I mean, besides the guardian. Who makes your lunch and helps you buy school supplies?"

"Nobody, I take care of myself," Willow said defensively. "I get homeschooled by a tutor. She brings the books and stuff."

Amy felt sad for Willow as she realized how lonely she must be. It was no wonder she didn't smile much. Amy wondered if she had any friends but didn't think so with these circumstances. If she had attended the local high school, she could have been playing sports or worked in after-school clubs instead of witnessing constant pain and illness in the hospital.

"Why is any of this important anyway?" Willow asked with her chin up.

"Well"—Amy sighed—"I have something to tell you, and I'm not sure how you're going to take it. Your mom is in the hospital, and I met her yesterday. She gave me permission to tell you that she's here. Apparently, she and your father have had some discussions about you lately."

"Not about me, more like my grandmother's money."

Amy was amazed that Willow was so savvy. "Willow, I'm not sure. But your mom is in the hospital, and I thought that you should know. I wasn't sure if you wanted to visit with her, and I didn't want you to be surprised if you ran into her."

"Is she all right?"

"Yes, I think that she's going to be okay. She was talking about you quite a bit."

"I don't know why. All she ever cared about was drinking. If she had to choose between me and a bottle, she always asked for ice, if you know what I mean."

Amy cringed at her analogy. "Well, maybe she's ready to give all that up now. Hopefully, she may want to turn her life around."

"And I should just run to her with open arms and scream, 'Hi, Mommy, where have you been my whole life?'"

Amy wasn't surprised at how angry Willow was. The whole family suffered in situations like these, and this one would be no different. Amy just wanted to open the topic of conversation in case Willow's father became an issue. "No, I don't expect you would want to do anything like that. I just wanted you to know that she is here. I really have no idea what your relationship with your parents is or when you had seen them last. I just don't want you to be surprised if you see them."

"I don't even remember my father. I wouldn't know him if I saw him anyway. My only memory is that he had a weird scar on his cheek. Grandmother said it was the mark of the devil."

"Willow, I didn't mean to hurt you in any way, and I'm sorry that I had to stir up such bad feelings. But sooner or later, you may run into them again, and you should be prepared. If you ever want help dealing with all those feelings, I can help you make arrangements for that too," Amy offered hopefully.

"They didn't want me, and now I don't want them, especially because I'm going to be rich someday. I hope they drop off the face of the earth."

Ouch. Amy thought this was going just about how she had predicted. "Okay, let's drop the subject. Just so you know, your mom is on the fifth floor for now. You can avoid going there if you want. Are we still friends? Are you still coming to the clinic tomorrow morning?"

"I guess so. None of this is your fault. You're just trying to look out for me," Willow said placidly.

Amy's heart broke, and she wished Willow would smile again. She committed herself to trying to bring a little sunshine into this girl's life. Amy remembered all the things her niece liked to do. Her niece was fifteen but was still in a coma. Amy began to get choked up. Time to move and get busy. Lately, distraction had become a way of life.

"Willow, the most important question of all. Do you like ice cream?"

Willow looked up at her. "Yeah, chocolate mostly."

"Come on then, let's go down to the cafeteria. There's lots of ice cream and hot fudge at the sundae bar. I'm buying." As they left the conference room, a small smile returned to Willow's pained face.

Chapter Thirty-Eight

Father Victor and Father Pat paused on the sidewalk outside of Hasco's Bar and Grill.

"Do you think we should go in?" Victor asked out loud, mainly to himself. "Do you think they would hang the posters?"

"It certainly wouldn't hurt to ask," Pat replied in an exhausted tone. "Lord knows, we've been to almost every other establishment on Main Street." Victor and Pat had parted with Florence after meeting with just two of the shop owners. Florence took a few moments to introduce the visiting priests and then spent another twenty minutes discussing how she had made all the arrangements for the upcoming carnival. Both priests thought that they would have a better chance of displaying more posters if they split into smaller groups, namely, Florence in one group and them in the other.

"Well, come on then, let's go in," replied Victor as he pushed open the heavy wooden door. They were immediately greeted with the aroma of stale beer and cigarette smoke. Behind the bar, they saw a large man wiping the counter with a white towel. As the two priests entered the bar, the bartender looked up and offered a warm welcoming grin.

"Welcome, come on in. We don't often get men of the cloth in Hasco's. As a matter of fact, this is the first time that I can remember. Have a seat, please. What can I get for you? On the house, of course."

"Diet cola, please?" Victor said as he straddled the bar stool.

"And you, Father?" Tony said as he turned to Father Pat.

"Ah, ice water. Thank you," Pat replied as he sat.

"So what brings you into Hasco's today?" Tony asked as he looked at the pile of posters in Victor's arm.

"Well, we are visiting St. Francis Parish," Victor began to explain. "They're having their annual carnival next week, and we were wondering if you would mind hanging some posters in your establishment."

"Be happy to help, Father. Small thing to do for the church. Do you need anything else? I can bring ice or soft drinks," Tony offered as he placed their drinks in front of them.

"I'm not sure, but thank you. I'll have to see what arrangements have already been made. Would it be all right if we ask and get back to you?" Victor asked hopefully.

"Of course, you know where I am. So how do you like Rocky Meadow so far?"

"It's quite peaceful. I'm from the streets of Chicago, so this is a real change of pace for me," Victor replied as he thirstily sipped his soda. "I didn't realize how thirsty I was."

"Here, let me refill that for you. I'm from New York myself, so I know exactly what you mean. You're a little out of sync when you arrive, but believe me, after a while, you don't want to go back."

"I believe that. By the way, what's your name?" Victor asked.

"Tony, Tony Noce. How about you?"

"Father Victor Cerulli from Chicago and Father Patrick Doherty from Allentown, Pennsylvania," Victor answered for both of them as Pat seemed to be occupied looking around the room.

"Well, welcome to Rocky Meadow. Please let me know if there's anything else I can do for you."

"Well, actually I do have a question," Father Victor said cautiously. "You may be just the person to ask."

"Great, ask away, Father."

"Well, you're a big guy."

"Not as big as you, Father." Tony laughed.

"Well, it looks like you stay in shape. You wouldn't know where I could find a good gym with a boxing ring, would you?"

"Do you like to box, Father?" Tony said with a sly smile and nod of his head.

"Actually, I do. I'm trying to find a good gym around here."

Tony chuckled. "Well then, you're in luck today. As it happens, I like to box myself. I usually go to Mickey's, right down the block."

"Mickey's? Is that the official name of the gym?" Victor asked excitedly.

"I'm not sure about that. We all just call it Mickey's, but I'm sure that you'd love it. If you want, I can go with you for the first time and show you around, Father."

"Really? How would you feel boxing a priest, Tony?"

"I'd try not to hurt you too much the first time around, Father."

Father Victor let out a hearty chuckle. "Is that so, Tony? Just remember, I won't be wearing my collar in the ring, but I'll still show you mercy when you scream." As Father Victor and Tony continued their conversation about boxing, Father Pat continued to look around the room. If he hadn't been in full view of the few patrons in the bar, he would have taken several deep breaths. Just being in the room, he was enticed by the smell of the stale liquor from the night before. He didn't ask for alcohol, but he really wanted some. Father Pat observed the local customers. Most were enjoying a lunch of cheeseburgers, potato salad, and cold beer.

However, one gentleman was sitting in a corner booth with his head on the table. As Pat watched, the man slowly raised his head and looked back at him. He blinked his eyes several times as if he were trying to clear his vision. Then the man just continued to stare at him with sad, deep-set eyes. Father Pat guessed his age to be around sixty. His desperate facial expression reached out to Father Pat, silently pleading for help. Without really knowing why, Pat got up off his stool and walked over to the man. The man raised his face to the priest and crossed himself. With a trembling voice he asked, "Are you real?"

Father Pat looked down at the poor man. "Excuse me?"

"Are you real? Did God send you to me?"

"Do you think God sent me to you?" Father Pat said softly as he sat in the chair across from him.

"Are you real, Father? Did God send you to me, or are you just another hallucination?"

"I assure you that I'm very real," Father Pat said kindly and squeezed the man's hand for reassurance. "What do you need, my friend?"

"I'm a boozer, Father. I've lost everything. Everything that matters to me anyway. My job, my wife, my kids, and now my self-respect. I was just laying my head on this table and praying for God to help me when you walked in. But that would be too easy, so I thought I must be hallucinating again."

"You're not hallucinating," Father Pat assured him. "I promise you that I'm very real, and I understand a little bit about drinking too."

"Then God did send you to me. Can you help me, Father? I feel like crap. Oh, excuse me, I shouldn't have said that. I'm not feeling well," the man said as he burped and laid his head back on the table.

"What's your name?" Pat asked softly as he sat down across from the man.

"Larry, Larry Kalosy," he replied as tears started to stain his weary face.

"Have you seen a doctor recently? Have you tried a support group?"

"No, Father, I didn't. My wife and family tried to get me to go. All the signs of alcoholism were there, but I didn't go because I was too stubborn to admit that I was a drinker. I couldn't hold it together anymore, but I was too proud to say so, and I didn't go."

"My son, when all the signs point to one path, God is directing your journey. Let your eyes be opened. Humble yourself and get the help you need. It'll be difficult, but you'll reap greater rewards when you do," Father Pat encouraged.

"Will you help me, Father?" Larry asked as he grabbed the priest's arm. Father Pat thought for a long, quiet moment as Larry stared up at him. He wasn't in his own parish. He didn't know what resources were available, but he knew this man was ready for help. He'd have to do something.

"Do you have a place to stay, Larry?"

"I got thrown out of my house, Father. Tony lets me stay here sometimes. I tried to lean on some of my friends, but they're tired of me too. I swore to them that I wouldn't drink anymore if they'd help me. But the minute I was alone, I would sneak all the alcohol I could."

"Closet drinking?"

"Yeah, I guess so. I'm stupid. As if I thought they wouldn't be able to smell it or anything."

Father Pat looked at the man with the gaunt face. He knew that he was in need of some serious help, support, and good food. He would speak to Father Michael and see what the church could offer for Larry. Tony would probably know of a local medical program. He could also ask at the hospital tomorrow when he had his physical. Ah yes, his physical was due. The physical where they would ask him questions and draw his blood to check his liver and cholesterol. What was he going to tell them?

Father Pat Doherty slowly looked up and saw his own reflection in the bar mirror on the wall across from him advertising a famous beer. The craving, the gaunt face, the closet drinking, the inappropriate actions, and the excuses were all there. But it wasn't Larry's reflection; it was his. He admitted to himself that he was a full-fledged alcoholic, and he knew that this was God's way of bringing him to that realization. He had known for a long time but didn't want to believe it until he saw Larry. As his throat tightened, he said with a choked voice, "You know, Larry, I think God has sent you to me. Do you have a phone number or an address where I can reach you? I have to make some inquiries, but I would like to try to help you." *And myself,* thought Father Pat.

"Tony will know where you can find me, Father. Let's just hope it's soon."

"As soon as I can, I promise," Father Pat Doherty squeezed Larry's hands and, in that moment, felt like he had a sense of purpose for the first time in a long while. He also knew that he needed help for himself. He wasn't as eager to get help for himself and admit to his complete dependence of alcohol, but he would find help for this man, and he would go with him. With the grace of God, they would both be saved. With a final squeeze of Larry's forearm, he said, "I will contact you soon. Stay here with Tony and wait for my call."

Father Pat stood up from the table and went back up to the bar where Father Victor and Tony Noce were still trading barbs. "Victor, I need to get back to the rectory and speak with Father Michael."

"Sure, is everything okay?" Father Victor asked as he turned around at Father Pat's tone of voice.

"Yes, but I think I need to get help for our friend Larry over there," Father Pat replied. He then looked at Tony and asked what he knew about Larry.

"Nice guy, but he's got a bad drinking problem. He's been cut loose by just about everyone. I was going to try to talk to him myself, but if you think you can do something, Father, that would be great. He's got nowhere to go but down. I've been watering his drinks and trying to get him to eat, but I haven't gotten much of a response yet."

"Well, I think he's ready now. I have to ask Father Michael what programs are in the area. Tony, is there a detox near here?" Father Pat asked quietly.

"We usually just bring them to the emergency room if they're willing and agree to go. We have a local AA group, but I think he needs something a little more intense at the moment," Tony replied, looking over at Larry.

Father Victor spoke up and said, "Well, we have a car, and we have the manpower, so let's just drive him over to the hospital now."

"You wouldn't mind, Victor? Larry could really use the help, and I think he'll go," Father Pat mused. "Let me go over and ask him. If he's willing, we'll go now."

"Father Victor, let me have the rest of those posters," Tony said with a smile. "I'll make sure they're up before sundown. I have plenty of friends who need to do a little community service in this town. The hospital is six blocks away, just follow the blue signs. Looks like you're going on a little road trip," Tony pointed out as Father Pat and Larry approached the bar. "I'll catch you in the ring at Mickey's."

Chapter Thirty-Nine

Amy dropped a stack of charts on the nursing desk and prepared to leave the emergency room. She had finished seeing her share of patients for the day, and Ernie was already seeing the next patient. Amy had a few more things to do before she could finally leave the hospital and go relax on her bench. It was a beautiful Thursday afternoon, and the sun was warm. The temperature still dropped into the forties at night, which was typical for Vermont in the spring, but this afternoon was bright and sunny, and Amy wanted to take advantage of it.

She left the emergency room after giving sign-out information to Ernie for the patients that were still waiting for test results and follow-up. Amy headed up to the fifth floor and entered Marty's hospital room. "Hi, how are you today?"

Marty looked up from the magazine she was holding and smiled weakly. "Okay, i guess. I haven't had any alcohol in two days. I feel like I've been here for three weeks even though it's only been a couple of days, and I think that I'm about to go out of my mind."

"Well, the good news is that your chest x-ray was normal."

"Thank goodness for that," Marty replied in a tone that was a little less than sarcastic. "I'm sorry. When I first came here, I was scared and bargained with God or anyone who would help me. Now, I'm really craving a drink, and I'm ready to scratch someone's eyes out if need be."

"This is the hard part. Remember, you can ask for medication if you get really shaky or anxious. I want you to try to stay as calm as possible," Amy pointed out.

"I know. It's just amazing how you swear to something one day and then completely change your mind after a few hours in the barrel," Marty said.

140

"I know it's hard. But you're going to do it this time. I have confidence in you, and don't forget you're doing this for Willow anyway. You need to protect her, remember?"

Marty's face blanched as her stomach turned with the thought of Bobby trying to contact Willow. "I know. I'll get through this if it's the last thing I do. That bastard is not going to hurt her again."

"He's actually hurt all of you. It's not just one person who gets hurt, and you know that. Most of our actions impact others' lives too, which brings me to my point. We spoke about Willow working in the hospital. I want you to know that I talked to her this morning, as you requested, to break the ice."

"You did? What did you say? What did she say? How did she take it?" Marty couldn't stop the rush of words, or her thoughts, pouring out of her mouth as they collided like falling bowling pins.

"Well, I just let her know that you are here for help and that you'd been asking about her. I told her that you are sorry about everything and hope that you two could talk someday."

"What did she say? Does she hate me?"

"Well, I'm not going to lie. She's angry, and she has every right to be. She feels abandoned. Your mom was her lifeline, and when she died, Willow felt like she was abandoned again. She's lost, lonely, and I think scared despite the fact that she's as tough as nails on the outside. But then, she'd have to be since that's been her coping mechanism all this time."

Marty shook her head as a tear slipped down her cheek. "I've been such a bad mother, it's amazing."

"Look, it's not going to help if you beat yourself up on this. What you need to do is get yourself in shape and then make this right between the two of you before you lose the next fifteen years. She could use someone in her corner right now, but it's going to take a while for you to earn her trust."

"I'm trying, I'm trying," Marty said as she shrugged and threw her hands up in the air.

"Has Tony said anything about Bobby? Did he ever come back to the bar? I just want to make sure that Willow is safe for now."

"No, there's been no sign of him yet. Although, I swear I must be hallucinating from the lack of alcohol, but for a brief second, I thought I saw him in the hospital corridor earlier today. When I turned around, there was nobody there. He's easy to recognize with that scar on his face, but I didn't see anyone. I must be skittish, I guess. Anyway, Tony and I talked to the lawyer that's taking care of Willow, and he said that he would get the police involved if he shows his ugly face. But there's nothing obvious going on, and that's how Bobby works. He's always in the shadows, manipulating someone or something for his selfish reasons."

"Well, just keep working on it. In the meantime, if Willow does come to visit, try to keep things light. You two have to work through a lot of emotion, and it's going to take a while. Just connect for now. I don't think either one of you is emotionally ready to handle fifteen years of hurt feelings. When you're back on your feet, we'll arrange the proper counseling. For now, just follow through with your floor counseling and support groups."

"Yes, boss lady," Marty said with a salute.

"Marty, I'm just trying to help," Amy said defensively.

"I know that, but I don't know how to be gracious because I've been out of touch for fifteen years. Just ignore me."

"No such luck. Just take care of yourself. Okay?"

"Okay. I promise," Marty replied.

"I have to go, but I'll pop in sometime tomorrow," Amy said as she turned and left the hospital room with a wave. She was thinking about what Marty had to say. Bobby had a strange scar on his face. Willow mentioned that her father had a strange scar on his face. The only person Amy kept seeing with a scar on his face was that priest who was always with Ben Lawrence in the intensive care unit. She really needed to find out who that priest was, but every time she went to the intensive care unit, he ran off. It was getting late, but she'd definitely had to look into that tomorrow. As she left the hospital to relax on her bench, she couldn't believe that she still hadn't heard from Lou.

Chapter Forty

Michael slowly walked through the woods and stretched his long legs. His calf was less sore today, but he knew that he wasn't ready to run yet. After lunch, he had sent Fathers Victor and Pat out with Florence. He had looked in on Father Juan, who was sound asleep in his room. It was getting harder for him to counsel priests these days. The pressures of the priesthood were difficult to begin with, especially since the world had become more difficult. Some priests were not up to the task of being responsible for a business as well. Priests were people with problems just like any others but held on to a higher standard. Michael usually identified with a little bit of emotion in each of his brethren. That's why he took their counseling, failures, and pain so personally.

Michael could keep working with Victor and Pat. He hoped there would be some treatment options left for Juan although he felt depression was a big part of Juan's problem at the moment. Hopefully, that would be confirmed after their physicals tomorrow. He was lucky when he called the hospital for appointments. He heard a rumor that the hospital clinic was scheduled to be closed permanently. Ready to beg for physicals if necessary, he was pleasantly surprised when he was given four appointments without a hassle. All the priests had some basic insurance, but finding primary care doctors was becoming a bigger problem these days. Tomorrow, they would all be examined, have blood drawn, and whatever other tests the doctor thought might be necessary. He included himself as he hadn't gone in quite a while.

As Michael drew near the edge of the woods, he glanced toward the bench and saw Amy sitting there with her face to the sun and legs stretched before her toward the Divide. She seemed like such a nice person, and maybe someday, she'd be smiling as well. As he approached the bench and got ready to sit down, he reminded himself not to ask so many personal questions. He couldn't help it, but for some reason, she just intrigued him. "Hi, mind if I sit down?"

Amy opened her eyes and looked toward Michael. "By all means," she replied as she shifted toward the left side of the bench. "How's your day going?"

"So far, so good. It's been pretty standard stuff. Beautiful weather, isn't it?"

Amy broke out in a loud, hearty laugh and looked toward Michael. "You're funny, you know that?"

"Hey, I didn't even get to ask you about your car yet."

"Well, we didn't finish with the weather. Yes, this is a beautiful day. You know how they say we only get six perfect days each year? Well, this would be one of them," Amy responded with true appreciation.

"It sure is," Michael agreed. "Okay, do I ask about your car next?"

"No, I think the next logical comment would be about the Divide. Then we can go to the car if we're looking for fill."

"You didn't mention the Divide yesterday, so I wasn't sure."

"I know, but today it looks fabulous with the sun sparkling on it like that. The river is high and strong. So much energy, it makes our problems seem small in comparison," Amy answered. "I didn't say that you could only talk about the car and the weather. It's just that the questions were getting a little too pointed yesterday."

"I'm sorry about that. I still want to be your friend. If I get too intrusive, just give me a signal and I'll stop. Sometimes, it's an occupational hazard," Michael replied with a warm, genuine smile.

"Truce," Amy said and extended her hand. As she shook hands with Michael, she noted again how soft his hands were. His grip was just right, not crushing like someone trying to prove their strength and not weak and sweaty. He had nice hands. Being a surgeon, Amy always concentrated on hands, hers as well as others.

"Here's my half of the olive branch," Michael said with a smile. "To be honest, I really can't even stay today. I have an appointment this afternoon. I just wanted to stretch my calf, say hi, and enjoy at least fifteen minutes of sunshine before I'm locked inside my office for another couple of hours."

"I know what you mean. Sometimes it's a shame when we realize how much time we miss being able to appreciate the day around us. I've had work days that started in the dark, ended in the dark, and I missed the daylight completely."

"Was that by choice or design?"

"Well, part of the problem is my profession, I suppose. But there are people who can spare a few minutes and still don't get out at all. They're glued to their computer or the television. I'd rather sit in the park."

"So you can appreciate nature and God's beautiful work?"

"Yes, sometimes we take too many things for granted," Amy said sadly.

Michael sighed and stood up. "I'd better get ready for my meeting. Otherwise, I'm going to start asking a lot of questions. I just thought of fifteen with that last statement." Michael chuckled.

"Well then, have a great day. Don't forget to stop and smell the roses."

"Hey, that's usually my line," Michael quipped as he stood and turned from the bench. "Maybe I'll see you tomorrow."

"Maybe, bye," Amy answered softly. At first, she had been upset because another person was invading her bench time. But today, she realized that she had actually been happy to see Michael even if just for a few moments. She had been isolated, hurting and lonely for such a long time. Maybe coming to Vermont had been the right move after all; maybe she finally found someone she could trust.

As Michael walked off, Amy's thoughts drifted back to Boston.

She was walking down the gray-painted cinderblock hallway until she reached the red plastic sign on the wall that said Autopsy. After taking a deep breath, she pushed open the door.

"Hey, Amy," the pathologist said. "What are you doing down here?"

"I understand you have a patient of mine. I, ah, wanted to see his body," Amy replied.

"Hey, it's okay, Amy. We all lose one or two. Well, actually I don't, but you can't save them all."

"I understand. I just wanted to see this one," Amy said quietly.

"He just came down from upstairs. He was a sudden death, so they had to send him down. Come over here, I'll move the sheet for you."

Amy moved over to the cold steel gurney and looked down at the scum. He was finally dead all right, but he looked peaceful. How dare he lie there looking so peaceful? She wanted him to look tormented. She wanted his death mask to reflect the fear her sister had felt when she was murdered. Amy wanted to pummel him with her fists and rip his unseeing eyes out. She purposely came to autopsy to feel triumph, but instead, all she felt was rage.

"Hey, are you okay?" the pathologist asked politely.

Her voice shaking, Amy said, "This is the bastard that murdered my sister and put a bullet in my niece's head."

"Really? I thought you were his trauma surgeon."

"I was. I didn't know it then, and I saved the scum's life," Amy said.

"Oh, crap. I didn't know, Amy. I didn't mean to be disrespectful."

"That's okay. I just wanted to make sure that he is finally dead."

"That he is," the pathologist said with conviction. Her emotional crisis didn't go unnoticed, and then everything just got worse.

Tears fell from her eyes as she sat on her bench. Today was just another day. Time to go home and get ready for tomorrow.

Chapter Forty-One

Amy hurriedly walked through the front doors of Rocky Meadow General. The weather outside was cold and rainy, but at least it was Friday. She wanted to change in the locker room at the back of the ER and then head over to the clinic for their first big day. They had five appointments scheduled, and the ER would also be sending any patients with simple problems. As Amy passed the central desk, Ernie looked up and called to her, "Amy, what's going on?"

Amy waved and walked over to him. "Hi, Ernie. Remember when I talked to you about helping with the new clinic? Well, today is technically the first day. I hope it works out because they'll be watching my every move."

"I think you have a great idea. Especially now when we're so overcrowded with routine medical issues."

"They agreed to give me three months to see how the program works. We may not be able to generate any revenue for the hospital, but at least, we can try to stop losing money in the ER. Since family practitioners are becoming scarcer, we can attract some patients with insurance as well as those without. Just keep your fingers crossed," Amy rushed on.

"You got it. I'm all for decreasing the volume in the ER. That way, we'll make fewer mistakes as well," Ernie said with a smile. "By the way, I have a potential patient for you this morning."

"Oh, really," Amy said cautiously, noting the large mischievous grin on Ernie's face. "Do tell."

"Well, in cubicle 2," Ernie said while chuckling, "we have Ms. Helen Coyle."

"Go on," Amy said slowly.

"Helen is a ninety-one-year-old female who's here for a fractured ankle."

"We both know that I won't be able to treat a fractured ankle in the clinic, so what's this all about?" Amy asked suspiciously.

"You're gonna love this. I don't think that you got cases like this in Boston," Ernie said eagerly.

"I'm sure that I haven't had a case like this in Boston, so out with it already."

"Well, this morning, Helen had taken her shower. She was in the bedroom wearing her birthday suit when she opened her underwear drawer. Much to her dismay, she found that a mouse had decided to give birth to a new family in there."

"I don't like where this is going already."

"Anyway," Ernie continued, "she pulls the entire drawer from the dresser and runs out to the backyard with it." Ernie began chuckling even harder, and when he saw the look on Amy's face, he said, "I know this isn't funny, but it is. Anyway, Helen runs outside and empties the entire contents of the drawer in the bushes out in the backyard."

"Please, you're killing me," Amy said.

"Oh, wait, it gets better. So now, we have bras and panties hanging off the bushes and Helen, in her birthday suit, standing there making sure the mice are all gone."

Amy started shaking her head as Ernie continued, "The problem is that the elderly next-door neighbor, Harold, had just finished taking the wrapping off some of the bushes that managed to survive the winter."

"Don't tell me Harold was standing there."

"He most certainly was. So without cracking a smile, he says, 'Gee, Helen, aren't you cold?'" Ernie said in the midst of hysterics now.

"He didn't, please tell me he didn't," Amy pleaded.

"He most certainly did. When Helen realized that he was standing there, she screamed and tried to run back into the house," Ernie said as he was wiping his eyes.

"Is this true?" Amy asked suspiciously.

"Cross my heart," Ernie said while laughing harder. "So while running, Helen trips over a bra that had fallen out of the drawer."

"You're making this up," Amy challenged.

"No, I'm not," Ernie insisted.

"Well, then what did Harold do?"

"He didn't know what to do. So he covers her with the blue tarp that he was holding and calls 911."

Amy was now holding her head and rubbing her closed eyes with her hand. "You can't make this stuff up."

"The paramedics arrived to find Helen lying naked on the grass, under the blue tarp, with a bra wrapped around her fractured ankle. Harold was standing five feet away holding the ropes that the bushes were bound with, talking to himself. The paramedics called the police because they weren't sure if Harold should be arrested."

"Oh my god." Amy was starting to chuckle. "You have to be kidding me. What happened next?"

"Well, they just transported everyone over to the ER. Helen is now dressed and being casted by Dr. Weber in orthopedics."

"And Harold?"

"Harold is the one who needs to be in the clinic because he needs counseling."

"Ernie, that's so sad," Amy said sympathetically. "The poor guy. He's traumatized, and he was just trying to help."

"It's too funny," Ernie said.

"Actually, I'd love to have full counseling available in the clinic. Everything from nutrition and exercise straight through to family counseling. I have a follow-up meeting with administration, and I'm making a list of everyone's suggestions."

"Well, let me know before your meeting. Maybe I'll go with you," Ernie said with a nod.

"That's a great idea. Perhaps we should make it an open staff meeting. I have to think about that," Amy replied.

"Speaking of staff, Lou Applebaum has been in here twice looking for you."

"Lou? I've been looking for him for two days. Do you know where he went?"

"I think he was on his way up to the CICU," Ernie said.

"I have to speak to him about a patient. Listen, Ernie, I'm going to run upstairs. If anyone from the clinic comes in, tell them that I'll be there as soon as I'm done in the unit," Amy asked.

"You got it. Get out of here," Ernie said. Amy heard him still chuckling as she left the emergency room.

Chapter Forty-Two

Michael slowed the car and turned into the hospital parking lot. All four priests were in the minivan. Jack was busy helping Florence with some final arrangements for the carnival, so Michael was in charge of the driving. The four priests concelebrated the morning mass, changed their clothing, and headed toward the hospital. Katie promised to have a full lunch waiting for them when they returned, and since they were already starving, Michael hoped it would be sumptuous. Katie also quietly mentioned to Michael that Father Pat had called her to help with disposing of his liquor bottles. Pat told Katie that he was given a new direction from God, then smiled and thanked her for her assistance. Michael had also been briefed about Larry's hospital admission when both priests arrived back at the rectory yesterday. Katie had kept their dinner warm, and Michael sat with them while they ate.

Michael turned into the circular driveway and took advantage of the special parking spot in front of the hospital that was usually reserved for clergy. As he turned off the ignition and set the emergency brake, the remaining priests poured out of the car and began to stretch. Once the car was locked, they all headed through the main doors of the hospital and stopped at the security desk.

As the security guard was giving them directions to the clinic, an old rusty station wagon pulled into the circular driveway. It slowly came to a stop at the parking spot for clergy, and Bobby noticed that the minivan was already parked there. After muttering several curses, he pulled up a little farther and looked toward the hospital. He noticed the crowd of priests talking with security and immediately broke into a sweat. He couldn't go in there now; the security would surely ask more questions or try to have him meet with the other priests. His disguise had suddenly become much more dangerous and transparent. As Bobby drove away, he was trying to think of another way to get into the hospital and up to the CICU. He was going to have to make his move soon and shouldn't have waited this long. Benjamin Lawrence would just have to die as soon as possible and that annoying doctor too just for getting him aggravated.

Chapter Forty-Three

Amy dashed out of the elevator as the doors opened and quickly ran into the cardiac intensive care unit. She looked around and saw that Lou was in Ben's cubicle. She checked her watch and noticed that she should have been in the clinic five minutes ago. Hopefully, Kathy was already there and had handed out the registration paperwork for the patients to fill out. As Amy entered the cubicle, she noticed that Lou was reading over the chart.

"Lou, I've been trying to get hold of you for two days," Amy stated with exasperation.

"Hi, Amy. I'm really sorry. I had an emergency with my parents. My partner agreed to cover for me, so all my calls were being transferred to him."

"I'm sorry to hear that. Are your parents all right?"

"They are now, but my mom is in a hospital in Burlington with a broken hip. My dad isn't really able to care for himself, so I had to arrange for someone to watch over him for now. At least I know that he won't spend the next few weeks eating boxes of cereal and wandering the neighborhood."

"I'm sorry, Lou. It must be stressful to have to keep a close eye on your parents when they live several hours away."

"You can say that again. Anyway, what's up, or did you just really miss me?" Lou said with a small grin.

"Oh, Lou, of course I missed you," Amy teased. "But actually, I wanted to tell you that I was checking on Ben the other day. He scared me because as I was standing at his bedside, he suddenly grabbed my arm and shouted, 'Rob Liz, Rob Liz.' He looked terrified. His eyes were wide open and staring. I feel like he was trying to send a message, but I have no idea what he meant. I thought that you might be able to figure it out since you've known him so long."

"'Rob Liz?' I have no idea what that means. You're saying that he woke up? That he showed activity?"

"Lou, he grabbed my forearm and started shouting. Then, I tried talking to him, but I got no response. I notified the unit doctor so they would recheck his testing. I'm telling you, I was alone with Ben for barely two minutes once that priest left. All of a sudden, he jumps up and starts screaming."

"What priest? Father Michael from St. Francis?"

"No, I don't think he ever gave me a name, but he's been here standing guard since Ben came in," Amy said.

"The only priest I know is Father Michael from St. Francis. I know that St. Francis has other visiting priests. Could it have been one of them?"

"I don't think so. First of all, Mrs. Russo told me the priests from St. Francis hadn't registered yet. Then, I had one of the nurses check his chart, and he definitely doesn't have St. Francis listed as his church. Also, this priest wasn't just someone who was visiting. He was holding a vigil. He gave the stink eye to anyone who walked in."

"What? What's a stink eye?" Lou asked as he chuckled.

"You know the stink eye. It's a certain look that tells you when you're not welcome or someone isn't happy with your behavior. It also involves raising the eyebrow a little bit too."

"I never heard of that," Lou replied.

Amy sighed and said, "Lou, I'll show you the stink eye later. Just listen to me, the priest that was here had a scar on his cheek. I'm telling you, something's not right with this picture." As Amy was pleading her case, Ben moaned and startled them both.

Lou turned toward the patient and said, "Ben? Mr. Lawrence, can you hear me?" He immediately put on his stethoscope and started checking Ben's vitals. Ben continued to moan ever so slightly. He was clearly agitated about something. His breathing was fine, but his heart rate was beginning to climb.

Amy interrupted him, "Lou, I have to go to the clinic. Today is technically the opening day of this new program, and I don't want to be late. Believe it or not, I think I have a couple of priests from St. Francis coming in. I'll ask them if they know a priest with a scar on his cheek. I'll send a nurse in here to help you, but for now, keep a close eye on Ben and call me when you're getting ready to leave the unit."

"You're really worried about him," Lou said seriously.

"I'm telling you, something isn't right. First of all, we still don't really know what happened to make him collapse."

"All right, let me take some time to check Ben over and go through the chart. I'll call you before I leave the unit. Go to the clinic and talk to those priests."

"Good plan. Let me get that nurse for you. I'll talk to you later."

After Amy left the cubicle and arranged for a nurse to help Lou reevaluate Ben's condition, she raced to the elevator. She was now twenty minutes late. As she watched the floor numbers slowly change on the elevator panel, she was thinking about getting a better description of Bobby's scar from Marty.

Chapter Forty-Four

Willow silently walked down the hospital corridor and looked into the patient rooms. Most of the patients in this area had been admitted for some sort of alcohol or substance abuse problem. Some were lying in bed; some were walking the corridors wearing street clothes. A few were in a group therapy session. The charge nurse was just finishing the admission chart for a guy named Larry, but the room Willow was interested in was 521B. She knew from the chart rack that her mother, Marty Davis, was listed as being the registered patient in 521B. There wasn't another patient listed for that room, so her mother must be in there alone and in the bed by the window.

Willow wanted to peek in at her mother before she had to report to the clinic. She really hadn't seen her in a while and wasn't even sure that she would recognize her mother. She didn't want to talk to her yet. After Dr. Amy told her that Marty was a patient, Willow went home and had a bad night. She slept poorly and had some weird dreams. Willow really missed her grandmother, Lizzie. She needed her more than ever now and silently talked to her as she walked down the hall. Willow asked her grandmother's spirit for strength and courage as she approached her mother's room. She wasn't sure why she felt so scared. Her parents never tried to hurt her physically, they had just abandoned her. She was getting use to being alone.

Willow stood quietly at the door to her mother's hospital room and gazed at the figure sitting in the chair by the window. Her mother was approximately thirty but looked older than her years. She looked tired, gaunt, and very sad. Willow thought she'd look a lot better if she had her hair trimmed, gained a few pounds, and added some makeup. She noticed that her mother didn't have the mean, angry face that she'd expected.

Over the years, Willow had practiced all the mean things she wanted to tell her parents, if she ever got the opportunity, but looking at her mom this way, she decided that it wouldn't really help her feel better. Her mother already looked defeated.

Sensing someone in the room, Marty turned and saw Willow standing in the doorway. She just stared for a few seconds as if she couldn't believe her eyes. "Willow? Oh my god, Willow, is that you?" Marty's voice started to choke, and tears were beginning to fall down her face. She grabbed the armrests of the chair and sat up straight, leaning forward to see better. Willow just stood at the door, frozen.

Chapter Forty-Five

Amy rushed into the back door of the clinic and almost straight into Kathy Wilson, the program director. "Whoa, take it easy there," Kathy cried after jumping aside to avoid a collision.

"I'm sorry, Kathy. I got caught up in the CICU. I didn't want to be late on our first day, but this was important."

"No problem, we're fine. Our four priests have arrived. They're busy finishing their registration sheets. We copied their insurance cards, and pretty soon, we'll start bringing them into the rooms and take their vitals."

"Great, so far, so good," Amy said with a sigh of relief. "I want this to work out."

"I'm so happy that you've helped me, you could be two hours late and I wouldn't complain," Kathy said with a laugh.

"Well, keep your fingers crossed. Who do we have as staff today?"

"Actually, I was able to get the same nurses and techs from the other day. They were all happy to come in. The only person that isn't here yet is Willow, our volunteer," Kathy said as she watched Barbara walk toward them. "Dr. Daniels, do you remember Barbara? She was one of our nurses on Tuesday?"

"Yes, I do," Amy replied as she looked toward Barbara. "Nice to see you again, thank you for coming to work at the clinic today."

"My pleasure, I'd love to see this clinic grow." Barbara smiled.

"From your lips to God's ears," Amy said. "How are things going out front?"

"Well, the first two patients are in the exam rooms. I took their vital signs and finished the initial assessments."

"Do they have any particular problems to report?" Amy asked.

"The patient in exam room one is a fifty-four-year-old Roman Catholic priest from Chicago by the name of Father Victor Cerulli. He's currently visiting St. Francis Church. He doesn't have any major medical problems and has had no surgeries. He loves to eat, but he's a big guy, so he probably can handle much more than the average guy. He was a pastor of his own church in Chicago and became very stressed, which led to his retreat at St. Francis. He likes to box and has just recently become aware of a boxing ring in town, which he plans to frequent. He's not on any prescription medications, has no allergies, and his blood pressure is perfect."

"When was his last physical?" Amy asked quietly.

"Actually, he hasn't seen a doctor in quite a long time," Barbara noted.

"Okay, then I'll go do the physical. In the meantime, let's order some lab work to check his sugar and cholesterol. If he hasn't had a stress test, let's order one before he gets into that boxing ring," Amy directed.

"Very good," Barbara agreed.

"What about the patient in the second exam room?"

"Okay, his name is Father Patrick Doherty. He's also a Roman Catholic priest, age sixty-two, who is visiting St. Francis. He admits to having a slight problem with alcohol, and that's what led him to St. Francis, for counseling."

"Is St. Francis a church or counseling center?" Amy asked with confusion.

Kathy turned to Amy to explain. "St. Francis is our local Catholic parish. It serves the community, but in addition, the pastor, Father Michael, also does private counseling for other spiritual leaders in a retreat fashion."

"That's funny because I recently met a psychologist in that area named Michael," Amy replied as she slowly shook her head. "Anyway, go on, Barbara."

"All right, Father Doherty is not on any prescription medications but may need something for mild to moderate hypertension. His blood pressure is borderline high."

"When was the last time he had alcohol?" Amy asked.

"Approximately twenty-four hours according to his history," Barbara read.

"Well, then the pressure may come down if he doesn't drink anymore," Amy commented. "Maybe we can just monitor for a week. How's he feeling?"

"Okay, he's seems a bit cranky, but I'm not sure if that's lack of alcohol or just him."

"What else?"

"He hasn't had any surgery, and he's allergic to penicillin. His family history is positive for heart disease and Alzheimer's disease."

"Last physical and workup?"

"Same as patient number 1. He's not seen a doctor for a long time. I don't really know why because both priests have good insurance," Barbara commented.

"We all make excuses. While I'm in room 1, get labs on Father Doherty, an EKG. Let's hold off on the stress test. See how much he drinks a day. I hope he doesn't need to go up to detox."

"You got it," Barbara said as they turned and walked down the hall.

Amy turned and called back to Kathy, "Let's get this party started."

Chapter Forty-Six

Bobby sat in his car in the parking lot and raged. He hadn't gone into the hospital yet. When he saw all those priests, he went home and changed his clothes. He was now wearing regular street clothes and had brushed his hair differently. Bobby was afraid to impersonate a priest with so many real men of the cloth inside the hospital. Even if he wasn't challenged about being phony, he would have to evade questions about his assigned parish. Bobby hadn't thought far enough in advance to make an intricate cover story, and it was too late to start now. As he left the car and approached the main hospital entrance, he decided that he would ask for room passes to see his lovely wife, Marty. He knew she was in the hospital, on the fifth floor, from hanging around the cardiac intensive care unit. As far as he knew, she hadn't recognized him in the clerical outfit he had worn. Once he got past the security desk, he could go to the third floor instead and stop in the unit. Benjamin Lawrence had to die, and it had to be today.

Chapter Forty-Seven

Amy left the exam room and headed over to the nurse's desk to write her notes. Since she hadn't had a chance to change, she was wearing a pretty spring dress that was partially hidden by a starched white lab coat with a Rocky Meadow General Hospital insignia emblazoned on the left arm. Her stethoscope was draped around her neck as if it were medical jewelry adorning the coat. Her long hair was swept up in a chignon that looked very soft and stylish. As she approached the nursing station, she was greeted by Barbara.

"Are you ready for the next patient?"

"Just a minute," Amy replied. "I want to complete the notes on the first two patients. You finished with their EKG's and lab, right?"

"Sure did," Barbara answered.

"Good because they wanted to go up to the fifth floor to visit a man named Larry. Apparently, they helped him get admitted to detox yesterday."

"Good for them," Barbara said. "Maybe Father Pat will get some help too."

"Okay," Amy directed as she placed the two charts on the desk and turned toward Barbara. "I'm ready for the next patient."

Barbara began to recite her assessment. "The next patient is a little more difficult. He's a Roman Catholic priest from New Jersey. He's young, thirty-six years old, and unfortunately, has metastatic stomach cancer."

"That's not good," Amy sighed.

"No it's not," Barbara agreed. "Several months ago, he had lost his appetite and some weight. He really didn't have a lot of pain, but he did notice some trouble swallowing his food. He assumed that it was from too much stomach acid. After he passed out at a basketball game, he was admitted to his local hospital. He had some testing done and was told that his biopsy was positive for stomach cancer. He had some positive lymph nodes as well."

"What a shame. So young, isn't he?" Amy asked with a concerned look.

"Younger than me, that's for sure," Barbara pointed out. "Anyway, he was removed from his active parish duties in order to pursue treatment. He received two chemo treatments in New Jersey but had a bad reaction. After that, he really got depressed, so his archdiocese sent him to St. Francis for counseling."

"When was his last oncologist appointment?" Amy asked.

"Two weeks ago in New Jersey. I believe that they scheduled him for an oncology consult here at Rocky Meadow after his physical. I didn't get the impression that he was happy with his program at home, but he still wants to go back to Jersey as soon as possible."

"You know, I have a good friend in New Jersey by the name of Dr. Amanda Chase. She's the medical director of a large hospice and palliative care program. Amanda is very connected down there. I could give her a call and make some arrangements for him as long as he wants to go."

"Well, I'd definitely talk to him while you're doing his physical. I don't know what his obligation is here, but I'm sure they'd let him go home to pursue active treatment."

"All right, let me talk to him," Amy sighed. "I'll go in and finish his physical and assessment. I don't want to get any scans until he makes a decision about what he wants to do and he sees our oncologist. They would just repeat it all in New Jersey anyway."

"You got it, boss. I'll go start with the next patient," Barbara said as she turned and headed for the waiting room.

Chapter Forty-Eight

Willow stood in the doorway and stared at her mother. Marty stood up from her hospital bedside chair and stared at her daughter. "Willow, is that really you?"

"Yeah, but I have to go," Willow replied as she shifted on her feet.

"Please don't go, not yet. You're beautiful, simply beautiful," Marty said as she gazed at her daughter with awe. "You're all grown up."

"And all by myself too," Willow said harshly.

"Willow, I'm so sorry," Marty said as tears started falling again. "Please give me a chance to explain. I know there's no excuse, but I knew you were in better hands with your grandmother than with me."

"How about after Grandmother died?" Willow rebuked her quietly.

"I know it was wrong. It's all confused in my head right now. Just give me a chance to make it up to you. I'm really trying to get help this time, I swear. I want to protect you."

"Protect me?" Willow said incredulously. "You're the one who abandoned me. Now you want to protect me? From what?"

"From your father. I'm afraid of your father."

"I have no idea what you're talking about."

"Willow, your father came to see me. He purposely found me to ask about you. He wanted to know how much money you had. He wanted to know how he could get his dirty hands on your money."

Willow started to laugh. "Is that what this is all about? I knew it. My money? Now, I'm just a meal ticket? That's rich, that's really freaking rich."

"Not me, I swear, just your father. I wanted to kill him. Tony almost did, and then we had to warn you."

"Who's Tony?" Willow asked suspiciously.

"He's my friend, and he's a retired cop from New York City," Marty said with enthusiasm as she pleaded with Willow for understanding.

"Knock, knock." Both women jumped at the sound of the male voice at the door.

Chapter Forty-Nine

Amy examined Father Juan's abdomen and felt the hard edge of the liver, indicating a problem. She then felt his spleen and checked his ankles for edema. She straightened the sheet covering his hospital gown and walked over to the counter.

"You can sit up now," she told Father Juan as she scribbled some notes.

"Doctor, how long until I die?" Father Juan asked softly.

"Pardon me?"

"How long do I have left?" He repeated the question while pleading with his eyes for a generous answer.

Amy turned to Father Juan recognizing the fear in his voice and walked over to him. She placed her hand on his upper arm and gave him a little squeeze. "I'm sorry that you have cancer, and I know that it must be very frightening for you," she said as he nodded his head and struggled to hide his tears. "I only did a limited exam, but you seem medically stable to me at the moment. I think you may be depressed, but medically, you're stable. Let me ask you, are you interested in trying aggressive therapy again?"

"I will put myself in God's hands, but I'm not sure what he wants me to do."

"I don't know the answer to that either. You'll have to pray to find out. Perhaps you should discuss things with your pastor. But you do have some options. You can try a different chemotherapy. Another option would be a palliative care program with an experimental treatment, or you can stay in a hospice program for supportive care. I know that you didn't do well with standard chemotherapy, but sometimes, the experimental treatments work even better."

"I'd be willing to try treatment again, but I want to go back to New Jersey."

"Actually, you could go back to New Jersey. That's where you're from, right?"

"Yes, and I miss my home very much."

"I know a good doctor by the name of Amanda Chase in Jersey. If there's an experimental program, she'll know about it. You may have to take a few extra tests to get started, but it may be worth it."

"Please call her for me. I'll speak with Father Michael. I'd like to know what's available, and then I'll make my decision."

"You got it. I'll call her in a little bit. What's the best way to contact you with the information?"

"I listed the number for the St. Francis rectory on my chart. You'll be able to get me there."

"Great, you can get dressed now, and I'll talk to you sometime later," Amy said with a supportive smile.

"Thank you, Doctor," he said with a small sliver of hope on his face.

"You're welcome, Father Juan. No promises, but I'll get the information for you," Amy said as she squeezed his arm and left the room.

Chapter Fifty

Bobby silently stood in the elevator until the car reached the third floor. The doors slid wide open. He entered the hospital corridor and walked toward the cardiac intensive care unit. His pass listed his destination as the fifth floor, room 521B; however, he had no intention of going to the fifth floor yet. He was determined to stop in and see Mr. Benjamin Lawrence one last time. Ben knew that Bobby had tried to kill him. Ben knew everything.

Bobby quickly slipped through the doors of the cardiac intensive care unit and into the familiar glass cubicle. The curtains were already drawn, which would help him immensely. He could inject Ben with the needle he had hidden in his coat pocket and then simply deposit the evidence in the red needle container in the room. Who was going to look in there?

Bobby held the side of the curtain as he quickly moved around the bed. The oxygen running at the back of the bed sounded like a sustained hiss. The heart monitor, measuring electric pulses, would be silent soon. He slowly pulled down the blanket from the sleeping patient, who snorted and turned toward him. Instead of finding Ben, Bobby was shocked when he realized he was looking into the face of a little old lady with blue hair. She blinked twice and started to smile at him. As her grin widened, he noticed that she only had two teeth in the top of her mouth. Her plate had been removed and placed in the denture cup at the side of the bed. As she reached out and tried to grab his hand, he jumped and dropped the needle he was holding. He bent over and wildly looked around for the syringe containing poison as well as his fingerprints. When he heard a nurse walking by the cubicle, he jumped to the corner of the room and stood still until she had passed. Beads of sweat started to fall from his temple, coursing down his cheeks. As soon as the nurse was gone, he exploded out of the cubicle and into the hall.

Chapter Fifty-One

Amy held the cell phone to her ear as she listened to her friend's voice give instructions about leaving a message at the tone. "Amanda, hi, this is Amy in Vermont. When you get this message, please call me about a patient that really needs to be in your palliative care program. You have my cell number. Talk to you soon." Amy pressed the disconnect button as Barbara walked over to the desk.

"How's Father Juan?" she asked in a quiet voice as she looked at Amy.

"Scared, shocked, but medically stable at the moment," Amy replied with a shrug. "He wants to go back to Jersey. He needs to sort this out emotionally and spiritually. I just don't know where the best place would be for him to make sense of it all."

"He needs to talk to Father Michael," Barbara stated simply.

"I think he's doing all that already," Amy said. "Anyway, it's completely his choice."

"Let's hope whatever he decides will bring him peace," Barbara said hurriedly.

"That's for sure. I'm getting some info for him, and then he just has to let me know. I can make arrangements for any program he wants in Jersey. Once he has all his options in place, he can decide what he wants to do. If he doesn't go back to New Jersey, he'll need to start with an oncologist in Rocky Meadow as soon as possible," Amy said as she finished her notes. "He's got a few decisions to make, and I don't envy him that. Sometimes it's easier to follow a solid direction than to try to figure out which way to go."

"That's true, very true. In the meantime, are you ready for the next patient?" Barbara asked with her eyebrows raised.

"Yes," Amy answered slowly as she looked at Barbara. "Why are you making a face?"

"Because, you're finally going to meet Father Michael. He's the pastor of St. Francis Church."

"Good because I have a lot of questions to ask him," Amy said.

"Okay then." Barbara looked at her chart. "Father Michael is a thirty-eight-year-old male in good physical health. He exercises on a regular basis. He doesn't take any prescription drugs, and he has no allergies to medicine."

"Good, just out of curiosity, what does he like to do for exercise?" Amy asked intently as her suspicions were raised.

Barbara consulted her chart. "Apparently, he's a runner," she answered as she looked up at Amy. "Why?"

"Because, I just recently met a man named Michael over by the Divide. He told me that he was a psychologist, but I'm a little confused on the priest thing. Oh yeah, he had a calf injury from running the Devil's Peak trail," Amy mused. "You don't think it could possibly be the same person, do you?"

"Was he rather good looking?" Barbara asked with a smile.

"Not that I really noticed, but yes, I would say that," Amy replied.

"Well, Father Michael is attractive, which can be an occupational hazard for a priest."

"Regardless," Amy said professionally, "was there a recent sprain or anything?"

"Well, it just so happens that our Father Michael states on his registration form that he recently sprained his calf. It sounds awfully coincidental," Barbara answered with a shrug.

"Why wouldn't he tell me he was the pastor?"

"Why don't you go find out?" Barbara said as she handed the chart to Amy. "He's in room number 2."

Amy took the chart and walked to the exam room. After knocking on the door and announcing herself, she gingerly opened the door. "Hi, Father Michael?" Amy called out and exaggerated the name. She observed him sitting on the exam table when she entered the room. He was definitely the man she had met several times during the week at the bench. As she extended her hand, she said, "Hi, I'm Dr. Amy Daniels."

"Hi, I believe that we've met," Father Michael replied as he took her hand. "I'm Father Michael Lauretta from St. Francis Church."

"Nice to meet you again, apparently," Amy said in a confused voice. "I'm sorry, but I didn't realize that you were the pastor of St. Francis when we talked earlier this week."

"Does that make a difference?" Michael asked.

"Well, yes, I think so."

"Why?" Michael asked kindly.

"Because there are a lot of reasons." Amy found herself starting to get defensive, especially when she couldn't list anything immediate.

"Does this mean we can't be friends anymore?"

"No, I mean, it's just that you took me by surprise. I have to think about this a little bit," Amy said as she tried to steer the conversation back to his physical. She was trying to figure out why this lack of information irritated her so much. Nothing had happened; there hadn't been a date or suggestions, just friendship. Yet somehow, she felt misled. "In the meantime, let's go over your chart."

"Okay," Michael replied with a smile.

For the next twenty minutes, Amy reviewed Michael's history and performed a complete physical. She drew blood, discussed the proper prevention for his age, and ordered the appropriate lab testing while trying to remain completely professional, detached, and calm. "Okay, that about does it. I'll call you when the results are in. Do you have any questions?"

"Yes, will I see you at the bench later today?"

"I don't know," Amy said with a little anger creeping into her voice. "Why do you ask?"

"Because I think we need to talk about this. I think we got off on the wrong foot, and I'd like to discuss it with you."

"Well, I'm just surprised that you didn't tell me you were the pastor."

"Do you tell everyone you meet that you're a doctor?"

"No, but that's different."

"Why?"

"Because, being a doctor is my profession, not my way of life."

"Do you really believe that?"

"What do you mean?"

"Well, if you saw a bleeding child sitting in the street or a man clutching his chest in the supermarket, would you just walk away because you're not on duty?"

"Obviously not," Amy replied. "Most of the health-care workers I know would stop and help."

"So morally, you're on call 24-7," Father Michael pressed the point.

"Well, I guess so if you put it that way."

"But you don't always walk around in greens and a stethoscope?"

"What's your point?" Amy asked.

"It's the same with priests. Our calling is within us 24-7, but we don't always have to carry a Bible or hold a cross out before us. At times, we don't have to wear our clericals either."

"Okay, but it's like forgetting to tell someone you're married."

"It's only a problem if you're dating. You're allowed to be friends with married people."

"You know, this really isn't the time or place for this," Amy said angrily.

"Fine, how about later at our bench?" Father Michael asked.

"I don't know," Amy said sharply. "In the meantime, I have two questions that I really have to ask you."

"Fine, ask away," Father Michael said.

"First, I want to ask about Father Juan. He seems medically stable, but he's very unsettled with his current situation."

"He's trying to work through the shock."

"Well, he told me that he wants to go back to New Jersey. If I'm able to get him into a treatment program, can he go?"

"What do you mean?"

"I don't know what his situation is here. He told me that he was sent here by the archdiocese. If he left, would that be breaking a vow or something?"

Father Michael chuckled. "You and I really have to talk one day. He's not in prison. He was sent here to have some counseling to help him deal with his anxiety about having cancer. If there's treatment out there for him or if being away from his home or family is making him worse, he's free to go."

"Good because I left a message with a friend in New Jersey. I think there's a good program for him, but I have to hear back from her first."

"Please let us know as soon as you find out," Michael said. "We'll make arrangements for whatever Father Juan wants to do."

"Okay, that I will," Amy said. "Next, we have a mystery patient in the hospital this week. We're not quite sure what happened to him, but he's in a light coma right now."

"Would you like me to go see him? I can offer prayers," Father Michael asked.

"Thank you for that." Amy smiled at the immediate offer. "Actually, that's part of the mystery. He's had a priest with him the entire time he's been here. Everyone assumed that this priest was from St. Francis since it's one of the only Catholic churches in the area."

"Well, you've met all my priests this morning. Right now, it's only the four of us at St. Francis. Fathers Doherty and Cerulli are scheduled to start visiting patients in the hospital tomorrow."

"Really?" Amy asked with a surprised voice. "Do you know any other priests living or working in the immediate area?"

"No, not really. Even if there are priests just visiting this area, they usually stop in at the church to concelebrate mass or touch base."

Amy's mind was starting to reel. She knew this was an important piece of information. "This priest has a scar on his right cheek. I think he said that his name was Davis. Father Davis," Amy said. Suddenly, the missing piece clicked into place. "Oh no. Have you ever heard of a Father Davis?"

"No, I can't say that I have," Father Michael replied curiously.

"I have to go, I have to call Lou," Amy said more to herself than Father Michael.

"Wait, when can we talk again?"

"I'm not sure right now. I'll call you with your lab," Amy shouted over her shoulder as she ran from the room. As Amy ran past the nurse's desk, she almost knocked Barbara over.

"What's wrong?" Barbara asked.

"I have to get to the unit right away," Amy yelled over her shoulder.

"Is everything all right? Did something happen to Father Michael?" Barbara asked. "Do you need help?"

"No, it's Mr. Lawrence. Just try to page Lou Applebaum to the CICU stat," Amy shouted as the elevator doors slid closed. After what seemed like forever, the doors opened again, and Amy ran out of the elevator straight into Lou.

"Amy, are you okay?" Lou asked anxiously, his arms holding Amy steady.

"Lou, I talked to the pastor of St. Francis." She breathed heavily. "There has not been a priest from St. Francis here all week. I also remembered something else."

"What? What's going on?"

"Willow told me that her father has a scar on his face. I think this guy is really Bobby Davis. He's only dressed like a priest. Marty told me she thought she saw him in the hospital. Lou, Ben is in danger. We have to call the police."

"I just got a call from the unit that a man was in Ben's cubicle. He ran out the door when a nurse came in."

"Is Ben all right? Did they call security?"

"Well, yes and yes. The guy might have been Bobby Davis, but he didn't get what he wanted because I transferred Ben to another room this morning."

"Ben isn't in the unit anymore?"

"No, he's not. Ben was slightly more conscious this morning. We have a small area of private rooms that we keep strictly for VIPs. The patients aren't even registered in the regular system to maintain confidentiality. After our conversation this morning, I convinced the administration to let me use one of those rooms until we sorted this whole thing out."

"I'm so happy to hear you say that," Amy said with a big smile.

"Sounds like we transferred him just in the nick of time. Security is notifying the police, and hopefully, we'll find him."

"Do you think he's still in the hospital?" Amy asked.

"I wouldn't be if it were me," Lou said.

"Marty Davis is upstairs. Maybe we can go get a better description of Bobby. That way, we'll have more information for the police when they get here."

"Sounds like a plan, and security is reviewing the unit videotapes to get a picture of the mystery priest. Come on, let's go," Lou said as he escorted Amy back into the elevator.

Chapter Fifty-Two

Marty looked up when she heard the male voice and was relieved to find Tony at the door. Willow just stared at the large man until Marty walked over and began the introductions. "Tony, I'm so happy to see you," Marty said. "I want you to meet Willow. This is my daughter, my beautiful daughter, Willow," Marty repeated in a choked voice.

"Nice to meet you," Tony said as he shook Willow's hand. "Your mom has told me a lot about you. She's so proud of you."

"She is?" Willow said incredulously. "I didn't think she even knew who I was."

"Your mom has kept an eye on you for a long time. I know that she hasn't been in close touch, but she's going to get some serious help now, and I'm pretty sure that you'll see a lot more of each other."

"That is, if you'll let me," Marty said anxiously to Willow. "I'd really like to be friends if we can."

Willow didn't get a chance to reply before there was another knock on the door.

"Hello? Anybody Home?" Father Victor Cerulli's voice boomed into the room. "Tony, what are you doing here?"

"I might ask you the same thing, Father," Tony said with a smile. "I'm visiting some of my good friends. How about you?"

"Well, we're actually looking for Larry," Victor replied.

"Larry, the new guy?" Marty asked. "I saw him in group therapy this morning, and I recognized him from Hasco's, but I didn't get a chance to talk to him yet."

"Yeah, you know Larry," Tony said to Marty. "The good priests were at the grill yesterday, hanging posters for the carnival, and Larry asked them for help. They were kind enough to drop everything and bring him to the hospital."

"He came up to the floor late last night, so he may be napping in his room," Marty said. "They have a pretty strict schedule up here. Right now, we have free time, but we have another group starting in twenty minutes."

"Well, maybe we should go look for him," Father Pat said.

"Wait a minute," Tony said. "Father Victor, did you get a chance to check your schedule for the boxing ring yet?"

"Not yet, but I will. Then I'll show what real boxing is all about," Victor said kindly.

Tony's deep laugh could be heard down the hall while the others watched the two spar with their words.

"Hello, oh, wow, the gang's all here," Amy said as she walked into the room with Dr. Lou.

"Dr. Daniels, hi, this is my daughter, Willow," Marty said happily.

"Yes, Willow and I have met several times," Amy said. "As a matter of fact, she's going to be helping me in the clinic."

"Oh no," Willow cried out as she looked at her watch. "I can't believe that I missed the first session."

"No problem, I assumed that you were busy elsewhere. Next week, we'll start fresh."

"This is like a party," Marty said. "I haven't had this much company, ever."

"Well, uh, Marty, Dr. Lou and I came up here because we wanted to ask you a few questions," Amy said. "If you don't mind, that is."

"Questions, about what?"

"Well, about Willow's father, Bobby," Amy said as gently as she could. "Although, I didn't expect all these people to be here."

"That's okay," Father Victor said. "We're on our way out to find Larry. Tony, it was nice seeing you again. We start visitations here tomorrow, so maybe we'll run into each other, and then we can make plans."

"Looking forward to it, Father," Tony said as he shook the priest's hand.

As the priests left the room, Marty spoke up, "Whatever you have to say about Bobby, you can say it in front of Tony and Willow. Tony knows him for the jerk that he is, and sadly, Willow will have to find out sometime."

"Okay, I guess," Amy said uncomfortably. "Why don't we all sit down?" After they had slid the hospital visitor chairs into a circle and were seated, Amy started the conversation. "We, that is, Dr. Applebaum and I, wanted to ask you some questions about Bobby. Marty, when you first came into the hospital, you had indicated that he had threatened Willow."

"That's right," Marty said angrily. "He was asking about the trust funds that my mother left her and how he could get his dirty hands on some of the money."

"Are you kidding me?" Willow asked while making a face.

"That's why I was so upset. Tony promised to help me finally straighten out so I could help you," Marty explained.

"I don't freaking believe it," Willow said.

Amy tried to steer the conversation back to her questions. "Anyway, there's been a man in the hospital for the last several days. He's been dressed like a priest, but when we talked to the pastor of St. Francis Church, he assured us that he didn't know who this priest was."

"Bobby is no priest, I can tell you that," Marty said.

"Well, the thing about this particular priest is that he has a scar on his right cheek," Dr. Lou said while pointing to his face.

"Bobby has a scar on his face. He was torturing a cat, who escaped by scratching his face. I'm glad too because Bobby would have killed him for sure."

"What was he doing to the cat?"

"I heard through the grapevine that Bobby had a thing about needles. He liked to inject things. He would inject anything he could get his hands on like fruit, rubber balls, and even animals if he could catch them," Marty said with a shudder.

"What would he inject them with?" Amy asked.

"In the beginning, it was nothing. Just air, I guess. He liked sticking the needle into things. That's why I got so nervous when he started working for that pharmacy," Marty said.

"Excuse me," Dr. Lou asked. "Can you tell me which pharmacy?"

"You know, Rocky Meadow Apothecary. The one that Mr. Lawrence owns?"

"Benjamin Lawrence?"

"Yes, that's his name. I heard that Bobby would get upset when he worked for him because Ben refused to call him Bobby. Ben wanted the pharmacy to always sound professional."

"What would he call him?"

"Robert, always Robert. Ben is very formal and proper around the drugs," Marty replied.

"Robert? Ben said the words 'Rob, Liz.' Could it stand for 'Robert'? 'Robert and Liz?'" Amy asked Lou.

"My mother's name was Elizabeth, but a lot of people called her Lizzie. She was Willow's grandmother and did a wonderful job raising her. Does this have something to do with my mother?" Marty asked angrily.

Lou turned to Marty to explain. "We really don't know. It's just that a patient recently came to the hospital in a coma. He was awake only briefly, but he kept saying 'Rob Liz.' Willow, I don't know if you remember, but I was your grandmother's cardiologist. When she died and they brought her to the ER, there were some things that had happened that we couldn't quite explain. The patient that just came in reminded me of your grandmother. Then, when the man kept saying 'Rob Liz,' we thought he might be trying to send a message."

Willow clutched her stomach. "Oh my god, I think I'm going to be sick."

"What's wrong, Willow?" Marty asked with concern.

Willow started crying. "It's just that Grandma died right after I gave her a needle full of insulin. You don't think that I killed her, do you?"

"Willow," Amy said gently, "we know that you didn't do anything, so please don't cry. Let me ask you, did you show the needle or the insulin to the police?"

Willow was crying harder now. "No," she whispered. "They never asked for it, and I was afraid that I did something wrong. I was even afraid to throw it away because I was worried they would search the garbage, like on those TV shows."

"What did you do with it?" Amy asked softly.

"I . . . I," Willow sobbed. "I buried it in a fruit jar in the backyard."

"Do you know where? Can you find it if you had to?" Amy asked eagerly.

"I think so. Will I have to go to jail?"

Marty grabbed her daughter and hugged her tightly while she placed her face against the top of her head. "You're going nowhere. Now that I have you, no one is ever coming near you again."

"Willow," Amy explained, "the reason we need to find the fruit jar is that we can look for Bobby's fingerprints on the bottle. We can also check the contents of the bottle to see if it was actually insulin or something else. You're not going to get in any trouble, I promise."

"I can try to find it for you," Willow said.

"Great, good girl. We're going to let the police help us with this, okay?" Amy asked.

Willow nodded her head but jumped at the sound of a loud clanging in the hall, followed by someone yelling. Amy jumped up to look outside the door. Amy looked to her left and found herself staring straight into Bobby's face. His expression of hate sent chills right through her. Then he pointed his finger at her and mouthed the words, "You're dead, bitch."

"Call the police," Amy yelled as loud as she could. "It's him, it's Bobby." As her words rang out, Bobby turned and started running for the stairs. Tony ran out of the room and started chasing him down the hall. Amy grabbed the hall phone and shouted to the operator to call a code black. A code black was the announcement that would alert the security staff and, hopefully, lockdown the hospital. As Amy hung up the phone, she ran to the opposite staircase to try to cut him off from the outside doors. She flew down flight after flight of stairs, hanging on to the railing so she wouldn't fall. As she reached the bottom step, she felt, more like saw, someone push into her and run out the fire door. As she got up off the floor, she ran outside and watched as Bobby jumped the small wall that separated the parking lot from the hospital grass. Her cell phone started chirping in her pocket. Amy grabbed the phone, hoping she could give direction to the police. As she opened the phone, Tony banged out the door and stood next to her, breathing heavily with Lou right behind. She put the phone to her ear, "Hello?" Amy panted, hoping it was the police.

"Amy? Hi, it's Amanda . . ."

Chapter Fifty-Three

Amy drove her car over the covered wooden bridge, but instead of stopping and walking to her favorite bench, she continued another two blocks to the church driveway. She found a parking stall, and after turning off her car, she got out and looked around. The church grounds were built on a hill at the base of one of the mountains. Amy looked toward the Divide, at her bench, and the splendid view of the mountains beyond and could easily understand why they had chosen this spot to build a retreat house. Turning back to the rectory, she climbed the steps and rang the bell. Within a few minutes, a handsome middle-aged woman opened the large wooden door and said, "Hello, can I help you?"

"Hi, my name is Dr. Amy Daniels. I'm here to bring some information to Father Juan."

"Oh, please, come in," Katie said as she stepped back from the door and offered a large, radiant smile. "My name is Katie."

"Hi, nice to meet you," Amy said as she stepped into the rectory foyer.

"Father Juan is resting upstairs. If you don't mind, I'd like to show you to the parlor, and then I'll go get him. It may be a few minutes."

"Thank you, I'd appreciate that," Amy said.

"Would you like a little tea while you're waiting?" Katie asked cheerfully.

"No, thank you, I'm not really a tea person."

"Coffee then? We have wonderful coffee in Vermont, don't we?"

"As a matter of fact, it's quite good, but I only drink decaf. My life is exciting enough," Amy joked.

Katie showed Amy to a group of couches near a marble fireplace. "Make yourself comfortable, dear, and I'll go get Father Juan."

"Thank you, Katie," Amy said as she sat on one of the couches. The fireplace was set with fresh wood. As she looked around the room, she noticed that the furniture, while not quite antique, was grand in design and very inviting. She could just imagine herself sitting near a crackling fire in the cold weather, reading a good book while curled up on one of these couches, sipping hot chocolate. The view from the large window was just as spectacular as being outside. In the winter, this room would be a warm, wonderful haven, a perfect place to watch the beautiful, pristine snow of Vermont pile up in silence. She could even imagine a horse-drawn sleigh coming up the drive.

Amy turned at the sound of the door and jumped up as Father Juan and Father Michael entered the room. They were both dressed in clericals and walked to the couch opposite from hers. Father Michael started the conversation. "Please sit," he said as he pointed to her couch. "Welcome to our rectory."

"It's quite a beautiful place," Amy said as she reseated herself.

"Thank you," Father Michael replied with a smile. "How can we help you?"

"I'm actually hoping that I can help you. I heard back from Dr. Amanda Chase in New Jersey," Amy replied as she looked at Father Juan. "I gave her a brief summary of your medical history, and I'm happy to tell you that she thinks there may be a program that would be a perfect fit."

"Really?" Father Juan said with surprise.

"Yes, of course, you realize that it's an experimental program. Dr. Chase said that she would be happy to contact your oncologist in New Jersey, with your permission, and make the arrangements if you're interested."

"Of course I'm interested," Father Juan replied. "Vermont is a beautiful place to think and visit, but I miss my home very much. If there's a chance that any program may help me, I'd like to be a part of it."

"How soon would Father Juan need to leave?" Father Michael asked.

"I'm not sure, but within days to a week by the time the necessary appointments are made," Amy replied.

"Fine, that will give me plenty of time to make arrangements with the archdiocese as well," Father Michael said as he turned to Father Juan and embraced him. "Godspeed, my brother. We only wish you the best."

"Thank you, thank you both," Father Juan said as a large smile spread across his face. "I want the treatment even if it only offers a small chance that I can live longer to spread God's message to my kids."

"That's the first time I've seen you smile since you arrived here," Father Michael teased.

"My heart is now full of hope," Father Juan answered. "Thank you again."

"I'll call you when I hear back from Dr. Chase so that you have enough time to make travel arrangements," Amy said to Father Juan.

"Thank you. I have a few calls to make. Would you please excuse me?" Father Juan asked as he stood and headed for the door, anticipation glowing on his face.

"Good luck, Father Juan," Amy said. "I'll be in touch."

"God bless you," he answered. As he turned toward the door, he almost collided with Katie bearing a large tray filled with a coffeepot, cups, and saucers.

"Oh my," Katie said. "I was just bringing in a fresh pot of coffee."

"I would love a pot of your coffee, Katie," Father Michael said.

"I have some fresh cookies too," Katie said as she set the tray on the table between the two couches.

"It looks delicious," Amy said as she watched Katie pour the coffee. The strong aroma was appealing after a long day.

"Cream and sugar, dear?" Katie asked as she held Amy's steaming cup.

"Just cream for me, thanks."

"Here you go," Katie replied as she handed Amy the cup. "You look like you could use a little pick-me-up."

"Thank you, this is very good," Amy said as she sipped the coffee.

"Father Michael, for you," Katie said as she handed him a cup.

"Thank you, Katie."

"You're welcome. Well, I'll be off to the kitchen. Dinner is almost ready, if you can stay," Katie said to Amy.

"Thank you, Katie, but I really can't tonight."

"Well, another time then," Katie said with a smile. "It was nice meeting you, dear."

As Katie left the room, Father Michael settled back on his couch and said, "So what was happening at the hospital? You were asking about a Father Davis and then just ran out of the room."

"I'm sorry for running out. As I mentioned earlier, we've had a mystery patient this week. He's in a coma, and we're not quite sure why, but something strange happened. Then there's been this priest by his bedside since he came in. No offense, Father, but he didn't look like he had the countenance of a typical priest."

"I would love to hear your definition of what that should be." Father Michael chuckled.

"That's another story," Amy said with chagrin. "Anyway, one day I asked this priest his name since I'm new to the area anyway, and he said it was Father Davis. Unfortunately, no one at the hospital had ever heard of a Father Davis. You'd never heard of a Father Davis. I also noticed that he had a scar on his right cheek."

"Priests have scars, physically and emotionally," Father Michael said as he drank his coffee.

"Obviously, but the rest of the story is that we've also had a threat against a young girl at the hospital by the name of Willow Davis. She told me that her father had a scar on his right cheek. For some reason, the two facts just clicked together for me when I was speaking with you this morning, and I needed to alert the unit and security."

"I know Willow Davis and her family," Father Michael said slowly. "As a matter of fact, her grandmother, Elizabeth, donated a lot of money to this church. Even now, we receive donations on a regular basis from a trust fund that she set up before she died. Willow helps us out on occasion when we need a volunteer."

"Our conversation is confidential, right, Father?"

"Of course it is, and would you please go back to calling me Michael?"

"Okay, well, Elizabeth is part of the issue here. Apparently, Willow had just given her an injection when she had that reaction and died. Willow's been secretly afraid that she was responsible for her death."

"Really? I wonder if she ever went to confession with that," Michael mused to himself.

"I don't know anything about that. She didn't mention confession. Personally, I haven't been to confession in so long I wouldn't even know how to do it anymore," Amy said.

"That's another discussion as well," Michael said. "So what does Lizzie's death have to do with Father Davis?"

"Well, we now know that Father Davis was actually Bobby Davis. We know that he threatened his daughter, Willow's life, to get access to her inheritance. We also suspect that he might have had something to do with Lizzie's death and possibly tried to kill our other patient."

"Very interesting," Michael said. "So what happened at the hospital?"

"We called security and the police. Bobby was there but escaped after running out of the hospital. Security is now on high alert. The police spent the afternoon getting statements from many of us at the hospital, and I believe they've put out a BOLO for him."

"What's a BOLO?" Father Michael asked.

"I believe it stands for 'Be On the Look Out,'" Amy answered as she finished her coffee and set the cup on the tray.

"Oh, I thought it was still APB, 'all-points bulletin.'" Michael laughed. "I guess I'm starting to get old. Anyway, so how is Willow dealing with all of this?"

"She's confused and scared. I gave her my cell, and I have all of her phone numbers in case there's any problem this weekend. The police department really doesn't have enough people to watch her, so she's staying close to home."

"She must be upset," Michael said.

"She is, I tried to talk to her, but she may need more professional help. Perhaps you can talk to her since she comes to the church," Amy suggested.

"She doesn't always come to mass. Maybe the two of you could come together on Sunday morning," Father Michael suggested.

"I haven't been to mass in a long time, especially not since . . . a long time," Amy said hurriedly.

"Amy, I sense that something is bothering you. If you ever want to talk about it, I'm here as a friend. I'm here as a priest if you need me to be, but I know that you're burdened," Michael said kindly.

Amy immediately choked up. "It's very difficult for me. Some . . . some of my family died, and it's been very hard for me to deal with."

"I'm a good listener, whenever you want to talk."

"It's different telling things to a priest than it is to a friend or a doctor."

"Why?"

"I don't know. Maybe because I was brought up with the idea that priests were in a position of authority. It's like telling your mother something instead of your best friend."

"We're not the police."

"I know that, but if someone is going to pour their heart out, they want to know what playing field they're on. The same story can evoke different responses depending on who you're telling it to, and as a psychologist, you know that."

"Yes, I do. I apologize for not making it clear that I was a priest. You know, it's difficult being a priest, especially with all the scandal that's come out in the last couple of years, but not all priests are bad."

"Neither are all doctors, but we get judged all the time," Amy said. "Some of us are very caring and sensitive and not money hungry."

"I understand completely. People get judged by their appearance, their weight, or their ethnicity, and most of the time, the judgment is incorrect. People have different reactions to being with someone in clericals. Mostly, they're comforted, especially in the church or in a hospital for instance. Some people have very negative reactions, depending on their beliefs or experience. Once again, I'm sorry that I didn't emphasize that I was a priest. But for the record, I have never touched little boys, or big ones for that matter, or women. I have never broken my vows. Sometimes, I have just as many questions about spirituality and God as others do. Yet I am a priest, a disciple of Christ. Priests are only human beings. There are many clergy that suffer from fear, greed, and addiction or who are afflicted with pain. We make poor choices just like all humans, and we pray for God's forgiveness. On a personal note, I get hungry, lonely, and depressed on occasion. I also laugh at times, enjoy beautiful sunsets, and I like to watch Bugs Bunny cartoons when I'm bored. I'm allowed to have friends and conversations about subjects other than the church." Michael paused to take a breath from his rant.

Amy couldn't help but grin. "And how do you really feel about that?"

"Very emotional, apparently," Father Michael said with a laugh.

"Listen, I'm a physician. I was a strong Catholic when I was young, but the only priests I've seen recently were on my surgical table. Death, disease, and trauma find us all regardless of position, power, or wealth. The patients that I saw were at their most vulnerable, stripped of their cloth and cloak. I realize that we're all just human beings trying to survive in this world. I thought I did a pretty good job at not judging anyone, but apparently, I haven't," Amy said. "I usually don't tell people I meet outside of the hospital that I'm a doctor because the response is overwhelming. They either assume that I'm rich and arrogant or ask me to diagnose them on the spot."

"Well, now that we got that out of the way, are we friends again?" Michael asked her with raised eyebrows and a grin.

"Friends," Amy said as she reached over the coffee table for a handshake. "Now, I really have to be going."

"You're sure that you can't stay for dinner? Katie is a great cook."

"No, I have an exciting frozen dinner waiting for me at home. Maybe some other time, but not tonight. I have some paperwork that I must get done," Amy said as she collected her things and started to leave.

As Michael walked her to the door, he said, "Amy, I'm really glad that you stopped by today. I'm happy that we straightened things out between us and for Father Juan. You've given him hope again, and that's priceless."

"I just made the connection. The rest is up to God," Amy said in a humble tone. "Thank you for the coffee. Please tell Katie it was delicious."

"I will," Michael said as he watched Amy go down the stairs and get into her car. As she drove away, Michael glanced to his right and noticed a man standing in the woods. Curious, Michael walked down the steps and started over to the trees. People from the community often visited the beautiful grounds of the church, but they were engrossed looking at the scenery or the Divide, not hiding in the trees. Just in case, Father Michael thought he should check it out. When the man saw Michael approach, he started running deeper into the woods. "Hey, wait a minute," Father Michael called out as he chased him for a few yards before his calf cramped up, and he had to stop.

Chapter Fifty-Four

Father Michael sat in the quiet confessional, waiting for parishioners. Confessions were slow today. It was a gorgeous spring Saturday, which he realized would compete with one's need to confess. He doubted that the art of sinning had decreased, but even he couldn't wait to get outside and enjoy the day. His calf had been feeling better after five days of ice, massage, and an elastic bandage, and his original goal had been to try a moderate training run. But after yesterday's encounter with the man in the woods, he had increased pain. Michael had debated calling Amy to let her know, but he didn't have her cell phone. Secondly, there was no sense causing panic if the man wasn't Bobby.

Michael couldn't believe that only one week had passed since he last heard confession. He still had no clue as to the identity of the woman that had come in and confessed to possibly killing someone. The woman had said that it was three years since her last confession. Thankfully, no dead bodies had been found recently although all this business with Bobby Davis was worrisome. But the person in the confessional was a woman, not a man. Michael was sure of that. She must have been referring to a past incident, or her self-imposed guilt was bothering her. He now knew that it wasn't Amy. He didn't doubt that she had witnessed many people die over the years, but that didn't mean she held herself accountable. Also, she said that she hadn't been in confession for a long time. Could it have been Willow? Maybe. Perhaps she was consumed with guilt after watching her grandmother, Lizzie, die after that needle was given. If she was at church this weekend, he would find some way to gently ask her about confession. Still, he wasn't sure that it was her voice, but he knew the voice was familiar.

He heard the old wooden kneeler squeak as someone rested their weight upon it. To start the confession, Father Michael slid open the small window screen.

"Bless me, Father, for I have sinned."

*   *   *

While Father Michael heard confessions, Father Victor and Father Pat finished the delicious breakfast Katie had made for them. "Katie, you're a fabulous cook. Food has never tasted this good to me," Pat said with enthusiasm.

"Oh, Father, it's the mountain air. You're getting a good old-fashioned appetite back again too," Katie said with a smile.

"Well, it was delicious. Thank you very much," Pat answered. "Could I bother you for some aspirin? I seem to have a bit of a headache this morning."

"Of course, Father Pat," Katie said as she retrieved a bottle of medication.

"Thank you, you're an angel," Father Pat said as he rubbed his temples.

"Katie, your family is very lucky," Victor said.

A shadow crossed Katie's face. "The church is my family now, Father Victor. I'm the lucky one. My husband passed a few years ago, and Father Michael was very kind to create a position for me."

"Katie, I'm sure that your being here is much more than mere kindness on Father Michael's part," Victor said. "It seems that St. Francis couldn't run without you."

"On the contrary, Father Victor, I think it would survive just fine if I left," Katie answered.

"I wouldn't be so sure of that, Katie," Victor said as he smiled. "Father Pat, we have to be going now. I promised Larry we'd be at the hospital for the group meeting this morning."

"Ah, so far, he's doing well there, isn't he?" Pat stated, more like asked.

"Well, so far, things are working out," Victor agreed. "But he has a long road ahead of him. I guess he was ready for a program and just needed the right shepherd to bring him into the fold."

"Let's go tend our flock then, shall we?" Pat said as he stood up to leave. "Katie, have a blessed day, and we'll see you for dinner."

"Same to you both. Have a great day," a blushing Katie said as they left the room. She turned to clean the table and planned on bringing a tray upstairs to Father Juan. He had stayed up late making plans to go home and, in the process, exhausted himself, so he was sleeping late today. The rest of Katie's weekend would be spent dealing with Florence and last-minute arrangements for the carnival.

Chapter Fifty-Five

Amy smiled when she turned into the long drive of Willow's home and saw her waiting on the doorstep. She was glad that Willow had agreed to go to church with her this morning but wished she wasn't sitting out in broad daylight in case Bobby showed up. Hopefully, church would do them both some good. Amy hadn't been to a mass in many years and then started feeling guilty when her sister had been killed. She used to attend mass and felt uplifted when the service was over, but that had been a long time ago.

She was surprised that Willow had agreed to come to church with her so readily, but she found out that Katie had also asked Willow to stop by and help with the carnival plans. Katie was a very nice woman, and Amy had taken a liking to her. The carnival was due to start in a couple of days, and there was much to be done.

Amy lightly tapped on the horn as she pulled the car to a stop. She opened her window for a quick wave and smelled the aroma of a fresh wood fire. Willow got into the car and began fastening her seat belt.

"Good morning, Willow," Amy said with a smile. "How are you today?"

"Good. I got up early so I could be ready on time." Willow smiled back.

"Well, you look great. We'll be there with time to spare," Amy said as she pulled out of the driveway and onto the road which led down to the base of Willow's property. "The view from your front door is absolutely gorgeous. Did your grandmother choose this piece of property?"

"My great-grandparents lived on this hill in a little wood cabin. They worked their farm until they died, I guess. When my grandparents inherited the land, they rebuilt the house. I don't know if they picked which direction it faced, though."

"The morning view with the sun over the valley is breathtaking," Amy said with admiration.

"The sunset at the back of the house is even prettier, especially when it reflects off the lake and the Divide. The whole valley looks orange-gold. Grandma said you can just about see the heavens from the top of this mountain."

"That sounds beautiful," Amy said.

"It is. We used to have tea on the back deck at sunset," Willow added, her voice choking up briefly.

"You really miss her, don't you?" Amy asked.

"A lot," Willow said as she sniffed.

"I know how you feel. My sister was killed last year, and my niece is in a coma. I miss them a lot too," Amy said quietly, wondering why she just admitted that to Willow.

"You do?"

"Yes, at first, I don't even know how I survived. All I could think of was my sister and my beautiful niece."

"Did you cry a lot?" Willow asked.

"All day, every day," Amy answered. "I know that they wouldn't have wanted that, but I missed them so much."

"I know what you mean. I miss my grandmother, a lot."

"I'm sure that your grandmother would want you to be happy. If you ever want to talk about it, you can always call me. You have my cell phone, okay?"

"Okay, maybe when I get really sad," Willow said quietly.

"On another note, did you come home with the police last night?" Amy asked as she turned the car onto the main highway.

"Yes, two of the officers drove me home," Willow said. "They spoke to my so-called guardian and then asked me to show them where I buried the fruit jar with the needle and the insulin bottle."

"Did they find it?" Amy asked curiously.

"Yes, they dug it up and put it in a Baggie. They took it to the lab for testing." Willow swallowed hard. "Do you think I'll be in trouble for doing that?"

"I don't think so, but why did you bury it anyway?"

"To be honest, I don't really know. When I came home from the hospital that day, there were so many people here. I was afraid that it was my entire fault. No one had asked about the bottle, not even the police, but every time I looked at it, I would get really anxious. I didn't know if I was allowed to throw it out, so I buried it."

"You weren't purposely trying to hide anything, right?" Amy asked.

"No, it's just that I didn't want to look at it," Willow said.

"You didn't have to show the police where it was. They don't suspect that you had anything to do with Lizzie's death, but it may offer a clue as to why she died."

"I hope it helps them," Willow said quietly.

"I'm sure it will. Try not to worry about it," Amy said encouragingly. After a few seconds of silence, Amy asked, "What does Katie want you to do today?"

"She said that people are already dropping off bottled drinks and prizes for the carnival. She wants me to help her sort them out."

"That sounds like fun," Amy said.

"Yeah, but there's a lot to be done. The carnival company will start setting up the booths and rides after today's masses, and we have to put the sponsor signs on each booth as well."

"Do you need a little extra help?" Amy asked.

"The more the merrier," Willow said. "Do you really think that he did all those things?"

"Who? You lost me there," Amy said.

"Do you think my father did all the bad things the police asked me about?"

"I don't know, Willow. Your mom indicated that he said some pretty mean things about you and your grandmother's money," Amy said as she looked at Willow briefly to gauge her reaction.

"Watch out," Willow cried.

Amy turned back in time to see the deer. She was able to swerve out of the way just in time. "You can't take your eyes off the road for one second around here," Amy said out loud.

"I get to start driver's ed soon," Willow said. "I can't wait."

Amy drove over the covered wooden bridge and down the road to the church entrance. As she turned into the church parking lot, she was surprised to see that it was packed with cars. The spaces were all taken. Some cars, as well as tractor trailers holding rides, were parked on the grass. Amy found a parking space near the back of the lot. "I guess we weren't as early as I thought," she said.

"We still have time," Willow said as they hurried across the lot to the steps of the church.

Amy and Willow found a seat in a pew near the front of the church. Amy had hoped to sit near the back of the church since she hadn't attended mass in years. She could just watch the people around her to know when to sit and stand and read the responses directly from the book. She used to have them memorized, but not anymore. As Amy waited for the mass to begin, she looked around the church. It was constructed of dark rich woods. The altar table and pulpit were made of smooth marble seated on a raised platform of marble. A golden tabernacle was set against a dark wooden background at the side of the altar. The altar candles were already lit and burning. Wooden beams with small prayers etched into them supported the high-vaulted ceiling. Sunlight was pouring through the glass stained windows, reflecting different patterns on the wood. The sun, behind the windows, made the transparent images shine with color. It was a beautiful church constructed years ago when the reverence of the house of worship was more important than the mortgage it would hold. Amy was always struck with a powerful feeling when she sat in a quiet church. Although there was no activity, there was an expectant charge in the air and feeling of anticipation and nervousness in her soul.

Willow was perched on the kneeler with her hands pressed against each other and her head bowed in prayer. After a few seconds, she sat back and smiled. As the clergy lined up in the vestibule, the leader of song announced the main celebrant and the entrance hymn. Rising, the parishioners joined in song with earnest. Amy couldn't help but smile as she turned toward the altar and sang the familiar hymn.

Relaxing as the mass continued, Amy thought she might start coming back to church on a more regular basis. Seated in front of the pulpit, she had a close view of Father Michael as he ascended the stairs and began his homily. She wasn't sure, but she thought he had a half smile on his face when he noticed them sitting there. She had never seen him serve mass before, and it felt strange, but familiar. His homily focused on new beginnings blessed with God's love after rising from the ashes of one's life. How important and appropriate that theme was. She herself had been trying to rise from the ashes for a while. The mass continued with the consecration followed by communion or sharing of the bread. At the closing prayers, she once again stood and joined in the recessional hymn as the clergy processed off the altar and toward the back of the church. Slowly the parishioners stopped to offer greetings to the priests on their way out. As Amy and Willow neared the door, Amy felt nervous but didn't know why. She stayed in line and was handed a bulletin as she walked out the door. She and Willow greeted Fathers Victor, Patrick, and Juan, standing in a row at the top of the stairs. After a few seconds, they reached Father Michael.

"Good morning, Willow," Father Michael said with a large smile on his face. "Hi, Amy. I'm really glad that you two made it to mass."

"Good morning, Father," Willow said with a small smile as she shook his hand.

"I hope you enjoyed the mass," he said as he then turned to Amy and took her hand in his.

"I actually did," Amy stammered. Their warm hands joined a little more tightly than the standard handshake after mass, and Amy found herself blushing when they let go. "I haven't been to mass in many years, but I think I was wrong to stay away."

"I'm so glad to hear you say that," Michael said with a big smile. "What about you, Willow?"

"To tell the truth, I haven't been to mass since Grandmother died," Willow said shyly.

"Not even confession?" Michael asked slyly now that he had his chance to sneak in the question.

"Not since she died, Father. I'm sorry, but she was the only one who took me to church. My so-called guardian doesn't go to church. She barely even talks to me."

"You haven't been here in a while?" Father Michael asked disappointedly.

"Not to mass, Father. I've come and helped Katie from time to time. But I haven't come to mass or confession. I'm sorry," Willow added meekly.

"It's okay, Willow. I'm not upset with you. You know, if you want to come to church, you can always call me or Katie, and we'll make sure you get here. I'm sure that Amy would bring you as well when she can come."

"Of course, I can bring you to mass, Willow," Amy said. "But there may be days when I'll have to work at the hospital. Then we could call Katie and make other arrangements."

"I'll have my driver's permit soon," Willow said a little too eagerly.

"Oh boy," Amy said. "You have to be careful on these roads. Let's not get too ahead of ourselves."

"I'll try, but I can't wait."

"Apparently not," Michael said as they all laughed.

"We'll see you later, Father. Amy and I are going to go help Katie with the carnival booths," Willow said as she tugged on Amy's hand.

"Really? You two are staying to help set up the carnival?" Michael asked.

"Evidently," Amy said with a shrug. "According to Willow, the more the merrier."

"Are you going to help as well?" Willow asked excitedly.

"Unfortunately, I have to go to another church to help with a baptism," Father Michael said. "But I wish I were staying here because it sounds like you and all the other volunteers are going to have a lot of fun."

"Well, that's okay. You'll be at the carnival later this week," Willow said brightly.

"That's a promise. We'll get some cotton candy together, okay?" Father Michael asked.

"Okay," Willow said. "We should go now."

"Amy, have a great day. Maybe I'll see you tomorrow at our bench?" Michael asked with a smile.

"Perhaps," Amy said shyly as they walked down the stairs and headed for the rectory.

Chapter Fifty-Six

Standing at the side of the parking lot, Bobby watched his daughter, Willow, talk to the priest and doctor. It was because of them that he couldn't find Ben Lawrence. It was also their fault that he was now on the Most Wanted list of the local police department. Looking for him everywhere, the police had come to his apartment and asked his neighbors plenty of questions. There was a police car parked in front of his place twenty-four hours a day. They had kept a patrol car in front of the Rocky Meadow Apothecary too. Now that stupid doctor was trying to be friends with his daughter and his money. He would fix that. He'd been watching the doctor meet that priest at the bench every afternoon. According to the church bulletin, which had been fluttering against his leg during mass, the priest was going on a bus trip with other parishioners to Burlington on Tuesday. The carnival would start on Tuesday as well. Bobby started to get excited as a small malicious thought ran around his brain. He would impersonate the priest and get her to meet him. The carnival would provide the perfect cover. In two days, she would be dead, and no one would notice with all the confusion.

Chapter Fifty-Seven

The hospital was bursting with the usual activity on Monday morning. In addition to visitors bearing flowers, balloons, and ice cream, there were many patients arriving for outpatient testing, procedures, and consultations. Amy made her way past the security desk and headed for the emergency room. Ernie had been on all evening and would be ready to leave as soon as she changed. Today, she was assigned to the emergency room, and tomorrow, she would be working in the clinic. For now, the clinic would run two days a week, and she hoped the program would be successful. From working at her last hospital in Boston, she knew that fast-tracking some of the patients would save them all time, money, and resources.

As Amy continued on to the ER, she thought about how much she enjoyed working with Willow and Katie on Sunday. They had worked hard but also had a lot of fun setting up the booths. They sorted the prizes that would be given away and placed the placards on the booths, indicating who the particular sponsor was. Some of the games were ready to be played, and just for fun, they spun the big wheels and tried their hand at tossing balls.

Katie made a delicious lunch, and the three of them told stories and laughed while they ate. It was the first time that Amy had socialized since moving to Vermont, and she really enjoyed herself. She was looking forward to the start of the carnival tomorrow.

Amy snapped out of her reverie when she was almost hit by an empty wheelchair being propelled toward the elevator by a technician on the run. "Sorry, heads up," the technician yelled out as he passed by. Amy jumped back and flattened herself against the corridor wall until he had passed by.

"Hey, slow down," Amy said with a laugh. "We have enough real patients. We don't need to make new ones." Amy turned and walked into the locker rooms. She changed into a fresh set of greens, put away her personal belongings, and got ready to start her shift. Monday was always the most hectic day of the week. A host of patients waiting for the weekend to end were the first group to show up in the hospital, eager and ready to push ahead with their treatments or exams. "Ernie, what's up?" Amy said as she walked over to the central desk in the emergency room.

"Hey, Amy. How was your weekend?" Ernie asked with a smile.

"Different, that's for sure," Amy said quietly.

"Well, I hope you rested because it's going to be hectic here today."

"Tell me something I don't know," Amy said with a grimace.

"Well, room 1 has a fresh fracture. We're just waiting for orthopedics to show up. Room 2 is an elderly woman with an exacerbation of her. We're waiting for her chest x-ray to come back. Room 3 is a kindly gentleman in acute kidney failure who needs to start dialysis today."

"Gee, Ernie, that's all you got?" Amy said with a grin.

"Well, in the waiting room, you have eleven people with various colds, coughs, and stomach aches. Oh yeah, there's a guy in room 4 who sliced his hand between his thumb and forefinger trying to cut his bagel. It looks like he'll need about fifteen stitches or so."

"Now, I'm sorry that I asked," Amy said.

"Be careful what you wish for. I'd stay and help, but I really have to get out of here. I need some fresh air," Ernie said with a tired smile.

"Go on, get out. I think that I have a physician's assistant coming in today anyway," Amy said. "I'll see you later."

"Actually, you'll see Art later. He's in the emergency room tonight."

"Good, just leave already and let me go to work," Amy encouraged kindly.

"I'm gone," Ernie tossed over his shoulder as he walked toward the locker rooms. Amy spent the next several hours examining patients, ordering tests, writing her chart notes, and trying to keep up to the Monday morning patient flow. The physician's assistant arrived before lunch and was able to cover the midday shift. Her arrival, combined with an empty waiting room, allowed Amy enough time to stretch and head toward the doctor's lounge for a well-deserved cup of coffee.

Amy chose the oldest but most comfortable easy chair in the room and enjoyed the aroma of the rich, strong brew. She had just started to relax when the lounge door swung open followed by the arrival of Lou Applebaum.

"Hey, Amy, I'm glad that I bumped into you. I was looking for you," Lou said with enthusiasm.

"Hi, Lou. Actually, I was going to call you later. The emergency room was busy this morning. This is the first break that I've had this morning," Amy said while taking a sip of her coffee. "Anything important?"

"Well, Ben is more alert. The police posted a guard at his door just in case someone figures out where we moved him. So far, no one's turned up."

"That's a relief," Amy said.

"As soon as he's coherent, the police will try to talk with him. Have you seen Willow today?" Lou asked while pouring himself a cup of coffee.

"No, not yet. I'm planning on going up to Marty's room when the shift is over. Maybe she'll be up there with her mom. I was with her yesterday, and I think she's just really overwhelmed with everything that's happened in the past week."

"I can imagine. The poor kid has a lot on her plate," Lou said while shaking his head.

"She said the police drove her home Friday and dug up the needle and the insulin vial she used to give her grandma, Lizzie, that last shot," Amy recalled.

"Yeah, I heard that. The officer that came in this morning told me that they found a partial fingerprint on the top of the vial. They're looking for a match. Also, whatever was in that vial, apparently, was not insulin, so they're running a toxicology screen," Lou said with raised eyebrows.

"If they can prove that the insulin was switched out, the police will open a homicide investigation for sure," Amy said with a grimace. "What a shame. I feel so sorry for that poor girl."

"I remember when Lizzie arrived in the emergency room that day. I knew something wasn't right, but I couldn't put my finger on anything specific. She had just had a physical and a stress test, and both were normal. She exercised all the time. In retrospect, I'm quite sure that she was murdered. I don't know exactly how or why, but she was too healthy to have an attack like that without help, if you know what I mean."

"Well, I'm sure that the police will figure it out," Amy said with a tired grin. "I just hope that they catch him soon."

"Me too," Lou said with a nod. After a small pause, he said, "I . . . ah . . . was wondering, maybe we could have dinner this week and talk it over a little more."

Amy smiled. "This week may be a little tough, Lou. I promised Willow and the good clergy of St. Francis Church that I would volunteer at the carnival. It starts tomorrow and runs all week. I thought it might be a good way to keep tabs on Willow while keeping her distracted," Amy rushed on.

"That sounds like fun," Lou said. "Maybe next week then when things calm down a little."

The overhead speaker exploded with sound at the same time Amy's beeper went off. "Code Blue, emergency, waiting room. Code Blue, emergency, waiting room." Amy jumped out of her chair. "I've got to go. If you have a minute, come lend a hand." As the coffee from her cup sloshed on the side table, they both ran out of the lounge.

Chapter Fifty-Eight

Father Michael stood on the steps of the church and greeted the morning parishioners. The mass had moved quickly this morning. Father Victor and Father Pat stood at his side and warmly shook hands with departing parishioners. Father Juan tried to attend mass but had to return to his room with severe nausea. They were still waiting for a final confirmation from the palliative care program in New Jersey, and Michael hoped it would come soon. Father Juan had been excited over the weekend when he learned there might be an experimental treatment for him, and he wanted to go home. Even if the treatment didn't work, he wanted to be with his family and his parishioners.

"Father Michael, can you believe that the carnival starts tomorrow?" Florence gushed with enthusiasm.

"Florence, how are you today?" Father Michael asked with a smile.

"Busy, Father, very, very busy. The carnival starts tomorrow, and there is so much to do."

"I'm sure that you and Ted are up to it," Father Michael said.

A quick shadow passed over Florence's face. "Ted gets a little cranky from time to time. Will you be helping us with the setup tomorrow morning?" Florence asked sweetly.

"I'm sorry, Florence, but I have to be at a meeting in Burlington tomorrow. I probably won't be back until late."

"Oh, that's too bad," Florence said with a mock frown.

"I'm sure that Katie and Jack will be able to provide you with whatever you need," Father Michael pointed out.

"I'm sure they will, Father, but I'll miss you," Florence said with a little whine.

"Don't worry, Florence. I'll see you and Ted during the carnival."

"Okay, Father. Have a good day," Florence called out as she reluctantly walked toward the parking lot.

"She's an interesting personality," Father Victor said as he came up to Michael's side.

"That she is, but she means well. She drives everyone crazy, especially Katie, but she does put a lot of effort into the carnival each year, and she gets great results."

"Somehow, I don't think her effort would be as great if you left the parish, Father Michael," Victor pointed out. Michael turned to look at Victor with a laugh.

"I assure you, Father, that our relationship is strictly spiritual. I appreciate her time and efforts, but our relationship will never be more than professional friendship and spirituality."

"That's a relief to hear, Father Michael."

"What are your plans for today, my friend?" Father Michael asked as he redirected the conversation.

"Father Pat and I plan to go back to the hospital. We're saying mass in the chapel, and then we'll visit the patients."

"I'm glad that you're getting involved over there, but be careful. I have an uneasy feeling about this whole situation with Willow and her parents," Father Michael said with a grimace. "The situation seems to be spiraling out of control."

"Well, I think Marty will be okay. Tony seems to be watching over her like a hawk. Speaking of which, Tony and I are going to spend a little time in the ring this afternoon. He may be retired from NYPD, but he's still pretty intense sometimes."

"I'm glad to hear that," Father Michael said as they walked back inside the church. "I know that Amy is watching over Willow as much as she possibly can, but I'll feel better when they have Bobby in custody. Keep alert and make sure you check in with Katie now and again."

"I will, Father Michael, I will," Victor said while he blew out the altar candles.

*　　*　　*

It was late afternoon, and Michael had been waiting for almost an hour at the bench. It was another beautiful day, but so far, Amy hadn't showed. Michael was a little surprised and hoped that she was just busy at the hospital. He was pretty certain that they had worked through their misunderstanding, but she really hadn't promised to be at the bench today. He was looking forward to discussing how the search for Bobby was going, and he wanted to hear about her day setting up for the carnival. Michael couldn't help but feel disappointed as he stood up, stretched, and slowly walked back to the rectory.

Chapter Fifty-Nine

Amy sat at her clinic desk and sorted through the incoming lab results. As she worked, her mind drifted back to the hectic day she had yesterday. Mondays were not usually that wild, but yesterday was busy. She had spent the entire day chasing down emergencies and then had to stay six extra hours in the emergency room as Art never showed up to take over the physician duties. Amy thought back to medical school and remembered working in the hospital during a blizzard. The rule was that you stayed until your replacement arrived. The unlucky workers who were on duty when the snow arrived would most likely have to stay for an extra shift. Art hadn't shown up yesterday, and there was currently no snow in Vermont. The hospital had managed to find a replacement halfway into the next shift, but she still hadn't found out what happened to Art.

Hoping to meet Michael at the bench to compare notes about Bobby, Amy was disappointed when she couldn't leave. She almost considered calling the rectory to tell him that she wouldn't be there, but that would have been somewhat awkward.

The police had been looking for Bobby for several days now. Amy knew that Father Victor and Tony were becoming close and hoped that some clue might come to Michael through them. Amy also knew that Father Victor was visiting the hospital, but she didn't know his schedule. She had decided to see Marty after her ER shift yesterday, but she didn't clock out until 11:00 p.m. By that time, it was too late to visit and gather information, especially if it would upset Marty. Hopefully, she'd have a chance to run up there once she was done in the clinic today. She knew that she'd have to be quick about it as she had promised Willow that she would volunteer with her at the opening of the carnival tonight. Willow was going through so much that Amy didn't dream of adding to her disappointment or giving her another reason not to trust someone. Besides, the carnival sounded like it would be pretty interesting. Amy hadn't been to a true carnival with rides, game booths, clowns, food tables, cotton candy, ice cream, and calliope music in a long time. St. Francis was also going to have horse and pony rides, artists drawing caricatures, and a garden show. She would've loved to go with her niece, but since that wasn't possible, she would enjoy Willow's company instead.

Amy looked down and started concentrating on the test results before her. She was noting the abnormalities so that Barbara could call the patient and make arrangements for follow-up care. The patient visits were light today since the community didn't really know about the clinic program being available yet. Maybe Michael would let her bring flyers to the carnival. She made a mental note to ask him about that tonight. Amy had a few months to build up the patient visits in the clinic and save money for the emergency room. If that goal wasn't accomplished, the clinic would be closed for good.

"Is that the sixth time that you've initialed that page?" Barbara asked with a sarcastic smile.

"Excuse me?" Amy asked as she looked up with a mock frown.

"You've been staring at the same lab report for fifteen minutes," Barbara pointed out with a smile.

"Well, my eyes are looking at the paper, but my mind is not comprehending the numbers at the moment," Amy admitted tiredly. "So much has happened in the last week, I was just trying to put it all together."

"Why don't you just take a break and go get a decent cup of coffee? There's no patient here at the moment, maybe you can clear your head."

"You're right. I'm not doing any good sitting here and ruminating, that's for sure," Amy replied. "I think I'll run upstairs and see how Marty's doing."

"Good, you can give the lab another try when you get back. By the way, this envelope was at the front desk for you," Barbara said as she handed Amy a plain white envelope.

"Who's it from?" Amy asked curiously as she turned it over in her hand.

"I have no clue. It just has your name on the front. No return address, no postage, and it's marked Personal. Maybe you have a secret admirer?" Barbara asked while raising her eyebrows a little.

"I think not," Amy replied with a sarcastic laugh.

"Well, I'll leave you alone so you can find out," Barbara said. "Then go and get some air. I'll page you if anything important happens."

"Thanks, Barb, I appreciate all that you do," Amy said as she smiled. When Barbara had left the cubicle, Amy opened the envelope and retrieved the typed note inside.

> Dear Amy,
>
>   Please meet me at the bench at 8:00 p.m. tonight. I have to tell you something important about Willow. I need to tell you in person, alone. It's very important. I think I have a lead on Bobby as well.
>
>   Father Michael

Amy turned the note over several times. There was no date, and it was typed on plain white paper. Amy wasn't sure if Michael knew that she would be at the carnival tonight. Maybe Katie had told him that she was planning on helping. *How odd,* she thought. *Why didn't he just call me?* Amy decided that this was important enough to call the rectory and see if Michael could talk to her now. Michael had never directly given her the phone number, so she looked it up in his patient chart record. After several rings, Katie answered the phone.

"St. Francis Rectory, can I help you?"

"Katie? Is that you?" Amy asked.

"It is indeed, and who am I speaking to, please?"

"Katie, it's Amy."

"Oh, Amy. How are you, dear?"

"I'm fine, how are you, Katie?" Amy asked nicely.

"Going out of my mind wouldn't quite explain it, but close. I think we've got about two thousand people here, and I've got horses trying to eat the garden show flowers."

Amy gave a nice hearty laugh.

"Katie, I'm so sorry that you're busy, but I'm sure it'll all be worth it tonight."

"Well, I'll let you know, dear." Katie laughed back. "What can I do for you?"

"I was wondering if Father Michael was there," Amy asked politely.

"I'm sorry, Amy. He's up in Burlington for the day at a meeting. He's supposed to be back by tonight, sometime, but I don't know exactly when," Katie replied.

"Oh, okay then," Amy said with a faint disappointment in her voice.

"Is there anything I can help you with?" Katie asked with concern in her voice.

"No, thanks, Katie. It's just that he left a note for me at the clinic, and I wanted to ask him about it."

"Well, I don't know anything about a note, but he'll be at the carnival tonight. Perhaps you can ask him when you see him there," Katie suggested hopefully.

"I'll do that, Katie. Don't get too crazy today," Amy suggested.

"Oh, Dr. Amy, thank you for the thought, but it's already too late," Katie lamented.

"Well, I'll be there with Willow to help you tonight," Amy replied.

"Good, we can use all the help we can get. I'll look forward to seeing you then. Bye now," Katie said.

"Bye," Amy said and hung up the phone. She was disappointed that she hadn't talked to Michael. Maybe he wanted to meet her later because he would just be getting back from Burlington. What time did he drop off the note? The clinic didn't even open until nine this morning. Amy scolded herself for not asking Katie when he had left for Burlington. Katie was busy enough; she couldn't call her back now. She'd just have to go to the bench at eight o'clock and see what he wanted to tell her.

Chapter Sixty

Bobby sat in his beat-up car and finished the cup of coffee he took from the hospital lounge. Visiting the clinic, he'd left the fake note with the clerk. He'd been afraid that he'd be recognized, but she hadn't even looked up. The doctor would get the note, and she'd come to the bench tonight. Bobby knew she would come if she thought she was meeting the priest. By 8:00 p.m., it would be dark enough that they wouldn't be seen. He'd tried to follow her home a couple of times, but she never went straight home. If he knew where she lived, he could have finished her off there.

He threw the empty coffee cup over his shoulder and into the backseat where he'd slept last night. A few remaining drops of coffee spilled onto the ratty blanket and papers that had kept him from freezing to death. It was spring in Vermont, but it still got chilly at night. He was tired of living out of public bathrooms and stealing the little money he could for food and gas. A hot shower would be nice too. He never divorced Marty because was sure that Elizabeth would leave her some money. Had he known she wasn't getting any part of the inheritance, Bobby would have taken off years ago. Elizabeth never liked him anyway. Bobby started the car and headed out of the parking lot. He had some time to hang around the park, and there was always an open purse lying around. It'd be a nice place to fantasize about how the good doctor would beg as he was draining the life out of her tonight.

Chapter Sixty-One

Amy walked on to the fifth floor just as group therapy was letting out. Several patients walked out of the group room with a small smile on their face as they looked forward to lunch and some free time. Smoking was no longer allowed in the hospital, and the patients were not allowed to leave the medical floor to go outside. If that were the case, a good majority would never return.

As Amy continued to watch the patients, Marty walked out with Larry, Father Pat, and Father Victor in a group. The two priests seemed to make a nice balance for the patients, and the group counseling would hopefully help Father Pat in the process. Amy didn't know how long their visit at St. Francis would last, but she hoped it would be for a long time.

"Dr. Amy, how are you?" Marty said with a smile. She stopped for a moment while the rest of the group headed over toward the lounge for coffee.

"Fine, Marty. How are you?" Amy replied as she thought that Marty had a nice smile. It was nice to see someone smiling. A smile on this medical floor usually meant good progress was being made.

"I'm doing well. I think they're planning on discharging me Friday."

"That's great," Amy said. "Have you told Willow yet?"

"No, not yet. Before I can go, I have to be registered in an outpatient program. I didn't want to tell Willow until I knew where I was going."

"But you're on your way to a new life, Marty. I can feel it. You're going to go all the way this time."

"Well, Tony has been a godsend for me. He's like my personal angel. If it weren't for him, I probably wouldn't have survived much longer. The hospital is making all the financial arrangements with the lawyer, Mr. Bradford, for the next part of the program, but if I wasn't lucky enough to have my mother's money, I'm sure Tony would have helped."

"He's very fond of you, Marty," Amy said with a smile.

"I know, and I don't know why," Marty said as her eyes began to mist.

"Because he sees the inner you like a beautiful flower that's about to bloom with a radiance beyond compare," Amy gushed. "You just have to see it too."

"I'm working on it. In the meantime, I can't thank you enough for helping with Willow. I hope to be strong enough for her one day, but I appreciate you watching out for her," Marty said.

"It's been my pleasure," Amy replied as she felt a wave of sadness. "She's a great kid. Speaking of which, she's walking toward us as we speak."

Marty turned and saw Willow walking toward them. Behind her, Tony was just getting off the elevator as well. Father Victor also saw Tony and was waving as he walked toward him for a chat. Father Pat and Larry stood by the coffeepot, having a discussion in low tones.

"Hi," Willow said as she shyly approached Amy and Marty. "What's going on?"

"Hi, baby," Marty replied as she gave her shoulders a little squeeze. "We just got out of group, and I was just telling Dr. Amy that I may be promoted to the next step of the program at the end of the week."

"What does that mean?" Willow asked.

"As soon as they find a good outpatient program, I'll be transferred there for about thirty days," Marty explained.

"Really?" Willow asked with surprise. "Do you stay there?"

"Yes, for the thirty days. While I'm there, they help me work on things like a job and my health. Just some of the things that I've neglected for the past fifteen years," Marty said as she touched Willow's cheek and began to cry. "I love you so much, and I'm so sorry, Willow."

"I am included in that neglected list?" Willow said as her tears began to fall as well. She gave herself a little hug and closed her eyes.

Amy felt like an intruder as the two began to break the bonds of anger and hurt that had separated them for so long. "I have to go back to the clinic, but I just wanted to touch base with everyone."

"You're still going to the carnival, right?" Willow pleaded with a sad face.

"Willow, I wouldn't miss it for the world," Amy said with conviction. "Once I'm done in the clinic, I just have to change."

"I'm going to go home and get ready too. You better wear sneakers and bring a sweater."

"What time do you want me to pick you up?" Amy asked.

"How about five o'clock at my house?" Willow asked softly.

"What about dinner?"

"I usually like to eat at the carnival. Once you get there, you're surrounded by all the smells of the sausage and popcorn. You have to be careful not to eat too much."

"Sounds good to me," Amy said as her stomach growled. "As a matter of fact, I think that I'm going to run downstairs for a quick sandwich now." As Amy started walking off, she called behind her, "I'll see you tonight. I'm sure that it'll be exciting." Willow and Marty were both talking and crying as she left the floor.

Chapter Sixty-Two

Amy spent the rest of the afternoon in the hospital clinic. She finished reviewing the labs and then completed her paperwork. When all was done, she said her good-byes and left the hospital to go home. Changing her clothes, she decided on durable sportswear. She had promised to volunteer but really had no idea what she would be doing. Willow had said they could be running a game booth or collecting tickets for the fifty-fifty. Either way, she would be ready.

At five o'clock, she drove to Willow's house and waited in the driveway. After a few minutes, Willow bounded out of the house with a big smile on her face. Clearly, she enjoyed the carnival and was happy to be going there. They exchanged greetings and drove over to St. Francis while chatting about various things that had happened in the hospital. Amy wanted to ask her how she felt about her mom's progress, but Willow was so excited that Amy didn't want to broach a topic that might upset her.

They entered the parking lot of St. Francis and were directed toward a separate parking area for the volunteers. They must have been expecting a lot of visitors as the entire area was roped off into specific parking lanes, and signs had been posted about a temporary police emergency. Amy and Willow locked the car and walked to the carnival area behind the rectory. On their way, they stopped to pet the horses and admire the wagons that would be used for rides. The food smelled delicious. As they walked down the length of the midway, they looked at all the different game booths and food tables. Amy particularly studied the little area they had set up for emergency medical care. Various nurses had signed up as volunteers to work the medical booth each night just in case there were any minor injuries. As they continued walking, they smiled when they saw the rides and the stage. The music and flashing lights from the rides and booths were already in full swing despite the fact that the carnival had just started.

"Do you like to go on rides?" Willow asked hopefully.

Amy paused for a few seconds. "I haven't been on a ride in a long time. Are they safe?"

"Who knows? They're supposed to be inspected," Willow said as she shrugged her shoulders. "Do you want to go on one?"

"Why not?" Amy said with a nervous laugh.

"Good," Willow said excitedly. "I can't wait. The rectory sent a bunch of ride tickets to my house, so we're all ready to go."

"Well, if we're going to do rides, we better do that first. Better to eat afterward just in case I get queasy," Amy said nervously.

"Let's go on the Ferris wheel first," Willow cried out as she grabbed Amy's hand and led her toward the ride. After standing in line for a few moments, they walked up the steel ramp and handed their tickets to the worker. They jumped into the swinging seat and pulled the safety bar down. As the ride slowly loaded additional passengers, they looked around at the sights and smelled fresh popcorn. The view from the top was amazing. Amy was able to look down on the church and the large rectory behind it. On one side of the church, she could see the large cemetery. On the other side of the church was the large grassy area, which currently corralled the horses. It was bordered by the woods and the entrance to various hiking trails, including the entrance to Devil's Peak. In front of the church to the left was the parking lot, which led to the road and wood-covered bridge that crossed the Divide. Against the woods near the Divide was her bench as well as the end of the Devil's Peak trail. The view of the mountains and hills from this vantage was beautiful, especially as the sun was setting. The day was still warm, and the glorious red and gold colors from the sunset were intense and seemed to stretch for miles from this height. She looked at the bench and reminded herself that she was due to meet Michael there in a little while. Amy had been hoping to run into him at the carnival, but then he probably wouldn't be able to talk to her because he'd be surrounded by parishioners eager to talk.

After the Ferris wheel, they stood on line for the Tilt-a-Whirl and the Graviton. After a few more rides, they bought sandwiches, soda, and cotton candy. "This is so good," Willow exclaimed while pulling large tufts of cotton candy off the white paper cone.

"That it is," Amy said, picking a small tuft off the cone. "The only cotton I get to handle usually has rubbing alcohol on the other end."

"Now, my hands are all sticky," Willow said, wiping her hands on a paper napkin.

"Come on, let's go wash up," Amy said as she wiped her mouth with a paper napkin and threw out her garbage.

They visited the bathroom, washed their hands, and tried their luck at a couple of game booths. Willow won a stuffed bear and a pillow. Juggling their prizes, they walked over and reported in as scheduled to Florence. They were given their assignments to help Katie and the Ladies Auxiliary at the cake table. "Are you having fun yet?" Katie asked as they arranged small plates of pie and brownies on the table.

"I'm having a great time so far," Willow said with a large smile. "I won some things at the booths. After we're done here, I want to go on a wagon ride. The horses are beautiful."

"Me too," Amy said as she looked at her watch. "Katie, have you seen Father Michael yet?"

"Not yet, my dear," Katie said with a smile. "He could be inside the rectory. I imagine he may want to take a rest before he comes to the carnival. He barely gets a minute to himself once he does."

"Well, he asked me to meet him for a few minutes, so I'm going to see if I can find him. See, Katie, here's the note I told you about," Amy said as she handed Katie the note, being careful not to let Willow see that it was about her.

"I don't know what this is about," Katie said. "But I guess it's important, so you'd better talk to him."

"You ladies will be okay if I leave for a little bit?" Amy asked.

"We'll be fine." Katie smiled. "Willow and I are in charge. You run along and do what you have to do."

"Great, I'll be back in a short while. Save a piece of strawberry cheesecake for me," Amy said as she waved and walked away. She had six minutes to get to the bench.

Chapter Sixty-Three

Flowing in the moonlight, the Divide was captivating. Amy could hear the water gurgling, and there was a cool breeze flowing off the water, but the small river looked different in the dark. The moonlight reflecting off the water looked beautiful, but mysterious and dangerous at the same time. She had been sitting on the bench for ten minutes now and still no sign of Michael. Perhaps he had been delayed in Burlington. She'd wait five more minutes and then go back to the carnival. She'd never thought to give him her cell phone number, and she would have felt awkward calling his even if she knew the number. With her luck, he would've been in the middle of a mass when she called. Amy was curious of what information he had about Willow. She had seemed so happy and carefree at the carnival tonight. Michael must have had some news about Bobby or about Lizzie's death. Amy hoped that they would find Bobby soon. Willow was in danger and didn't even know it. Amy was reasonably sure that Bobby wouldn't do anything drastic until Willow had complete control over the money, but he was getting desperate. Amy hadn't seen Lou at the hospital today, so she couldn't ask if any progress had been made with the police. She made a mental note to page him tomorrow and find out if Ben had become fully conscious yet.

As she continued looking at the water, Amy felt a sting at the back of her neck. When she raised her right arm to check for an insect, a gloved hand grasped her wrist and jerked it backward. Immediately she felt a sharp pain in her right shoulder and a cold sharp object in the left side of her neck. As she yelped in pain, she felt hot, moist breath against her left cheek. "I wouldn't scream if I were you," the voice whispered in her left ear. "Not that anyone would hear you over the carnival noise." Amy's stomach lurched into a hard knot. Where was Michael? "I've been waiting for this little meeting for a long time," he hissed as his lips brushed Amy's earlobe and traveled down the side of her neck. Amy immediately lurched forward, but her right arm was pulled back further, which caused her to slam her body back against the bench. Her attacker was leaning over the bench from behind. His left arm was now across her shoulders and breasts. He let go of her right arm and switched the knife into his right hand. As he fondled her breast, he traced the edge of the knife over her right cheek and down into the creases of her neck. Amy's right arm was free, but she was unable to move it as pain tore through her shoulder and down the length of her arm. His hot breath was now in her right ear and down her neck as his mouth moved over her right cheek. "I was planning on killing you quickly," he whispered. "All I need is a small slit over the carotid artery. It wouldn't take too long to die, would it, Doctor? We could sit here, and I could hold on to you for a while. No one would come near the bench. After all, they would think we are two lovers, sitting here just taking advantage of the moonlight."

Amy started yelling. He immediately clapped his left hand over her mouth and pulled her head backward. She felt sharp pains in her neck and felt dizzy for a few seconds. Her heart was pounding. *Please, God, don't let me pass out.* She knew that she would never wake up, and her mind whirled in terror. Amy thought about her sister's death and wondered if she had been as scared and terrified as she felt right now.

"Shut up, bitch," he said as he pushed the blade against her neck and released his other hand. "As much as I want to kill you right now, we have to take a little walk. They won't find your body for a while when I'm done with you. I can't take any more heat, and they won't be able to pin your death on me once the animals pick you apart for a couple of days."

Amy had a vision of her dead, lifeless body lying in the woods with blank eyes staring up into the sky, insects landing on her face. "Bobby, don't do this," she panted. "Killing me isn't going to change a thing, you know that."

"I do know that. But I'm so pissed off killing you would just make me feel better. You know, share the misery. If nothing else, it'll give me something to do tonight. I already injected you with a tiny bit of sedative, but not too much because you have to walk a bit. I'm impressed that you figured out who I was."

"Well, I don't think there are too many random murderers wandering around in this area, and none of them would know I was a doctor," Amy said hoarsely in a shaky voice.

"True, that's true. I was actually surprised that you caught on to me in the hospital. You're just a suspicious little bitch, aren't you?" Before Amy could respond, he started pushing a piece of cloth into Amy's mouth, and she started choking. "Stop moving," he said and slammed his fist into the side of her cheek. Amy immediately saw stars and started to get nauseous. "I wouldn't throw up right now if I were you. You might choke to death." Bobby started laughing as he pulled her into an upright position by her hair. He quickly grabbed her limp arms and yanked them behind her back. Using a piece of plastic tape from the parking lot, he tied her hands behind her. "You can breathe through your nose for now, bitch. We're going to start walking toward the woods. I have no problem sticking this knife in your side because I have nothing to lose at this point. So just play nice, and maybe we can even have some fun before you die." As he put his arm around her waist and half pulled her toward the woods, Amy started to cry. "Come on, honey, I want to see the moonlight from Devil's Peak."

Chapter Sixty-Four

Katie and Willow continued to serve the parishioners at the cake table. They arranged plates of cookies, pumpkin bars, brownies, apple pie, cherry pie, doughnuts, chocolate-covered pretzels, and cheesecake. As several people left the table with small plates of dessert and juice, Tony walked over. "I'd like a piece of that apple pie, please," he said with a smile.

"I'll get that for you," Willow said in a professional voice as she expertly cut the pie and placed a piece on the dish for him. When she had collected his money and placed it in the shoe box they were using, she gave him a big smile. "My mother may be leaving the hospital in a few days."

"I heard that. I'm proud of her," Tony said as he put a forkful of apple pie into his mouth. "This is delicious."

"Thank you for helping her," Willow said shyly.

"You're a very brave girl. I know this must be difficult for you since you don't really know your parents, but it'll get better," Tony said with a grin. "We'll get through this."

"I'd really like a soft pretzel," Father Juan exclaimed as he approached the table with Father Pat.

"Would you like it with salt?" Katie asked as she picked up a plate and waited for his answer.

"Not too much," Father Juan answered.

"Here you go, Father," Katie said as she handed him the plate. "There's no charge for the good priests of the parish." Katie then turned to Father Pat. "What would you like to try, Father?"

"Well, those brownies are looking very tasty," Father Pat replied. "I've seemed to develop quite a sweet tooth lately."

"Oh, please, Father," Katie said as she handed him a plate with a large fudgy brownie. "Enjoy yourself."

"Thank you, Katie," Father Pat replied as he stood with the other men and enjoyed his brownie.

"Would you look at this," Katie exclaimed as she laughed. "The gang's all here." As she spoke, they all looked up and saw Father Victor and Father Michael stroll over to the table. "What dessert would you two like to try?"

"Do you mean what would I like to start with?" Father Victor asked as his gaze traveled over the entire table. "I think I'll start with those chocolate chip cookies."

"Me too," said Father Michael.

"Keep it up, Victor, and I'm going to have to bring you back to the gym," Tony said as he finished his pie. Everyone laughed as Willow offered plates to the two priests.

"Did you two just arrive back from Burlington?" Katie asked with surprise.

"That we did, Katie," Father Michael replied. "There was a tractor trailer that lost a tire and blocked the roadway for an hour or two."

"So you haven't even eaten dinner yet?" Katie said.

"No, but these cookies make a great appetizer," Father Michael replied.

"Keep it up and you'll have to go running twice tomorrow," Katie said as she waved her finger.

"I'll have double vegetables tomorrow, I promise," Father Michael said as he bit into a cookie.

"Good, I'll start steaming them first thing tomorrow morning," Katie said with her hands on her hips. "By the way, Father Michael, did you ever meet Dr. Amy at the bench?"

"No, Katie. I haven't seen Amy. Is she here?"

"She went to meet you at the bench. She had the note you left at the clinic to meet her at the bench at eight o'clock."

"Katie, we've just arrived here," Father Michael said with a serious tone to his voice. The whole table became quiet as they listened to the conversation. "I didn't write a note. Did you actually see it?"

"Yes, I did," Katie said with a nervous voice. "It was typed, but it said it was from you."

"Katie," Tony said with a serious tone, "tell me exactly, what did the note say?"

"I don't remember exactly," Katie said as she fiddled with her apron. "I feel bad saying it because Willow is here, but it said something like

'Meet me at the bench at 8:00 p.m. Come alone because I have to tell you something important about Willow.'"

"This is bad," Tony said with a grimace. "Katie, this is important. How was it signed?"

"I don't remember," Katie said as she started to get tears in her eyes.

"Think back to when you saw the note. Did it have a regular signature with a pen, or was the name typed like the rest of the note?" Tony asked again.

"Now that you mention it, the name was typed. I thought it was strange that Father Michael didn't sign it because he has such nice penmanship," Katie said weakly.

"We better get over to that bench," Father Michael said. "What time is it?"

"Eight twenty-three," Father Juan said as he looked at his watch. "Just so you know, I walked around the church on my way over, and I saw a couple near the bench. To be honest, I didn't go near them because they were going toward the entrance of Devil's Peak and I thought they wanted to be alone, if you know what I mean."

"Katie, find the police that are assigned here or, better yet, just call 911," Tony said as he looked around. "C'mon, let's go."

As Tony, Victor, and Michael took off at a trot toward the front of the church, Willow got out her cell phone. "You can use my phone to call 911," she said as she offered it to Katie with tears flowing down her cheeks.

Chapter Sixty-Five

Amy couldn't breathe as Bobby dragged her deeper and deeper into the trail leading to Devil's Peak. She had trouble getting enough air into her nostrils and started to get dizzy. "Don't pass out on me now, bitch. We still have a little way to go here," Bobby said as he stopped on the path. He could see that she was having trouble sucking in air, so he removed the dirty handkerchief from her mouth. "I'll let you breathe a little," Bobby said, "but only because I'm not carrying you to the top. You're going to walk to your own death."

At that moment, Amy let out an ear-splitting scream. Bobby was so taken by surprise that he punched her in the mouth. She fell to the trail and just nearly missed hitting her head on a large rock. "Shut up," Bobby yelled. "No one's going to hear you up here anyway, but I swear I'll knock you out and drag you up there by your hair if I have to."

Amy's head was spinning, and she rolled over and vomited into the trail. She tried to stay on the ground as long as she could to catch her breath, but within seconds, she could feel Bobby's hands at the back of her shirt pulling her upright. "Come on, let's get this over with. You're really starting to piss me off," Bobby spit at her. Being pushed forward, she would have fallen again if he hadn't been holding on to her shirt. With her mouth bleeding, vomit in her throat, and her head pounding, they continued on the trail to the top of Devil's Peak.

When the three men reached the bench, they saw that no one was there. Tony ran forward and tried to scan the banks of the river. "See anything?" Father Michael asked with concern.

"No, but it's dark," Tony said. "Even if she was here, she could have washed down the river by now. We better spread out."

"Dear Jesus, let us find her alive," Father Victor said out loud as they all looked around the woods.

"Did you hear that?" Michael shouted as the men searched as well as they could in the dark.

"What?" Tony asked.

"It sounded like a scream," Michael answered. "Up ahead, on the trail to Devil's peak.

"How far is it?" Tony said as he tripped over a rock. "Ouch."

"Still a ways up, but these woods can play games with noises," Michael yelled as he ran toward the trail. "There are a couple of turns coming up. Be careful, there are some sheer drops over the side of this trail."

"I can't see a thing," Victor yelled as he followed the men in front of him.

"Your eyes will get used to the dark," Michael shouted back. "There's enough moonlight to see the path. Just don't go to the sides." Michael had run this trail at night on several occasions, but he didn't remember the woods looking as sinister then.

Chapter Sixty-Six

"We're here," Bobby said as they reached the top of the peak. He gave Amy another hard shove, and she fell to the ground. Her face hit the rough dirt as her hands were still bound behind her back, so she couldn't protect herself. "The moonlight is beautiful tonight, isn't it, bitch?" Bobby started chuckling as he turned to stare at the entire valley and river far below bathed in the clear moonlight. "I have to say, this is really a gorgeous view. You'll get a closer look on your way down, though." Bobby gave a hearty laugh as he started to pick her up again by the arm. "I feel so good right now. I don't think I'm going to take the time to beat the crap out of you first. I want you to stay alert as you tumble down the big hill with your hands tied behind your back."

"You're such a bastard," Amy said as she spit in his face. "I hope you die and rot in hell." She had never been so frightened and angry at the same time. She could only imagine how her sister and niece felt when they had been assaulted. Amy had never been terrorized before, and she now clearly understood the feelings of the patients she had seen who were victims of violence.

Bobby laughed even harder as he wiped her bloody spit off his cheek. "I'm sure I'll see you when I get there, love." Holding her with his left hand, he slapped her with the back of his right hand. "Next time, mind your own business. Oh, that's right, there won't be a next time."

"Bobby, that's enough," Tony shouted with all of his training from the NYPD at its sharpest. "Let her go."

Bobby turned and saw the three men hurry to the top of the peak. "Well, well, it's the big, scary policeman and his friends," Bobby said sarcastically. "Do you think you're going to stop me?"

"That's the idea," Tony said as they slowed down to a few feet of Bobby and Amy.

"Don't come any closer or I'll snap her neck," Bobby said, pulling Amy in front of him.

"Just calm down, Bobby. Hurting her isn't going to change anything," Father Michael said. "Let us help you."

"What are you going to do, pray for me?" Bobby said with a sarcastic laugh.

"They may, but I won't, and that's a promise," Tony said with a venomous tone. "Now, let her go. The Rocky Meadow police are right behind us. You're going nowhere, Bobby, this is over."

"Then, I really have nothing to lose, do I?" Bobby said as he looked around at the three men.

"Not really," Father Michael said. "But we'll pray hard for your soul. You're a troubled man, Bobby. Let us help you."

"I'm beyond help. You know that, Father," Bobby said with a laugh.

"We don't have capital punishment in Vermont anymore," Michael said. "We can help you, just don't hurt her."

"Gee, Father, are you more worried about her or me?" Bobby asked.

"Both of you," Father Michael said as he noticed Amy's leaning form. "Don't make things worse than they are."

"Bobby, let her go," Tony threatened with a stern voice. "We're done here."

"We'll be done when I say we're done," Bobby said as he dragged Amy closer to the edge of Devil's Peak. Her foot slipped off the side of the peak, and Bobby held her up by her arm. Tony started to run forward, and Bobby yelled, "Don't move or I swear I'll drop her right off the side." Tony stopped where he was, breathing hard and clenching his fists at his sides.

"What do you want, Bobby?" Father Michael asked. "We're at an impasse here."

"I guess you're right, Father," Bobby said with a deep sigh. "We're at an impasse. What I want is a lot of money and to kill the good doctor. Isn't that enough?"

"You're evil, pure evil," Victor said in a deep, threatening voice.

"I think you're kind of right about that." Bobby giggled.

"Bobby, there's nothing we can do?" Father Michael asked.

"No, I don't think so," Bobby said. "I'm not gonna stand here all night either."

"Tony, I think I hear the police," Michael said as he turned around and looked down the trail. "I'm the most familiar with the trail. I'm going to go back down and lead them up here. You and Victor watch him." Bobby turned and headed back down the trail.

"Do what you have to do, Father," Bobby yelled after him. "Light a candle for me when you get back to the church." Amy couldn't believe that Michael was actually leaving. By the time he came back with help, she would be dead or off the side of the peak. She didn't know what he could do, but at least he could have stayed and tried something. Father Victor seemed to keep moving toward the side of the path that Bobby was standing on, and Tony was standing six feet away, ready to pounce as soon as he had the opportunity. Bobby had pulled her back to the edge of the cliff and let go of her arm.

"Bobby, you know, if you drop her, Victor and I are gonna take you down so hard we'll have to throw you off the side just to hide the damage," Tony spit.

Bobby laughed and said, "Well then, Tony, let me ask you a question. If I go to jail and I'm still married to Marty, do I get to keep half of anything she inherits?" Bobby asked with a sneer.

"What the hell are you talking about?" Tony asked with an incredulous face.

"You know, what if one of my friends pays Willow a visit? And if something were to happen to Willow while I was in jail and I was still married to Marty, do I get to keep the money?" Bobby started laughing at his sick joke.

"That's it you bastard," Amy yelled in his ear. "I swear, you killed her once, you're not going to do it again." As she screamed at him, she lifted her leg and kicked him as hard as she could in the crotch. Bobby yelped in pain and started losing his balance. He grabbed on to Amy to steady himself but instead pulled on her arm, and Amy toppled toward him. Her added weight caused him to lose his balance, and they both went over the side of the peak. Tony and Victor ran forward and tried to grab them before they fell, but it was too late. They stood together and stared over the side of the peak into the black darkness, feeling sick at the sound of the screams.

Chapter Sixty-Seven

Amy's body slid backward down the rocky slope of the mountain. Bobby had lost his grasp, but she heard him screaming somewhere in the distance. With her hands tied behind her back she was unable to defend herself against any of the rocks or trees that she hit as she bounced backward. She remembered thinking that she felt really calm for someone who was about to die. She felt no pain except for a sharp, sudden jolt in her leg. Then there was nothing. She was just hanging except she still heard screaming and shouts somewhere around her. As she struggled to stay conscious, she felt someone grasp her legs and then her knees. Who was squeezing her knees? She slowly felt herself being pulled upward and then shifted onto a small rocky ledge. When she opened her eyes, she was staring into the pained face of Father Michael. Father Victor and Tony were on top of the hill, shouting up in the air, but she didn't know why. Were they shouting up to God? Amy turned her head toward Father Michael's smiling face. "Am I dead? Are you an angel? Is that why you left me, to get ready for when I died?"

Michael held her in his arms and whispered, "You're not dead, Amy. I caught you and pulled you up to this ledge. Help is coming, and you'll be okay." As he spoke, he was able to get the plastic tape off Amy's wrists.

"Really?" Amy asked with a strange smile as she stared into his face, unable to move.

"Really," Michael said as he traced his finger over her bruised cheek. Amy laughed and then started to sob uncontrollably. Michael tightly held her against his chest and softly gave thanks to God while they waited for more help to come.

Chapter Sixty-Eight

Father Michael sat quietly in the confessional booth waiting for a parishioner to arrive. As the minutes ticked by, Michael thought about what had happened at Devil's Peak for the thousandth time. It had been four days since Amy had almost been killed. The police and rescue squad were near the top when Amy and Bobby went over the side. Apparently, they had used their GPS tracking program on the cell phone that Tony was wearing to pinpoint their exact location. Since there was a tower located somewhere on the top of the mountain, they had received a strong signal and were able to find them immediately. Tony and Father Victor had stayed on top of the mountain to direct them to the location where Father Michael was holding Amy. They had to lower a basket to pull Amy up to complete safety. Father Michael was also lifted off the ledge with the aid of a safety belt. Everyone had been transported to Rocky Meadow General for evaluation, and Amy had been admitted for observation for head trauma for two nights. Her outward cuts and bruises had been cleaned and stitched. During the two days, she had a parade of visitors including Willow and Marty, as well as hospital staff, wishing her a speedy recovery. Ernie had even stopped by and spent an hour telling her more funny stories about the ER. At one point, she had four priests praying over her bed and offering blessings. Michael held a vigil in her room just as Bobby had watched Ben. Michael watched her physically improve and just hoped that she would heal emotionally. She had promised to meet him at the bench next week, and he was eagerly looking forward to it. He really hadn't been able to talk with her much since she was discharged from the hospital. Katie and Florence had made a schedule of people eager to help care for her in her home. The carnival had continued and was even more crowded as the news traveled around town, and people wanted to see the sight of the crime. Thank God, the carnival would end tonight.

Michael heard the wooden kneeler squeak, and he slid the small window panel open.

"Bless me, Father, for I have sinned," the familiar voice said.

"How long has it been since your last confession?" Michael asked softly. His mind was racing. It was her. After everything else, it was the woman who thought she killed someone, and he knew that voice. Amy was home in bed, and Willow was with Marty at the rehab, but he knew that voice.

"Two weeks, Father. It's been two weeks since I was here." The woman was crying now. "But I'll never find peace until I confess, Father Michael, and I'm too ashamed to tell you face-to-face in the rectory."

"Katie?" Father Michael said with disbelief. "Katie, is that you?"

"Yes, Father," Katie said through her sobs. "I love this parish so much I'll be sorry to leave, but it's time. After what happened this week, I know that you can't be free until you face your fears and responsibilities."

"Katie, let's talk about this inside," Father Michael said. "I'm finished here for now."

"But I want to confess, Father," Katie said with sincerity. "I think I killed my husband. He was in pain from the cancer. I gave him the narcotic medicines, and he died."

"Katie, I promise that I'll take your confession once I know what you're talking about," Father Michael said. "Please, let's just talk first."

"If you wish, Father Michael," Katie replied.

"Good, I'm coming out now," Michael said as he slid the window closed and walked out of the confessional. He walked with Katie to his office library, and they spent the next hour talking about her husband.

Chapter Sixty-Nine

"You mean, she thought she killed him?" Amy asked after she listened to Michael's story.

"Apparently," Michael replied as he explained Katie's fear to Amy. "She was only following directions when she gave her husband the medicine the hospice physician ordered, but since he died a short time later, she was convinced that she had killed him."

"We often use medications to ease a patient's suffering. It's a difficult situation even for nurses sometimes," Amy replied softly. "I'm glad she let you tell me. It must have been painful for her."

"It was a hard decision, but she's been living with the guilt all these years," Michael said as he shook his head.

"Well, I'll talk to her. From what you've told me, she followed the directions perfectly. The proper amount of medication was accounted for. I don't think she did anything wrong, but she needs to talk about it. Then, she'll feel better. Maybe a good support group as well," Amy said as she grimaced.

"Are you okay?" Michael asked when he saw her pain. Her bruises were healing, but she still looked frail.

"Much better now," Amy said. "It's a beautiful day, we're sitting on our bench, and I'm alive. I couldn't be better."

"Our bench?" Michael asked with a grin as he took her hand.

"Well, in the beginning," Amy began, "I was a little upset with you trying to horn in on my thinking time, my private bench time. But after all we've been through, you're welcome to sit on the bench with me whenever you'd like."

"Thank you, I'm honored." Michael laughed as he claimed his half of the bench.

"Honestly, thank you, Michael," Amy said as she looked into his face with tears in her eyes, "for saving my life. I wouldn't be here now if you hadn't crawled out onto that ledge. I thought you were leaving me to die, and my heart really broke inside."

"The times that we feel most alone are the times we are truly watched over," Michael said softly. "That's when your faith has to be strong. I would never have left you."

"You knew about the ledge?"

"I did from running on that trail. I figured that if you went over the side, you would slide right by that ledge, or at least, I hoped you would. I had told Tony about it on the way up, so he knew I was going to go out there. I prayed that God would give me the strength to catch you, and he did."

"I was so scared. I've never been that frightened in my life except when my sister died, and I knew that I couldn't go through anything like that again," Amy cried.

"I was crouching on the ledge, and I heard you yell at Bobby, that he had already killed her once and he wasn't going to do it again. What exactly were you talking about?"

Amy laughed and shook her head. Tears continued to fall down her face, over her cheeks and lips. The bruising and swelling of her face hadn't gone completely away yet, and she looked tired. "You know, by then, I had been punched and hit in the head so much that I was starting to get a little confused. The reason that I came to Vermont was to run away from Boston after my sister and niece were attacked. I think that I was confusing my sister with Willow at that point, but it's the same situation."

"What happened, if you don't mind my asking?" Michael said softly.

"My sister had met someone on the Internet. They e-mailed for a long time and then finally arranged to meet each other. At first he was real smooth and polite, but little by little, you could see an inner personality starting to emerge. He began to pay too much attention in an inappropriate way toward my fifteen-year-old niece. My sister realized things weren't right and tried to break it off with him." Amy paused for a long moment before she could compose herself and continue. "One day, my sister was out shopping and heard screams when she got back to the house. She called the police and ran inside. That bastard was trying to rape my niece. My sister struggled with him. It didn't end well, and he managed to hurt them both. The police arrived, and in self-defense, they shot him, but he didn't die. They transported him to my hospital, and I was one of the trauma surgeons on call. I saved his life and was told he was shot during a home invasion. I thought he was the victim. I didn't know that he had killed my sister and put my niece in a coma. The bastard hurt my family, and I saved his life."

"Now, he's in prison?" Michael asked gently.

"No, the bastard is now dead," Amy said with conviction.

Michael didn't know what to say. "Do you want to tell me about it?"

Amy thought back to the day she was called into her chief's office.

"Amy, I wanted to tell you again how sorry I am for your loss. The trauma of losing your sister and then being responsible for the life of her tormentor must be eating you alive."

"I did what I had to do," Amy replied stoically.

"I'm sure that you did," her chief had replied. "It's just that since he died within ten days of the surgery, we had to have a coroner's inquest."

"I understand that."

"Well, we have the final autopsy report. The medical examiner has ruled his death as natural causes."

"I'm glad, sir," Amy replied. "How did he die?"

"From a cerebral hemorrhage. He had police stationed outside his door the moment he came into the hospital. At some point, he told the nurse he had to go to the bathroom. When they unlocked his handcuffs, he tried to escape. In the process, he fell and slammed his head on the floor. That's what led to the hemorrhage."

"I see. I have to leave, sir," Amy said.

"You can go home. I know this is all too much for you at the moment."

"No, I mean I have to leave the hospital. I have to leave Boston," Amy explained. "I can't work here anymore, it's all too unsettling."

"Amy, you're too upset to make rash decisions. You're a fine surgeon. Don't make any decisions now. Get some help. You can take a leave of absence if you need one, but we'll just leave things open."

"Thank you, sir" Amy said as she left his office.

Amy finished telling Michael her story.

"You did the best you could, it was in God's hands." Michael tried to comfort her.

"No, you don't understand. He died of natural causes, but I wanted to kill him. I even went into his room with a needle one day. I'm no different than Bobby," Amy said.

"Amy, you are different. You didn't kill him. You were angry and upset, but you made the right choice."

"It's been haunting me ever since." Amy started to cry. "My sister is dead, and my niece is in a coma. I thought seeing him dead would help me, but it didn't."

"It's going to take time," Michael whispered softly.

"I heard they found Bobby's body," Amy said softly. "The police haven't told me too much since that night."

"Yes," Michael said, "they found him in the Divide. He slid down the mountain and straight into the river. The river washed him over the waterfall where he got wedged into a group of rocks. A couple of local boys saw the body and called the police."

"Lou Applebaum called me," Amy said. "Ben Lawrence was able to give a full statement to the police."

"I didn't know that," Michael said. "How did he tie into this whole thing?"

"Well, years ago, Bobby had a part-time job at the pharmacy. That's how Bobby learned about needles and injections. Ben fired him long ago but never changed the locks to the pharmacy. When Ben began to keep his inventory on a computer, he realized that things were missing, and he was really worried when he heard that Lizzie had died under strange circumstances. Ben waited for a while and then confronted Bobby, but he couldn't prove anything. To keep Ben quiet, Bobby tried to kill him by injecting a whole bottle of blood thinner into him, but he wasn't successful. Bobby stayed with him in the intensive care unit to try again, but the unit had constant video monitoring, and Bobby knew that he would be filmed. As long as Ben didn't wake up, there wasn't a problem."

"But he did wake up?"

"He started to come to consciousness and warn us. When Ben was moved to an undisclosed location, Bobby lost control of the situation and blamed everything on me."

"Thank God you're safe, and Bobby won't be bothering anyone ever again," Michael said. "I'll pray for his soul. Now, it's time for the healing to begin for you, but you have to heal from the inside, you can't run away from it."

"I know that now," Amy said with a sad smile. "But it's hard. There's been so much pain."

"You just have to keep your faith, Amy. Think of all the people you've helped. Father Juan is leaving for New Jersey tomorrow, and he looks like a new man already. Katie has agreed to stay at the rectory as long as you talk to her about the medicine. Marty gets out of rehab in three weeks, and she wants to help Father Pat run a new support group for anyone who needs help with alcohol addiction. Tony has been a big help to her already, and I'm sure that he'll keep her strong. Speaking of strong, Tony is still boxing with Father Victor, who'll be staying here at St. Francis and helping me run the parish for a while. Willow has already blossomed with your help. All that time, she thought she had killed her grandmother. What a horrible burden to bear. She had no way of knowing that Bobby put atropine in that insulin vial. Willow can't wait until you're well enough to spend time with her. We explained to her that none of this was her fault, but she'll need support for a while. She's excited about working with you in the clinic. So you see, one life can touch and change so many others," Michael said.

"Like you've changed mine?" Amy asked with a smile.

"I'm just doing God's work, but I've been putting in a little overtime lately." Michael laughed. "We have to realize that every day is a gift from God and that we're all God's angels. We do what we can, and he takes care of the rest as he sees fit."

"Now, you sound like a trauma surgeon. Welcome to the club," Amy said with a smile as she raised her face toward the sun and soaked in the warmth. It was a beautiful, sunny day. Michael and Amy continued to sit on the bench side by side in deep, bonded friendship. Together, they watched the river rise and fall, ebb and flow, and just continue to move forward.

10651992R0

Made in the USA
Lexington, KY
27 August 2011